He didn't believe in her psy
drawn to him?

Cal lifted Brie into his a
hard she closed her eyes. But
rain-slicked arms even though ne, too, was drenched by the run
around the Jeep. His scent lifted from his neck, his clothing. In
his arms she felt the oddly familiar strength and promise of
protection as he slogged through the muck and stomped up the
three steps.

Brie was breathless by the time Cal scooted them under the
porch roof. The wind-driven rain no longer pelted her skin, yet
she didn't open her eyes. She wanted to hold this moment of all-
encompassing security. She wanted to hold tight to the man who
made the moment possible. "Brie?"

Had she heard Cal whisper her name? With the background
rumble of thunder and the steady drum of rain on the porch roof
she couldn't be sure. One thing for certain, he still held her aloft.
Maybe that was the problem. After all, she clutched at his neck
as if he were a life preserver.

Brie lifted her eyelids. Cal's face hovered only inches from
hers.

Her next breath brought with it his scent, a rich blend of
clean skin, rain water, and male earthiness. Brie's heart picked
up speed until she felt the pulse in her neck flutter. It was
happening again, just as it had earlier on the way to the ranch
for dinner. She was slipping under the spell of Cal Porter's vital
presence. His soul might be in agony, but physically he hummed
with life. Never had Brie felt such conflicting energies roll off a
man. But never had she been so lured by a man's essence that
she allowed those energies to touch her in return.

Slowly, gently, he released her legs. Cal eased her down the
length of his body, a graceful sensual slide, until her toes and
heels touched the planks.

Brie's insides quivered with an eagerness so wanton she
didn't recognize herself. "Cal," she murmured, "what's going
on here?"

Cal leaned closer, pinning her gently to the post with his
solid body. His mouth, warm and scented with the residue of
brandy, hovered over Brie's lips. "Beats the hell out of me."

Brie could hardly take more than quick, shaky gulps of the
heavy, humid air. "I...I think you're going to kiss me."

"Good guess, Madame Psychic. Are you going to stop me?"

This book is dedicated to the following people:

My California girlfriends who are heroines of their own stories—Jodie Durnerin, who stands alone with dignity and grace, and Kristy Jue, who blossoms where she's planted.

The godmothers of all my books, Jan Hunsicker and Elysa Hendricks, with gratitude and affection.

And my husband, Craig, as always with love.

Other books by Barbara Cary

Marista

Miracles and Magic

***

Barbara Cary

Miracles and Magic
Published by ImaJinn Books

ISBN: 1-933417-03-X

10 9 8 7 6 5 4 3 2 1

PUBLISHER'S NOTE:
This book is a work of fiction. Names, characters, places and incidents are products of the author's imagination or are used fictitiously. Any resemblance to actual events or locales or persons, living or dead, is entirely coincidental.

Books are available at quantity discounts when used to promote products or services. For information please write to: Marketing Division, ImaJinn Books, P.O. Box 545, Canon City, CO 81212, or call toll free 1-877-625-3592.

Cover design by Rickey Mallory

ImaJinn Books
P.O. Box 545, Canon City, CO 81212
Toll Free: 1-877-625-3592
http://www.imajinnbooks.com

One

Myles palmed the bowl of his wine glass and stared into the midnight sky. This hour always made him tense, as if life was balanced on a cusp between ignorance and knowing.
Prologue, *Murder, My Love—From the Files of Myles Daemon, P.I.*

* * * *

Lightning bolts chased each other across the night sky, silhouetting the baggy thunderheads and filling the air with scorched ozone. Wind-driven, needle-sharp rain drenched Brie's hair and face. The light jacket, that two hours ago had fended off cool night breezes in Los Angeles, clung to her arms like a cold second skin. Muck seeped around the edges of her strappy pink sandals and squished between her bare toes.

Yet she hardly felt the chill or flinched at the crack of thunder. Brie teetered on the bank of a flooded creek bed and stared with morbid fascination into the roiling water illuminated by her dimming headlights. Blind intuition had compelled her to slam on the brakes scant yards before she and her car plunged into the swollen creek. The wild current could have easily battered them both against the rocks and she'd have drowned.

Just like in the dream.

Brie shivered with a new cold that pushed up from her soul. She might have escaped physical drowning, but the terrible lifelike dream still dragged her down with the weight of impending doom. The same intuition that saved her warned she hadn't cheated Fate, only received a preview of the future as it might unfold.

The Universe is open to change, Aunt Sophie was fond of telling her. *You have more free will than you realize, Little Moon Child, if you only listen to the whisperings of your soul.*

"I did listen, Sophie," Brie muttered through chattering teeth. "I listened and drove right into my nightmare."

Brie hugged herself for warmth and comfort. If only she had read the road map more carefully and paid more attention to the exits off the highway. How many of those seedy hotels had she passed by when the first, fat raindrops fell on her windshield half an hour ago? Anyone who lived in Southern

California knew summer monsoon rains sometimes struck with unexpected ferocity in the semiarid foothills.

And once she'd gotten turned around why had she blindly headed for that bright, flickering light in the distance? It might have been nothing but scrub grass set ablaze by the lightning and then doused by the downpour.

But reason had never had anything to do with this flight back to New Mexico and Aunt Sophie. Brie had let fear of the unalterable past and panic over a vision of a possible future drive her into this present danger.

Suddenly, the rush of water seemed louder. The crack of thunder deeper. The pelt of rain on her face more violent. Behind her the car lights dimmed, brightened, and dimmed again. The battery was giving out, either from stress or soddenness or both. As another deep chill wrenched her upright, Brie shook off her paralysis. She had to think. She had to...

"Get the hell away from the bank!"

The shout, angry and male and close, scared the remaining air from her lungs. Preoccupied with her escape from doom she hadn't felt the approach of another human. Clearly not all wildlife out here in the middle of nowhere slithered or walked on all fours. Brie spun toward a source of approaching lamplight and put the water to her back. Never a wise strategy according to Darien, her dear friend and *feng shui* mentor.

The move proved Darien right. The leather soles of her sandals hydroplaned on the sodden dirt. Brie went down hard on her left hip and arm. But the scrape of rock against her palms and knees felt as nothing compared to the constriction in her chest when she realized her whole body was sliding toward the raging creek.

Clawing at the stony ground only spackled her face with fetid earth. Her fingertips barely penetrated a half-inch before hitting rock-hard clay. The creek bank sloughed her off like it did the downpour, and the slippage became a slide toward the waiting abyss. The stuff of her nightmares.

A scream tore from her throat, a hoarse and pitiful sound against the continual explosions of thunder and the keening of the wind. She tried to scramble forward, but the thrashing of her legs only drew her down. The arch of her foot scraped rock then skimmed the cold, gushing water. Instinctively Brie held her breath.

"Son-of-a..."

A large, strong hand clamped her right arm just above the elbow. The sudden yank upward almost wrenched muscle from bone. Brie's shins dragged along the rocky ground for a second before she flipped around and landed on her backside.

The stranger hunkered down to eye level. But with the hood of a black rain slicker writhing in the wind around his face, she only glimpsed fierce eyes, thick rain-clumped eyelashes, and a teeth-barring snarl. "What the *hell* are you doing way out here on a night like this? Are you crazy?"

Winded, Brie squinted into the harsh light of the hurricane lamp he held high in his free hand. Some soul-deep, dark emotion fueled a different kind of storm, a turmoil that rolled off this man and assaulted her psyche. A painful sadness, harsh and bitter and old, penetrated the carefully constructed barriers of her unconscious mind and called out to her. In his grasp Brie glimpsed leashed anger and whorls of danger.

The man's touch and his powerful psychic intrusion had suddenly become as treacherous to her soul as the floodwaters were to her body. Brie yanked against his hold. "Let me go!"

Instantly he did so and sat back on his heels. "No, problem! And you're welcome!" he shouted over the storm.

Despite the concession Brie scuttled backward beyond his reach, as if that alone could repel his stark emotional tug on her soul. Rocks clawed at the hem of her jacket and snagged the silk skirt of her sundress. Her breath came hard and heavy as she tried to shout above the weather. "I...I didn't mean to sound ungrateful or rude. I..."

She almost admitted her fear, but that wasn't wise. Brie swiped at a clump of hair that clung to her wet cheek and retrenched. "I'm not familiar with the highway this side of the mountains. I made a wrong turn, that's all. Perhaps you could point the way out of this canyon."

The electrical bolts overhead cast his features in natural strobe light. Brie thought he frowned, then smiled without humor as he perused her legs and hiked up skirt in a way that made her already skittish insides cramp with tension. "A city girl, huh?"

She resisted giving him a taste of her city-girl survival skills. "Los Angeles," she called out. "And I know how to take care of myself."

"Yeah, I bet you do." He rocked backward and balanced a moment before hefting to his feet with an easy male grace.

"Thanks for the warning." Then he waved in the direction of her car. "U-turn and go back up the way you came. Make a left at the fork of the road and drive five more miles. You can get back on the main highway from there. Just move away from the bank fast before the creek floats *you* back to some Los Angeles storm drain."

As he loomed over her, his face all but obliterated by the snapping slicker hood, Brie realized her heart pounded with a reaction other than fear. For some reason her heart hurt for him!

Brie cast aside her confusion and gave the water a quick look. The stranger had a point. Foamy spray already licked at the edge that had given way under her slight weight.

She had to get up. She couldn't appear helpless. If nothing else she had to actively defend herself against his overwhelming tow on her psyche. Brie dug in her heels and tried to roll to her side for balance. Once again the leather-soled sandals betrayed her on the wet rock and slimy clay. Her right hip and hand took the full force of the jarring this time. Her palm was so raw from abrasions she flinched and fell back on her elbow.

Pain shot up her arm and straight into her neck and shoulders. Worse, she twisted her right leg and felt a disheartening "pop" in her knee. If she was lucky—very, very, very lucky—the joint wouldn't start to swell until she could get to a motel that had an ice-vending machine.

The stranger loomed over her, backlit by the storm, waiting. *For what*, she wondered.

Yet Brie knew the answer before she finished the thought. Raw intuition told her this man offered only his help. He hadn't imposed himself on her. He'd even given way when she'd pushed him back, though he was strong enough to do otherwise.

Still that was little enough evidence with which to judge a man. A strange man. With scowling dark eyes and a quelling way of taking stock of a woman. Not to mention the surge of strong, bitter emotion that had compelled her to let down her guard and let him inside her head. Better be safe than sorry.

As quickly as the blinding rain, muck, and her strained joint permitted, Brie tucked both legs beneath her, braced her palms on the ground and scrambled to her feet. Her body quavered. It took a moment to test the sturdiness of her knee. It ached, but held her weight. Brie dusted the chips of stone and goo from her hands and sidestepped away from the bank. "Sorry if I inconvenienced you," she yelled into the storm. "I'll be on my way. Thanks."

Her headlights flickered and died.

The stranger swung his lamp toward the darkened car and then back toward Brie and the creek. "You think?" he called out.

His sarcasm made her feel all the more vulnerable. Brie put up her hand, fending him off and saying farewell at the same moment. "I'll call for help on my cell phone."

"It works in these foothills?"

Well, no it didn't, come to think of it. She'd found out that much when she tried to call Darien just before she made a wrong turn into wilderness hell. "All right, fine! Then...then maybe you would call someone for me. I'll go back to my car and wait."

"The storm cut power and phone lines," he answered. Then he waved the lamp to his left. "My cabin is just up this path if you want to wait out the storm there."

There wasn't a hint of warmth or welcome in his voice. He made the offer out of duty. Ironically, Brie trusted his reluctance.

Yet she still felt the aftershocks of his psychic assault and hesitated. Perhaps she hesitated a few moments too long.

The stranger stood still for another couple of lightning strobes then shrugged. "Suit yourself." He turned on his heel and started up a gentle slope into the dark, taking the steady light of the hurricane lamp with him.

In the midst of the storm, Brie swore she heard, or at least felt, silence. Even her heart didn't seem to beat as she watched the violent dark swallow the stranger first, then start to dim the beacon of light.

Brie didn't feel the air fill her lungs or consciously open her mouth. "Wait!"

The lamp swung around. At least the stranger heeded her call.

Wasting no more time, Brie dashed back to her darkened car as fast as she dared on her injured knee and fumbled with the rain-slicked driver's side handle to yank open the door. First she retrieved her keys and then grabbed the roll bag stuffed with her belongings from the front passenger's seat.

All the while the stranger didn't move from his place on the pathway. Brie slogged her way through mire that made her skid and turned her ankle twice before she got close enough to make out the details of the tall, sturdy man holding the only illumination besides lightning for miles around.

"A woman's got to have her makeup, right, Miss L.A.?"

Desperate to get out of the rain and away from the creek, Brie ignored his snideness and trudged past him. In the near distance she could just barely discern the outline of a cabin dark as the stormy night around her.

Dark as the psychic energy of the man who lit her steps from behind.

* * * *

Brie rode a gust of wet wind across the knotty wood threshold and into the small cabin. She ground to an awkward stop and stood dripping rainwater off the sleeves of her jacket and the hem of her thin sundress. Heat from snapping flames in a stone hearth across the room embraced her chilled body. The burning wood gave the air a warm, homey smell, though the fire did little to illuminate the dark wood plank floor and walls. The soft glow did, however, reflect well off the glassy eyes of several wall-mounted trophy animal heads staring down at her from all sides.

Clutching her roll bag to her chest, Brie peered up at the posed, lifeless heads and could almost hear Darien murmur, *Bad feng shui. Very, very bad feng shui.*

Behind her the door slammed shut. Forgetting about her twisted right knee, Brie started and spun in place. The joint sent out only a small lick of pain. Brie sighed in relief for that much good fortune, as the cabin's owner pushed away from the door he'd closed with the force of his broad shoulder. With deliberation, he set the lantern on a table by the door and snapped his arms impatiently, sending a shower of water into the room and onto her.

Brie back stepped, whether to avoid the spray or keep her distance from the surly man she wasn't sure. Either way, it was time to establish some kind of defensive social link. "I apologize for being such an imposition," she said. "But I must have seen your lights before the electricity went out, so I just headed this way. Thanks for coming out to help me."

Having made the overture Brie waited for him to turn around. She could always tell much by looking straight into a person's eyes.

With his back still to her the man stiffened. "What was I supposed to do? I saw those headlights of yours bounce down the road. Thought you'd end up on my front porch." He slipped back his hood, glanced over his shoulder without really looking at her, and started to shrug out of his slicker. "How is it you didn't realize five miles back you were on the wrong road?"

The accusation in his voice frustrated her attempts at civility. Still, she had to try. She was stuck with this man's hospitality— or lack thereof—until the power and telephones came back on. "I told you. I took a wrong turn. Then in the downpour I could barely see the side of the road to make a turn even if I knew what direction I was going. My tires started to skid on the wet gravel and dirt."

For a moment, Brie actually felt as if her car had swerved out of control, gone airborne, and then plummeted downward. Her stomach dropped, and she had to hiccup a breath to halt the roller coaster ride in her imagination. She squelched a shudder that had nothing to do with her sopped clothing.

He didn't respond as he paced two steps to a row of pegs near the door and carefully hung up his wet slicker. Brie admired the way his long-fingered, wide hands accomplish the task without fuss. Amazingly, the brush with disaster hadn't shut down her ability to appreciate a man on some basic level, and even pushed the images of the persistent waking dream temporarily to the back of her mind.

In shadow, with his back to her, this dark-souled stranger did cut an imposing figure. He probably wasn't quite six-foot, but a faded green T-shirt outlined solid shoulders and torso and exposed strong forearms. Generic blue jeans fit snug over lean hips and legs. For some reason Brie was surprised to see this surly cabin-dweller wore thick soled, heavy leather black shoes that were the *choice de jour* for Los Angeles males who wanted to appear in style but still ruggedly masculine. On this man, those sturdy, rugged "hip" shoes looked anything but pretentious.

Brie realized she'd spent far too much time admiring the stranger from behind and too little time trying to figure out a way to establish some neutral ground. "I guess I was lucky I didn't drive off the road and into a ravine."

"No, you almost drove off the road into Milagro Creek."

His censure raised her hackles again fast. The least he could do was graciously accept her thanks. Brie decided to make one last try to be friendly. "Milagro. Doesn't that mean 'miracle' in Spanish? Maybe there was some magic at work tonight after all."

He finally turned. Flickering hearth light cast the spare angles of his face with the same harshness as his manner and voice. A thick ruff of short-cropped, medium brown hair added to the almost military composure of his expression. Even so, the unflattering shadow couldn't disguise the natural appeal of his well-defined features. If he could break a smile, he might even be handsome.

Instead, his narrowed green eyes threw out sparks of challenge. "I never have believed in magic. And miracles seemed to pass me by. Let's just say I was in the right place at the right time to save your tail tonight."

The angry grumble jarred her, but not as much as the soul-deep sadness that had begun to roll off him again and seep into her awareness. He squinted, perhaps to see her better since she was backlit by the hearth fire. But as he emerged from the shadows, he made no effort at even a meager social introduction.

Brie steadied herself and took the initiative. Thrusting out her hand she lifted her chin. "Then thank you for saving my tail. My name is Brienne Quaid."

He ignored her hand. "Name's Cal Porter." He nodded at her roll bag. "Hope you have a change of clothes in there."

Brie snapped her hand back and clutched the bag tighter. "Along with my makeup?"

For a moment he smirked, the sort of expression that fueled her irritation. But after he came a step closer to Brie his features froze, and his green eyes searched her face in a way that made her feel as if she were a bug in the sights of an entomologist.

Had she stumbled into the lair of a mass murderer? Brie took another step backward. Her right knee twinged a protest, but she didn't flinch. "Mr. Porter?"

He blinked. For a second he looked perplexed, but shook it off. "I *mean* you need to dry off. Your teeth are chattering."

Then he trudged past her toward the hearth. At the fire he grabbed an iron poker and started to prod a flame. "Bathroom's that way." He tipped his head to the right, indicating one of two plank and mortar doors, but kept his gaze steady on the fire. "Take the lantern. I have a couple flashlights in the kitchen. I'll have some coffee ready when you come out."

Until Cal Porter mentioned it, Brie didn't realize her teeth really were chattering. And her knee had begun to throb in earnest. She sidled to the table by the door and grabbed the lantern per his instructions. "Thank you, Mister Porter, but if it's all the same, I'll take just a cup of hot water. I prefer herbal tea."

He swung his head around to look back at her. "All I have is leaded coffee. Don't have too many tea parties out here."

Brie smiled as sweetly as she could, given the circumstances, and patted her roll bag. "No problem. I carry my own supply. A cup of hot water will do."

"Fine. Hot water it is."

But he was staring at her again in that odd, half-stunned way that sent shivers down Brie's spine. That's when she heard a trill of feminine amusement. Brie cocked her head.

"What is it?"

Cal Porter's gruff demand broke her concentration. When Brie looked back to the fire, she discovered he'd set down the poker and stood facing her, legs apart.

She stifled a chill that came from inside and listened hard. But all she heard now was the rattle of the wind and rainfall on the windows, the dying rumble of a storm almost spent, and the pop of kindling in the fireplace.

"I thought..." she started to say, then shook her head. "It's ridiculous. I thought I heard a woman's laughter."

Cal Porter's handsome face went suddenly dark as the violent night sky. "You're right. That's ridiculous." He jerked his head once again toward the bathroom before turning back to the fire. "Your hot water will be ready in five minutes. You better move."

Though she didn't want to appear intimidated by the command in his voice, Brie did move, and she moved fast. Once behind the bathroom door she could finally shut out the dark psychic energy rolling off Cal Porter's person.

Now if she could only figure a way to stay locked in the bathroom until she could leave.

Two

"Mr. Daemon, my name is Selene."
Myles stared into her perfect face and the words ran through his mind: "She walks in beauty like the night..."
But the night held danger.

Chapter 1, Murder, My Love—From the Files of
Myles Daemon, P.I.

* * * *

Cal swore under his breath as he dumped the instant coffee out of the mug and back into the jar for the third time. Some of the granules escaped and ricocheted to the floor. Later, when he could see by more than the two flashlights on the counter, he'd take care of the gritty mess. Now, with that woman in sight just beyond the kitchenette, it was all he could do to keep a steady hand or a straight count of scoops.

Okay, Cal admitted he was unnerved. A car careens down the hillside in a toad-strangler storm and almost lands in the rain-swollen Milagro Creek. That much had happened so often in the seven years he'd lived in the cabin that county officials put warning signs every thirty feet amid the cactus and sagebrush along the road's ill defined and badly maintained shoulder. But what were the odds that this particular careless driver would bear a striking likeness to a woman who existed only in Cal's imagination?

He lifted his gaze just enough to peek at Brienne Quaid. No, reality hadn't shifted in the past five minutes. As she sat in the horsehair upholstered chair in front of the fire, Miss L.A. Lost still looked like the doppelgänger of Selene, the *femme fatale* he'd created to complicate the life of his fictional detective, Myles Daemon. If Cal were less certain of his sanity, he'd chalk up this woman's appearance as a waking dream, formed and executed by a brain in the throes of a month-long writer's block.

But there she sat, her back to him and her gaze fixed on the water filled kettle dangling over the snapping fire. The deep brown hair that had been plastered to her head and face ten minutes ago was now combed and drying into thick, soft waves around her shoulders. Firelight reflected gold off her smooth neck and arms. Her hands, with their long, sensuous fingers, lay nested in her lap, palms up.

She'd changed from her drenched clothes into another flimsy dress. This one was pale yellow and better suited to a walk along the boutique-lined streets of Palm Springs than a trek through arid backcountry. Like the elegant Selene she looked crisp despite the fact that she must have pulled the new clothing from the dark purple roll bag that rested at her feet. And, after her initial skittishness, Miss Quaid now had a self-possessed stillness about her that unnerved him. Sitting straight but relaxed, she didn't seem to breathe, though twice since he had been spying on her she tilted her head a degree, as if listening.

Yes, Miss L.A., with her chicory blue eyes, long legs, and full womanly curves was Selene as he'd first envisioned her in college when he wrote just for kicks and relaxation. How had Cal described Myles's latest dalliance? *She had the face of a farmer's very pretty daughter, and a body suited to please a man on hot, lonely summer afternoons or cold canyon nights. Innocent and temptress.*

This woman, who warmed herself at his fire, even had some of Selene's city-girl sass, though not his fantasy's orange-red manicure, fashion-streaked hair, or dramatic way with makeup. In fact, Miss Quaid didn't seem to wear makeup at all. No need to. Her skin was flawless as if it wasn't exposed much to the outdoors. And jewelry? She wore only a wristband made of worn brown leather clasped with a tarnished silver disk...

What the hell was he doing, comparing a real woman with one he'd created nearly twenty years ago? The resemblance—superficial resemblance at that, he decided—between Brienne Quaid and the fictional Selene was nothing more than coincidence.

"Yeah, coincidence. Plain and simple. Get over it," Cal muttered, and set his attention back to counting scoops. How hard could the chore be? Miss Quaid didn't even want coffee, only hot water for her prissy herbal tea.

Cal smirked to himself. Selene liked coffee, spoon-melting black and caffeine charged.

Somehow, that knowledge steadied him. Cal finished the task, grabbed the mug handles in one hand and made for the fireplace.

Miss Quaid started as he came up behind her. She looked

up at him with those wide blue eyes that were so familiar, and Cal almost missed a step on his way to the kettle over the fire.

"Didn't mean to make you jump," he muttered, and concentrated on this new task of pouring the heated water into the mugs. "I figured you'd hear me walk up from behind you."

"I...I guess I just tuned out for a moment," she answered.

Her voice was low and even, but breathy. Cal glanced sideways and caught her massaging her right knee. The movement pulled the flimsy yellow material across her thighs. For one stark second Cal recalled how the earlier rain-soaked dress had molded to her body, outlining a great looking pair of legs.

But there had been enough distractions for one evening, and Cal needed and wanted the female sort of distraction even less than Myles Daemon. He clung to his pique at being forced to play rescuer-protector, and shoved the mug of hot water at Miss Quaid. Then he backed away and sank into a worn plaid couch across from her. "Thought you might be hearing more voices. Does that happen often?"

She stiffened and cast him a quick, quelling Selene-like glare that made him catch a breath.

He shrugged with a nonchalance he didn't feel. "Okay, let's try again. So, what the hell are you doing driving around the backcountry on a night when even the frogs duck and cover?"

She shifted on the edge of the chair and reached into her luggage to pull out a tea bag. Cal noticed her hand trembled slightly, but there was no gooseflesh rising on her slender arms. Obviously she was more on edge than she let on and was trying hard to cover it. "I'm going to visit my aunt in New Mexico."

He nodded at her bag. "Short trip?"

"I don't know...that is, I wasn't sure. I packed in a hurry."

"Family emergency?"

She avoided his eyes. "Yes, you could say that."

She looked a little more ruffled. Whatever the case Miss L.A. didn't want to be here in front of his fire sipping tea. Cal sensed loud and clear she wanted to be off and running to her aunt in New Mexico. Or maybe she was running from something. Yet she didn't look the part of someone on the run. He'd learned to spot the type during his years as an officer of the California court system. Of course, people ran from lots of things, not just the law. How well he knew that, too.

"Need sugar for the tea?" he asked in a begrudging

monotone.

She shook her head, and set about steeping the herbal brew. "I've been enough trouble to you this evening, Mr. Porter."

"The evening's still young," he grumped.

She arched one perfect winged brow in a way that would have made Selene smile with approval and Myles steam. "Meaning?"

Though he didn't need the extra jolt to his zinging nerves, Cal took a long swallow of hot coffee before answering. "Meaning when a storm shuts off the power like this at night I'm usually down for the count until noon the next day."

When her brow rose higher, Cal forced a nonchalant shrug. "I'm too isolated for the utilities to give me priority service. Even if the power comes back on in the next five minutes you couldn't get service on your car tonight. The nearest garage closes at six."

She looked up at him through long, dark, Selene-like lashes. "I'm stuck here until tomorrow?"

He bristled at the shock and displeasure in her voice. "Or you could say *I'm* stuck with *you.* Fact is, I get my best work done at night and I like my privacy. You've made both impossible."

Miss Quaid held his glare. "I am sorry, Mr. Porter. Believe me, I don't like this situation any better than you do."

Cal wondered why she didn't appear the slightest bit intimidated. Maybe after years of absence from the courtroom he'd lost the "prosecutor's" voice and demeanor that often made other lawyers jump at cutting deals rather than face him at trial. He took a deep breath and spoke from the diaphragm. "Yeah, well, kinda makes you wish you'd paid more attention to the warning signs, huh?"

Her blue eyes went icy. "I have no excuse except my own inattention. I've already said I'm sorry, and I'm grateful for the shelter. Considering I'm costing you a night's work, I'll be happy to pay for food and accommodations."

More of that Selene-like sass. "Pay for what?" He snorted. "A cup of hot water, and the three-day-old bagel you'll get for breakfast? Forget it. Besides, I don't take major credit cards."

She didn't miss a beat. "I have cash."

Why did this woman's stubbornness irritate him? Maybe he'd lived alone too long and was used to the quiet. "Fine. Leave a tip on the kitchen counter tomorrow before you leave. We'll be square. By the way, do you think it's smart to tell a stranger you're carrying cash?"

Now she seemed to look not at him but through him. "Despite your lack of social graces I know you won't harm me. You're safe."

Cal nearly laughed. "Sure. Safe. That's what every man wants to hear about himself."

She sighed. "Nevertheless, it's true. I know."

"You know," he echoed. "You know the work I do at night isn't animal poaching or serial killing."

"Of course it isn't." She scanned the animal heads mounted on the walls. "These poor creatures weren't victims of your trophy obsession."

Her sudden confidence made Cal wonder if she recognized him from the days of saturation news coverage eight years ago. His defenses went up. "That so? Some kind of urban sixth sense?"

Now she looked away to the fire and once again started massaging that right knee. The cheek she'd turned to him in profile flooded scarlet. "For one thing, those heads all look older than you. For another, well, I'm...I'm quite intuitive. I can read people easily." She sighed deeply. "My aunt tells me I have a gift, though I've always had my doubts about that."

Cal leaned forward. "Are you telling me you can read people's minds, like some carnival fortuneteller?"

That brought her face forward. "I'm not a fortuneteller, Mr. Porter. I'm...intuitive," she repeated, though less surely. "I pick up strong impressions about people. But I do 'know' things, whether or not I want to." She fixed him with that beguiling, blue-eyed gaze. "Like I know you won't hurt me."

Her certainty made him twitchy. Didn't conventional wisdom teach women to have a natural fear of strange men, no matter how benign they appeared? And he certainly didn't appear benign with his height and weight advantage, not to mention a two-day growth of dark beard, and scruffy clothing.

Cal sank back into the couch. "Maybe you're just good at reading expressions and body language."

She let out a breath. "Yes, I'm sure that's part of it."

For a moment, Brienne Quaid looked truly lost and so alone Cal had to resist the urge to get up and go to her. He didn't like the strange tug this woman's mere presence had on his rusty protective instincts, so once again he went on the offensive.

"Great. You trust me without proof. That works, considering there are no guest room doors to lock yourself behind tonight." He thumped the cushion next to him. "This is your crash pad." He pointed upward. "My bed and workstation is in the loft. No one goes up there but me."

She nodded absently and let her gaze trail up the frame stairs to his private sanctum. "Guess that proves me right. It would be pretty hard to poach game or mass murder from a workstation. But just to put my mind at ease, how do you spend your evenings?"

That settled the question of whether or not she recognized him. Cal took a moment to stir his cooling, bitter instant coffee. "I'm a writer," he finally said.

She cocked a brow and nodded. "And you create best in isolation, and generally at night in your private loft. It all fits now. Have you had any success?"

"Some," he admitted laconically. "I write detective stories that blend mystery and true crime."

"I seldom read mysteries. I always figure out the endings halfway through the book."

"Because of that intuition thing, huh?"

A muscle in her jaw twitched. His questioning was getting under her skin. Though Cal hadn't intended it, he'd allowed the dead and buried prosecutor to rise from the grave.

Finally, she looked over at him, her face placid, though the serenity had come hard. "No, doubt."

And who was he to dispute her claim? While Cal had been a crack lawyer who could ferret out legal weaknesses in the opposition, he'd never been good at "reading" people outside the courtroom. That went double for female people. A change of subject was in order.

"So, Miss Quaid, what is it you do up in the big city?"

"I'm an interior designer."

"Bet business is good in La-La Land."

"Steady," she allowed. "Because I have a natural intuitiveness about people and places I can custom design functional as well as visually pleasing environments suited to the individual. I can create and be useful at the same time."

"The hope of every true artist."

"If you will. Isn't that why you write?"

Why did he write? The answers banged around inside Cal's head. *To fill my life with people who won't betray and desert me at the end of the day. To have an excuse to be alone. To hold on to my sanity while I wait. And wait. And wait...*

Cal merely lifted a shoulder. "To make ends meet until I'm forced to go out and get a day job."

Brienne Quaid tilted up her chin. Her cornflower blue eyes spoke eloquently of her disbelief. "Of course you do."

Intuitive or not, Cal wasn't sure he liked the way this woman seemed to have his number. He waved his arm in a circle. "This room must be an interior decorator's worst nightmare."

She clutched the mug in both hands as if trying to draw warmth from it. "Trust me, there are worse nightmares."

For an instant, Brie Quaid's soft features twisted with the same horror he'd seen as she had knelt on the creek bank and watched the flash flood surge by her. Horror. Utter horror, as if she were peering into the pit of watery hell.

"But whatever suits your needs, Mr. Porter," she went on. "Still, you don't strike me as a person who would actively choose the company of dead animals."

"Maybe you aren't as intuitive as you think."

"And I'm guessing you aren't as forthright as you could be. If you're trying to unnerve me, it won't work."

Despite the snap of their conversation she insisted on the truth. Cal took a swig of the almost cold coffee, winced, and shrugged. "I'm impressed, Miss Quaid. You nailed it again. I'm just a long-term temporary squatter in this taxidermy warehouse. My sister and her husband own the land we're on. They run a dude ranch further down the canyon. This cabin is the site of the original owner's homestead. It used to be a vacation home." Cal went icy inside. "But that was a long time ago."

"Well, I can see why you write upstairs," Miss Quaid commented. "I certainly couldn't concentrate with all these glassy eyes staring down at me. But neither is it wise to have your sleeping quarters mixed in with your workstation."

"Interior Decorating 101?"

"Basic tenant of *feng shui*. I'm studying the concepts with a master of the art. It's helping me with my designs."

Mystical bunk, Cal thought. But he'd already tried to keep his distance with smartass quips that only backfired. "I think I've heard of the concept."

Miss Quaid peered at him as if she could sense his skepticism. "I'm always amazed at how application of *feng shui* principles transforms living space. Flow of *chi* or energy around and through a home affects the way people inside live and interact. And I always advise against working in the bedroom."

Cal smirked. "Depends on what you work at."

She went bright pink, something Selene would never do. No way. Uh-uh. Then she flashed him a very pretty, if wobbly, smile. "Well, of course, I meant your writing."

She was good at looping around a double entendre, even if she couldn't control her blush reflex. Yes, Miss L.A. had some basic street smarts underneath that innocent façade.

Cal shrugged to disguise the fact that he found her the slightest bit interesting. "I've managed to crank out three books and am contracted for a fourth. Since the energy seems to be flowing okay I'll stick to the old scenery." Why should he mention the stubborn writer's block that had seized him by the throat and gave no sign of releasing him?

"As I said, whatever suits your needs."

Left unsaid was that the cabin wouldn't suit her needs. In fact, she looked distinctly uncomfortable.

"Sorry about the dead animal energies floating around, Miss Quaid. You'll only have to suck it up for one night."

She shook her head and hugged herself. "It isn't the animal energies that..." She wet her lips. "Never mind."

Cal came forward again on the cushion. "No, go ahead," he prodded. "Tell me what 'energies' you detect with that acute intuition of yours."

"I don't think that's wise."

He opened his hands. "Since I think this is all a crock anyway, consider it something to amuse the innkeeper."

Anger flared in her blue eyes, but quickly morphed into something approaching worry. She paused, and bit her lower lip as if weighing her next words. "Very well. I...I think it's been a long time since this cabin has heard laughter or housed joy. I feel restless, unrequited energies here that have nothing to do with these poor creatures. But I..." She narrowed her eyes and shook her head. "There's something else. A lighter energy that winks on and off. It feels, well, feminine."

"Bullshit!"

Cal didn't realize he'd sprung from the couch until he found himself staring down into Miss Quaid's startled blue eyes. Coffee sloshed from his cup onto the braided hearth rug. His fists were both clenched so tight his knuckles hurt. And in the middle of his chest was an ache so deep and sharp he could barely draw breath.

"Mr. Porter?" Selene—no Brienne Quaid—called up to him.

Cal sucked back air and forced his shoulders to relax. It did nothing to relieve the pain near his heart. "It's bullshit, Miss Quaid. Your interior design magic and mysticism, or whatever it really is. Sorry I asked."

Cal couldn't look into her face any longer. He tossed the remains of his coffee into the fire but didn't turn back to her. "Don't mean to be a rude innkeeper, but this isn't the Hilton. There are blankets in the closet over there." He jerked his head toward the door next to the bathroom. "I'm going upstairs to try and salvage some night's work."

"In the dark?"

"I have a battery lantern. I can write longhand."

"Of course. Thank you for the hot water. And the night's lodging."

She was probably glad to get rid of him.

He dared a sideways glance at her. "If you need anything help yourself."

"I will. Thanks again."

Cal turned and stalked to the kitchenette to retrieve a battery lantern. Then he made his way to the stairway. Three steps up he halted to look over at Miss Quaid. She'd resumed her unnerving stillness and didn't seem to notice anything but the snapping flames of the hearth fire. Even his outburst didn't seem to give her pause, though his own heart still beat double-time.

Cal stomped up the remaining stairs, set the lantern on his desk, and dropped heavily into the workstation chair. A darkened computer screen stared back at him. Work? Who was he kidding? Tonight would be like every other night in the past few weeks. Selene would elude his efforts to place her on the page. Myles would speak nothing but sarcastic clichés that sounded less witty than pathetic. The plot would stall in the middle of chapter ten. And if e-mail had been accessible he'd find another one-sentence message from his agent reminding him a first draft of this new book was due in six weeks.

Outside the storm had subsided. It blew out as fast as it blew in, but not before it stirred up a whole lot of distraction and trouble for Cal.

But the storm in his heart was just starting to brew.

Three

Selene Carter peered at him with the bleak steadiness of someone who had faced down hell and survived. "The police tell me you stayed at my brother's side while he was dying, Mr. Daemon."

Gut feeling told Myles trouble had just walked in the front door on two gorgeous legs. "Your brother was my client, Ms. Carter. Situational compassion is part of the service. Besides, he paid me through the end of the month."

Her brow twitched. "Good. Since you're still on retainer, I want you to help me find his killer."

In the back of his mind Myles heard his deadbeat father's words ring loud and clear: "My boy, always remember no good deed goes unpunished."

Chapter 1, *Murder, My Love—From the Files of Myles Daemon, P.I.*

* * * *

She couldn't breathe. A terrible weight pressed down on her chest as her body whiplashed side-to-side. Her head spun, as if she cartwheeled through the air. But she was enclosed. Enclosed in a death trap with water rushing in on all sides. Behind her a woman screamed...

Help me! Callan, please help me! I'm here!

Brie gasped and listened to the hammer of her heart. Behind her closed eyes she sensed the brilliant sunlight. Despair enveloped her for a moment. The dream had come to her again, as it did every time she had put head on a pillow for the past four weeks. Only this time it allowed her to sleep until morning. On the other hand, this time she was more than a horrified observer. She felt what the victim felt. She had called out a name in her mind. Callan?

The jostling from her dream resumed, not as hard but just as persistent.

"Hey. Wake up."

Cal Porter's voice came from above. The fragrance of soap and a more unfamiliar scent of man teased her nose. Slowly, Brie opened her eyes. The first thing she saw was the deer head lording over the hearth. With a groan she tried to close her eyes again.

"Wake up." Porter poked her arm again.

"Huh?"

The single syllable came out a croak. Brie rubbed her gritty eyes with her palms. When she could finally focus her eyes, she saw that Cal Porter was staring down at her, his eyes narrowed and his mouth turned down into a deadly serious frown.

"Why did you call me..." He blinked once, and seemed to brace himself. "You called me 'Callan.'"

She blinked hard three times to better focus. "I did?"

"Yeah, you did," he snapped back. "How did you know that was my given name? Why didn't you say 'Calhoun, or Calvin? Why Callan?"

"I didn't know," she answered. "I...I don't know why I said it. I think I might have been asleep."

His chin went up. "Well, don't use it again. It's just Cal. Got it?"

The searing pain and sadness she felt last night enveloped him again. "No, of course not, Mr. Porter. If that's what you prefer."

"It is," he snapped again, then stood tall. "The power's back on. Phone's working, too. There's hot water on the stove for tea. The bagel's in the cupboard over the stove. I called the garage. A service truck will be here in fifteen minutes. Good thing you're still dressed. Once the car's jumped you can be on your way."

Struggling to make sense of the terse monologue, she turned her head. But he already had his back to her and was headed for the door.

"I'll wait for the service truck outside." He raised his arm halfway before slamming the door behind him.

Brie supposed that was the abrupt counterpart gesture to his less than hospitable wake-up call.

One more hour's slumber would have been wonderful. She didn't remember falling asleep on the ratty couch in front of the hearth. She did remember feeling warm and comfortable under the blanket from the storage closet and deciding to enjoy a moment of drowsy relaxation instead of changing into a sweat suit. Brie figured her dress was now probably creased way beyond the help of the average household iron.

It didn't matter. Considering his borderline rudeness Porter obviously wanted her gone. She had no problem with that. The sooner she got up the faster she could be off his list of life's irritations, on her way out of this desolate canyon, and back on the road to Aunt Sophie. Reluctantly, she rolled to her side and swung her legs over the edge of the cushion.

"Ahhhh!"

Pain spiked in all directions from her right knee and stole her breath. In the throes of familiar agony, Brie recalled ruefully that she had intended to ice the joint last night before falling asleep. Laziness had its price this morning. Her leg felt frozen at a ninety-degree angle. She knew from experience that even gentle flexing would be excruciating.

Gingerly, she laid her hand on the knee. Even through the dress material Brie felt the heat of inflammation and could see the joint had swollen to nearly double its size. The last time she aggravated the old injury she'd spent a week propped in the comfy chair in her living room. Driving was an exercise in forbearance for nearly two weeks after that...

Driving! How was she going to get out of here with a knee that might not flex enough to work the accelerator and brakes? She had to find a way around this.

Clenching her teeth, she edged her right foot forward. The rip of pain brought tears to her eyes. She covered her face with her hands and tried to stanch her frustration.

This wasn't happening! She had to get to Sophie. She had to find some respite from this ugly dream that was stealing her life.

Suddenly a door slammed open. "Cal?" A woman shouted from the direction of the kitchenette. Brie hadn't even known there was another entrance to the cabin besides the one in front. "Cal Porter, get your sorry butt out of bed and make me some coffee. I'm *not* in a good mood today!"

What now? Did Porter have a drop-in girlfriend? If that was the case, Brie sincerely hoped the woman was less judgmental than her beau.

Brie wiped away a smattering of tears with the back of her hand. In reflex she started to rise from the couch. Pain brought her back down in a hurry and turned her reply into a whimper.

Boot heels pounded on the kitchenette floor, announcing the appearance of a woman who stood almost tall enough to look Cal Porter straight in the eye. She stopped at the loft stairway, set one booted foot on the bottom step, and grasped the rail with her gloved left hand. Expelling a hard sigh, the woman tilted back her wide-brimmed straw hat. Wisps of short, thick hair the color of brown sugar stuck out from beneath the hat. A few strands brushed the collar of her long-sleeved white chambray shirt.

"Cal, do you hear me?" the woman shouted, loud enough that Brie felt certain Porter would be able to hear outside. "Good grief, if I slept the day away like this..." She shook her head, and in doing so turned just enough to spot Brie. "Whoa, what have we here?"

Brie braced her weight on her left arm as she turned in place on the cushion. "Mr. Porter's outside, across the creek, seeing to my car," she rasped out. "I...I got stranded here last night in the storm, and the service truck didn't get here until just now, so I slept on the couch. I can assure you I'll be gone just as soon..."

The woman pushed away from the step, turned toward the couch, and held out her hands, palms up. "Hold on there, Miss. I'm picking up about every third word of that babble. Slow down to a gallop, okay?"

Brie choked back the rest of the wobbly words and nodded quickly. To her surprise, the woman smiled as she dropped her arms to her sides, ambled toward the couch, and gentled her voice. "Sorry if I startled you coming in the back door like that. I take a trail up from the valley around the other side of the hill that ends behind the house, so I can't see up the canyon. I tie my horse by the shed while I'm in here harassing Cal."

Again, Brie nodded, as if she understood what was happening. Obviously this woman knew Porter well enough to barge through his back door without so much as knocking. Yet, she didn't seem threatened by the presence of another woman in the cabin. In fact, Brie had the distinct impression there was a glint of amusement in the woman's eyes.

The woman came to the edge of the couch and peered down at Brie as she started to remove her riding gloves. "I'm Elaina Sutter." She extended her hand.

Brie wet dry lips. "Brienne Quaid." She stretched to shake hands, but winced and jerked upright. "I'm having some trouble with my knee this morning. I fell last night on the creek bank."

Elaina Sutter frowned and tilted back her hat a bit more. "You were out on the creek bank in the storm?"

"Long story involving a wrong turn off the highway and a

dead battery. Mr. Porter was kind enough to put me up for the night, but as soon as my car's back in shape I'm leaving."

"You think?" Ms. Sutter pointed at Brie's leg. "Looks like you've got a small melon under that skirt, young lady. Better get some ice on it before it locks up."

Brie lifted the hem of her skirt to expose her right knee. "I've seen it worse." That was probably stretching the truth, but she had to think positively. "Maybe I could just take some aspirin and the swelling will go down. I appreciate your concern though, Miss Sutter."

"Call me Lain," the woman said, as she removed her hat and set it and her riding gloves on the back of the couch. Then she came around it and stood in front of Brie, studying the swollen joint. "Did Cal leave you high and dry like this?"

"Oh, no," Brie rushed to say. "He just woke me up and flew out the door."

Lain raised a brow.

"That is, he's outside waiting for the service truck."

"He couldn't wait in here? Jeez, he didn't even get you breakfast?"

"He offered me a bagel." Why did Brie find herself defending someone who had been so eager to get her out of his space?

Lain sniffed. "Yeah, well don't eat 'em. Those bagels date from the last time he was in New York City three months ago."

New York? Cal Porter didn't seem like the kind of man who would vacation in the Big Apple. "I'm...I'm sure he stored them in the freezer until now."

"Don't bet on it. Sometimes I wonder how that kid stays healthy."

"Kid? Mr. Porter?"

Lain Sutter got down on her haunches for a closer look at the swelling. She cocked her head, but didn't touch the area. "Yeah, he hates it when I call him that, but it's a big sister's privilege."

"Sister?" Brie must have sounded relieved, because Lain Sutter glanced up at her with that amusement in her eyes. Green eyes, Brie noted, just like her brother's. "I thought...that is when you came in and started up the stairs..."

"You thought Cal had a honey," Lain finished, and snorted. "That's what I thought when I saw you bright as a buttercup on this old couch." She sighed hard. "At least, I was hoping."

An odd comment coming from a sister who seemed gruffly protective of her brother. But now it all fit. Porter had told Brie his sister and her husband owned this land and worked a dude ranch. Lain Sutter had every right to come flying through the window or sliding down the chimney if she chose.

Porter's sister stood with an agility Brie envied at the moment. "You sure as hell aren't going anywhere for at least a couple days, Brie," she announced as if she were an old friend, not a brand new acquaintance. "Even then you'll be lucky to walk without help, much less drive a car."

"But I can't stay here," Brie insisted. "I have to get to my aunt in New Mexico."

Brie made the last half of her plea to Lain Sutter's back as the woman marched to the kitchenette and started banging around in the cupboards. "Well, call your aunt and tell her you'll be a little late." She looked over at Brie. "And don't reverse the charges. Cal can afford it."

Before Brie could counter the suggestion, the front door banged open and Porter charged in. Brie wondered if making loud entrances was an inherited family trait.

He looked almost happy as he hurried to the couch. "Car's running, Miss Quaid. I'll help you with your bag."

He must have seen Brie shift her gaze to the kitchenette at his back and stopped dead in his tracks. Before he could react Lain slammed a cupboard door shut and waited for her brother to spin in place.

"Lain! What are you doing here?"

Cal's sister stood, right hand on hip, while she waved at him with a plastic bag she'd retrieved from the cupboard. "I came by to make sure this old wreck of a cabin didn't fall down around your ears in the storm last night." She stalked to the small, battered refrigerator and tore open the freezer. "But now I'm trying to prove to Brie over there that all our kin aren't inhospitable jackasses."

Lain jammed her hand into the ice bin and scooped out several cubes which she stuffed into the plastic bag. "You're pitiful, Cal. Just plain pitiful. You've been out here alone way too long." She repeated the process, only this time louder. "That poor girl hasn't even had breakfast, and you're ready to herd her out the door."

Porter glanced at Brie, then back at his sister. "She can get something to eat on the road. She's in a hurry to get to New

Mexico."

"Yeah, well," Lain accused as she swung the makeshift ice pack at him, "if you weren't in such a damned big hurry to get back to your self-indulgent isolation you'd have noticed she's got a knee swollen so bad she can't move off the couch."

"What?"

Porter watched speechlessly as Lain marched back to Brie and knelt down in front of her. With a gentle touch that belied the implied strength of her large hands, Lain applied the ice pack to the inflamed joint.

Unable to help herself, Brie gasped but nodded her thanks and let Lain transfer the pack to her care. Then Lain stood again and faced her slightly taller brother, matching his implacable stance while mirroring his scowl.

"She didn't say anything about her knee," Porter defended himself.

"Did you bother to ask if she hurt herself while she was crawling around on the bank?" Lain fired back.

"No. She looked fine."

"And you made her sleep on that lumpy couch? No wonder she's crimped up this morning."

"*I* should have slept on the couch?"

"If you were half the gentleman you used to be..."

Brie shut her eyes as their battle raged on above her. This wasn't happening! If her gift of "knowing" was so great, why hadn't she foreseen the past horrific twelve hours?

"Stop!"

The immediate silence made Brie realize that she'd done more than just wish the angry command. Lain, hands still on her lean hips, peered down at her in semi-shock. Porter glowered, but not in real anger, Brie realized with a start. The dark expression masked...fear?

Convinced that pain, hunger, and exhaustion had clouded her sensitivities, Brie held Porter's glare to nearly a count of ten. The roiling, gray aura of fear didn't dissipate. He *was* afraid. Perhaps that Brie really would impose longer on his privacy. Or, as Lain insisted, his isolation.

"Well, you're not quite as fragile as you look, are you, Buttercup?"

Lain's soft-spoken comment snagged Brie's attention away from the seriously aggrieved Cal Porter. Though she understood Lain was just calling the situation as she saw it, Brie took umbrage at her judgment.

"I'm hardly fragile," Brie ground out. "I've dealt with this bad knee for over half my life, and I'll deal with it now."

She shifted her gaze back to Porter. "I have no intention of staying here any longer than I absolutely have to. Maybe I can't drive all the way to New Mexico, but at least I can try to get back to Los Angeles. If you can spare half an hour more out of the morning I'm sure that will give me enough time to walk around and limber up before I leave."

"Not gonna happen," Lain warned.

Porter said nothing, yet Brie fixed her own glare on him as she dropped the makeshift ice pack on the couch. "Watch me."

Shifting her weight to the left side Brie managed to push off the cushion and slowly stand. The right knee protested with new shafts of sharp pain. Her left leg, which had to take the unbalanced weight of her body, groaned with its own morning stiffness. Sweat broke out on her forehead. Yet, she made it upright. True, she had to throw out her arms to the side to maintain her equilibrium, but she was off the couch.

Lain crossed her arms and smiled wryly. "You got grit, Buttercup, I'll hand you that. But don't let pride make you stupid."

With a deep breath, Brie managed to stand a little straighter and shift her right foot forward without causing too much of a spasm further up her leg. The minor success gave her confidence. "I'm not being proud or stupid. I'm just being practical. Your brother wants me gone, and I mean to oblige him."

"Hey, wait a minute," Porter piped up. His expression was now one of impatient concern as he watched Brie inch forward with her right leg. "Maybe Lain's right. You shouldn't push it. Maybe you can't stay here..."

Lain shot him a poisonous glare.

"Well, hell," he defended himself, "she can't sleep on the couch. You said so yourself. And how would she get up those stairs?"

"I'll send over one of our rollaway beds," Lain countered.

"How about you just find Miss Quaid a room at the ranch?" Porter argued.

"She needs quiet and space to get that knee working again. She'd get neither at the ranch. You know we're overbooked for the next two weeks, Cal. Or you would know that if you'd bother to stick your finger in the air once in a while and test the wind direction."

"Don't start, Lain."

The bickering was almost comical, but Brie didn't have time to be the focus of a sibling spat. "Hey, do either of you notice I'm doing okay over here?"

She got their attention. With both pairs of eyes on her, she smiled sweetly. "I'll be okay..."

And that's when Brie's right knee buckled. Woozy from pain she lost her bearings and started to pitch forward.

There was a blur of black, a rush of air, and Brie's body thudded against the solid wall of Cal Porter's chest. With two strong arms he braced her weight and then lifted her off the wooden floor. Her head spinning with pain, Brie clutched at his shoulders and laid her face against his neck. His skin was warm and smelled of sun-filled fresh air. The wiry dark beard on his chin chaffed her forehead, an abrasion that sent unexpected tingles radiating out to every part of her body.

He handled her with the same surprising gentleness she'd felt in Lain. But Porter's hold surrounded her with something more. She felt safe in his grasp, as if she knew this man would never let her come to harm. And for a blink of time she sensed he let down his guard. The anger and sadness that seemed embedded in his presence cleared, as if the sun had punched through a bank of thunderheads.

More amazing still, Brie found herself snuggled in a pocket of rare contentment, her soul cushioned in spiritual down ticking. For one miraculous moment Brie's heart was no longer seized with the images of horrific nightmares that had begun to invade her days. She felt light, aware, awake.

And when Cal Porter swung around and lowered her to the couch, Brie clung to his neck, unwilling to let go of the bliss.

Then she opened her eyes and found him staring at her. His eyes were wide, and his expression confused, almost troubled. But neither did he back away nor let her go, though he knelt on the hard floor and had placed her on the cushion. He felt something pass between them, too. Brie saw it in his gaze, felt the draw of his powerful psyche.

Lain cleared her throat and the link between them severed. Warmth shot through Brie, a potent combination of raw sensual energy and embarrassment. She pulled her arms inward, as if shielding herself. Porter practically jumped up and took two steps back, as if he'd been singed.

"Like I said," Lain muttered, "I'll have one of the hands bring over the roll away bed and some food."

Cal Porter's gaze jumped to his sister. For a moment Brie feared there might be bloodshed.

Lain only laughed, a guffaw as mellow as her speech, and she shifted her amused gaze from her brother to Brie. "I'll throw in a pair of crutches I saved from when I sprained my ankle, 'cause you better stay off that knee for a couple of days, Buttercup. Course, with the kid over there so able to carry you around that shouldn't be a problem."

Cal looked ready to charge his sister and flatten her.

Lain Sutter seemed completely unconcerned, and she held out her hand again to Brie. "Nice to meet you. I'll be back in a couple of days. Take care." She leaned closer to stage whisper. "And remember, don't eat the bagels."

Without bidding her brother a similarly gracious farewell, Lain turned on her boot heel and ambled out the back door.

A thick silence fell over the cabin. Brie gave Cal Porter a sideways glance and found him staring after his departed sister. A jaw muscle jumped double-time.

Brie picked up the ice filled plastic bag from the cushion next to her and laid it back on her knee. "Mr. Porter, I really think I could leave..."

"Forget it." His growl cut her off. Once again his expression was dark and forbidding, but he didn't look at Brie. He kept his eyes locked on the back door. He'd closed off the part of his soul Brie had glimpsed for just a moment. "Lain's right. You can't drive with your knee swollen like that. I'll bring your car up closer to the house."

He started to walk to the front door. "You better call your aunt. Don't worry about the charges."

Brie opened her mouth to acknowledge Lain had already told her as much, but decided discretion was in order considering the beating this prickly man's ego had already taken from his sister. "Thanks. That's thoughtful of you to offer."

Porter's hand already strangled the front door knob, but he halted. In that moment, his shoulders relaxed, he gave a quick impersonal nod, then let himself out and yanked the door closed behind him.

The cabin was quiet again. Brie glanced up into the glassy eyes of the dead deer over the fireplace. It was true. Misery loved company.

Four

Myles looked into her eyes. Deep blue eyes full of sadness and knowing and secrets. His secrets as well as hers. Lost in those eyes, he couldn't look away. Didn't want to look away...
Chapter 3—*Murder, My Love—From the Files of Myles Daemon, P.I.*

* * * *

"Do you need more tea? I could send a package overnight. What about a poultice? That always helped bring the swelling down in the past."

Clutching the handset of the portable phone Brie held back tears. Aunt Sophie's soothing, weathered voice caressed her soul, but it did little to stop the impatient flutter of her heart. "I still have plenty of tea with me, thanks. That, along with the ice packs, should bring the swelling down in a couple of days. At least I'm hoping."

Banging from the kitchenette interrupted her. For the past ten minutes she'd been on the phone to her aunt, and Cal Porter had been putting away the groceries Lain sent over along with the bed and crutches. Annoyance with her invasion of his privacy rolled off the man like a thick coastal fog in winter. He'd served her a breakfast of juice, toast, and canned peaches in efficient but sullen silence, and then he'd gone upstairs to eat by himself. Brie got the point, loud and clear. She didn't need sound effects for emphasis.

Glancing at the remains of the meager, lonely meal still sitting on the scarred pine coffee table Brie clutched the phone tighter and lowered her voice. "What I need is to be with you! Instead, I'm stuck in this gloomy cabin out here in wild west hell with an insufferable man who wants me gone as much as I want to be gone."

Sophie drew a deep breath and expelled it slowly. "You are where you need to be. Remember, Little Moon Child, there are no coincidences in life, only moments of opportunity bestowed by a generous Universe."

Sometimes Sophie sounded like an overoptimistic New Age guru. But Brie knew better than to blow off her aunt's placid platitudes, as she once had in her adolescence. Sophie didn't have the "gift of knowing" that had never been anything but a burden to Brie, but her aunt was always amazingly on target with advice. "Does the Universe have any kind of opportunity exchange policy?" she quipped half seriously.

Something thudded on the kitchen floor. Cal Porter muttered what sounded suspiciously like an expletive.

Unaware of the background noise Sophie chuckled. "No returns or refunds. You have to make do. Besides, you know the official cosmic rule. You get what you ask for."

"I'm pretty sure I didn't ask to wreck my knee again. Or be stranded with Prince Uncharming."

Whose keen gaze and deep sadness draws me in. Whose embrace makes me feel safer than I've ever felt in my life.

Brie cleared her thoughts with a mental shake. "This isn't cosmic delivery day, Sophie. It's more like a nasty cosmic prank."

"Don't be so sure."

There was no arguing with Sophie, but Brie had to try one more time. "I didn't ask for the dreams."

For a moment her usually glib aunt fell silent. "They still disturb you?"

"They're getting stronger. In the last one I was right in the middle of it myself. I was drowning. And I heard..." She swallowed hard at the memory. "A woman. I heard a woman cry out." *And, for some reason, use Cal Porter's given name, whatever that was about.*

Sophie exhaled a long sigh. "Even if I were at your side I couldn't help. You own those dreams, and you'll keep owning them until they play out in real time."

"But I don't want them to play out!" Brie insisted for what had to be the twentieth time. "The visions are horrible. Someone dies. I know it isn't one of my friends, or you. But I can't be sure it isn't me."

You've been given this message for a reason," Sophie answered as if that much should be obvious. "I knew someday the gift would break through all your attempts to control and deny it. This is that day. You have to reconcile the message with reality before the visions will leave you in peace."

Her aunt spoke the truth. Deep in her soul, Brie understood as much. Still, she held her defenses in place. "I won't let this 'gift' as you call it consume me, like it did Mom."

Another one of Sophie's sighs came across the telephone connection clearly. "No, you've swung the opposite direction. You've managed to control the gift and use it at your whim. Nancy never had your discipline."

"It cost her dearly," Brie whispered fiercely. "It cost mom

everything that made life worth living, including her mental balance."

There was a long pause, and then Sophie drew a deep breath. "Are you any less troubled right now, in spite of the tight rein you keep on yourself?"

The answer was obvious and painful.

When Brie said nothing Sophie pressed her point. "Your innate abilities are just as strong as your mother's ever were, but you've suppressed those abilities. Dammed them up. You let them only trickle out whenever you need them in your work. But like water behind a dam your gift has built to a pressure beyond which you can no longer deny or control. For once honor your gift fully, Brie. Let it spill over and carry you away. Or it will crush you with its awful weight."

Like the water tried to crush her in the nightmare.

A chill shot up Brie's spine. "What if the dream is carrying me away to a meeting with my own fate? Believe me, last night when I looked into that flooded creek I felt closer to death than I did sixteen years ago."

Sophie groaned her dismay. "Oh, Brie, my heart hurts for you. But all I can do from this distance is try to give you some assurances. You already know the message isn't meant for anyone in Los Angeles. Or for me. And if the dream was a premonition of your own death, you'd be telling me a far more harrowing tale about last night."

Her aunt seemed so certain. Still, Brie could even now feel the aftershocks of the dream. "I felt the pressure on my chest and the air leaving my lungs," she insisted. "And the woman's cry. Sophie, she was so afraid."

Brie paused and clutched the telephone handset tighter. "I really think I might be losing it," she confided, her voice shaking despite her best efforts to keep it steady. "Last night, when I came into the cabin, I know I heard faint laughter. A woman's laughter. It wasn't like the waking dreams. It was real. At least it sounded real. But there was no one here except Mr. Porter."

Sophie was quiet for a moment. Brie could almost see her aunt's salt-and-pepper eyebrows knit in rumination. "I don't know what all this means," she finally answered, adding weight to the already suffocating heaviness of Brie's frustration. "Just let the future unfold in its own time," she advised. "For some reason you've been given a warning. Or perhaps a sign."

The crunch and crackle of paper grocery bags nearly drowned out Sophie's soft words.

Brie rolled her eyes and tried not to grit her teeth. "I missed the signs, Sophie. That's why I'm sitting on this couch with my leg propped up, in the company of dead animals and the man-who-would-be-a-hermit."

"Dead animals?"

Brie could almost see her Mother Earth vegetarian aunt cringe. "I'll tell you about it when I see you. And with any luck that'll be by the end of the week."

"Don't push yourself," Sophie warned. "From what you've told me that knee took a bad beating. The last time that happened you were laid up for two weeks, practically immobilized."

"That was right after college. Since then I've grown up a little," Brie reminded her. "I'm doing my exercises faithfully, and I haven't so much as strained the joint for almost two years. I'll make a fast recovery."

"Well, whatever the future holds I'll be here," Sophie promised. "And if you decide differently I'll send along more tea and the makings for a poultice."

"Thanks. Oh, by the way, your birthday present landed back on my doorstep just before I left home yesterday. I forgot to put clear tape across the address, and the box must have gotten wet so the writing was smudged. But don't worry. I brought the doll with me, so you'll get your gift late but intact."

"I can't wait to see it." The bright lilt of excitement in Sophie's voice made Brie smile. "From what you describe it's a lovely piece."

"It is," Brie assured her. "I can't tell whether it's meant to be an angel or a fairy. But it's pretty and petite. I suspect if it didn't have that spider web fracture on the left cheek I probably wouldn't have been able to afford it."

"I don't care what it's worth in dollars, Brie. I'm sure it'll be a perfect addition to my collection. In fact, the way you talk about it I'm beginning to think you'd like to keep it for yourself."

Though she chuckled softly at Sophie's chide, Brie did feel a niggling of regret that she had promised the twelve-inch, porcelain-faced doll to her aunt. The pretty but irreparably damaged toy had caught her eye at an upscale resale shop a month ago. Iridescent blue-green wings and a harlequin patterned purple frock had leapt out at her from the midst of much larger and gaudier companions heaped in a haphazard pile. Though the doll's face was damaged, the delicate porcelain hands and slippers were merely scuffed.

Something about the doll's Mona Lisa smile had intrigued

Brie. She thought the expression was far too sophisticated for a child's toy and decided it would be a perfect addition to Sophie's collection. But ten days ago, when she packed the doll for shipment to New Mexico, Brie felt an unexpected pang of loss. Ignoring the stab of emotion, she shipped the gift to her aunt, only to have the box return "undeliverable" minutes before she fled Los Angeles late yesterday afternoon.

Now she carried the doll with her, snuggled safely between the folds of her clothes inside the roll bag. Late or not Sophie would receive her birthday present. And one way or another, Brie knew she'd again feel the sting of loss.

"Now I think you should go and get some rest."

Brie shook herself out of the reverie. "I'll try. I love you. Sophie. See you soon."

"What happens happens, Brie. I'll see you when you get here. And I love you, too, dear."

Brie closed her eyes tight. "Take care. 'Bye."

The line went dead. Brie switched off the portable handset, and laid it on the couch beside her. She took a deep breath and tried to calm herself. A couple of days. That's all she had to endure on this couch, in this cabin, with this rude man...

A cupboard door slammed shut.

Forgetting to be calm, Brie reached around and pulled the set of crutches over the back of the couch. Even though her right knee protested, she hoisted herself up with practiced ease, got her balance, and started to make her way across the room.

* * * *

Cal jerked the refrigerator door open and bent to peer inside the cold depths. Where was he supposed to stash all this food Lain had sent over? He wasn't feeding a football team for a week, just some city-woman who was inattentive enough to make the wrong turn into his life, and only for a couple of days.

Anyway he hoped she'd be gone by Thursday. With a deadline looming and writer's block crushing down, he was distracted enough. He couldn't afford uninvited company that needed waiting on hand and foot, much less someone who called out his given name in her sleep.

The hair on the back of his neck stood up, and gooseflesh rose on his arms. Why had she called him "Callan?" How had she guessed his name out of so many others that would have been a good bet? No one called him that, not anymore. And the only two people who ever did were gone.

Though not forgotten, and still able to make him ache to

the core of his being.

Cal shook his head hard to dispel the old pain and an odd sense of foreboding. Enough of that. Enough of the past. He focused his attention on the butcher-wrapped beef roast in his right hand, all three pounds of the stuff. From the looks of the slender Miss L.A., Cal doubted she would even eat meat, much less half this slab. He tossed the package onto the top shelf next to the gallon of skim milk. He hated skim milk. If Lain wanted him to eat healthy then she better buy him food that at least had some taste and texture.

The sound of a throat being delicately cleared distracted him from finding a place for a big hunk of cheddar cheese he still held in his left hand. "Excuse me, Mr. Porter."

Brienne Quaid had found her way into the kitchen. Maybe the fact that she was up and walking was a good sign.

Cal lifted his head high enough to see over the edge of the refrigerator door. What he saw dashed his hopes. Miss Quaid balanced on the crutches Lain had sent over with the groceries and rollaway bed. Though she looked steady, her eyes were tired and her face was etched with lines that hinted at her pain. He noticed she didn't let her right foot touch the floor, which must have taken strength and will.

Still, he didn't let his grudging admiration show in his voice. "What?"

She hobbled closer. "Could you possibly find a way to bang those cabinets a little louder? I can still hear myself think."

He lifted his head higher at the sass in her voice. "I'm used to living alone," he snapped back.

"You still *are* living alone," she pointed out. "I just happen to be occupying the next room. I don't expect you to be social, but maybe you could manage courteous, especially when I'm talking on the telephone within earshot."

Irritated by her presumptuousness Cal stood tall. But a terse rejoinder stuck in his throat when he gave her a once over. She had bathed and washed her bedraggled hair. The dark strands brushed her shoulders and curled inward at the ends. Despite her weary eyes and pained expression her skin glowed with blushing vitality, emphasizing her long dusky brows and lashes. She tilted her chin as if she were a schoolmarm waiting for a response from a naughty student. If she hadn't been on crutches Cal imagined she might have tapped her toe.

He didn't mean to stare. But once again the woman's preternatural resemblance to his Selene bemused him. More disturbing, a rush of raw attraction in his gut sent heat curling

upward into his chest and neck. Before he let himself begin
blushing, he scowled. "Should you be up and around?"

She exhaled her exasperation. "I doubt my voice would
have carried over the noise."

Too late he tried to hide his amusement. "It's carrying just
fine right now."

Miss Quaid cocked her head. "Right now you aren't
banging cabinet doors and crackling paper bags."

In answer, Cal eased the refrigerator door shut. "True. I
guess living alone has made me forget my manners."

The tilt of her head softened, but her eyes remained wary.
"Is that an apology?"

He shrugged. "Sort of. Guess I've forgotten how to do
that, too."

She sighed. "I really don't mean to be a nuisance. I...I'm
just very tired and eager to be on my way."

The weary blink of her eyes sent a shaft of compassion
and shame through Cal. He had behaved like a boor, all because
this woman had interrupted his week-long self-pity party and
abraded emotional scars with her uncanny good guess about
his name.

Brie Quaid turned awkwardly on the crutches and started
back across the room to the couch. Unwittingly, Cal found
himself admiring the sway of her hips beneath the thin cotton
dress, and the shape of her long, slender legs. Forgetting about
the rest of the groceries, he followed her to the fireplace.

"You get around pretty good on those crutches," he said
when she was almost to the couch.

She looked over her shoulder as if surprised to find him
right behind her. "I've had lots of practice over the years," she
replied, as she expertly set the crutches aside and lowered
herself onto the cushion. "I haven't had problems this bad,
though, for quite a while. I'm more frustrated right now than in
pain."

From the grimace she gave when trying to find a
comfortable position Cal doubted that. He stood across the
breakfast-messy coffee table and peered down at her. "How
did it happen?"

She was silent for a while as she massaged her thigh just
above the injured joint. "I was in a car accident when I was
sixteen."

The terse statement made him wonder if he should probe.
Innate curiosity overrode his concern. "Must have been bad."

She nodded. "It was. I lost both of my parents."

His conscience bucked. He'd been unsocial, no downright rude, to a woman who still carried the physical pain of a terrible loss. But Cal crossed his arms and reminded himself he didn't know of her circumstances until now, and it didn't excuse her inattentiveness that had led her to the creek bank in the first place.

"So, you've been on your own since you were a teenager?" He tried to sound objective, almost clinical. From the way she kept her gaze focused on her leg Cal supposed he succeeded.

"No, my Aunt Sophie in New Mexico raised me," she answered softly. "She's been like a second mother."

There was a sweet yearning in her quiet voice. Cal tightened the fold of his crossed arms to resist its allure. "So, instead of Miss L.A. I should call you Miss New Mexico, huh?"

She looked up with those chicory blue eyes. "My name is Brienne. Why don't you call me Brie?"

She extended her hand along with the verbal olive branch, probably to make the next few days bearable in his company. Even though Cal didn't want familiarity he'd been rude enough for this decade. He did have some sense of social rectitude left.

Slowly, reluctantly, he unfolded his arms. "All right, fine." He stuck out his hand as if they were meeting for the first time and clasped her long fingers. "Call me Cal." Despite the coolness of her skin, heat pooled where his palm touched her palm, and he pulled away fast.

She allowed her mouth to quirk at the right side. "I got that message loud and clear."

"I just never liked the name 'Callan,'" he said, wondering why he felt the need to explain himself. Besides, it was the truth. Mostly.

Brie eased back against the couch. Cal drew his arms back across his chest, but his right hand still tingled from the brief touch. "Is that who you were calling? Your aunt?"

She bit her lip and some of the wariness crept back into her gaze. "Yes, I...Sometimes I just need to connect with her." She chuckled self-consciously. "I suppose it sounds ridiculous for a thirty-two year old woman to be admitting this, but Sophie is my touchstone of reality. She... grounds me when I'm feeling at the end of my rope."

Cal eased himself onto the horsehair lounge chair across from Miss Brienne Quaid. "Is that why you pressed your luck on a rainy night? You're at the end of some rope?"

She looked away to the remains of last night's fire in the

hearth. "Let's just say the end of the rope slipped out of my hands a few days ago. I'm not sure I can find it. Or even if I want to find it."

Though her voice was quiet Cal picked up the desperation hiding inside the terse words. He knew about losing life's moorings—the lonely sense of being adrift in a stormy sea and scared as hell there would never again be a safe, welcoming port. If Lain hadn't come to his rescue seven years ago...

"So rest assured, I have no reason to bother you any longer than it takes for the swelling in my knee to go down."

Cal jerked his attention back to the conversation at hand. "Huh, oh, yeah, okay. You said a couple of days?"

She eyed him with wary curiosity. "I doubt it will be longer than that. I just need enough flexibility in my joint so I can drive safely."

That's all he wanted to hear. Cal spread his hands wide. "Fine. I'll stay out of your way as much as possible. If you want a radio I have a portable in the kitchen. It pulls in only a couple of local stations, but at least you'll have some entertainment. There's a portable TV upstairs, too, but out here it doesn't receive much beyond snow and static."

She lifted one soft brow. "I see we have something in common. We both appreciate peace and quiet."

Again she made her point with targeted words. Just like Selene. Sudden restlessness propelled Cal out of the chair. "Yeah, quiet. Right. Whatever floats your boat."

His curt reply made her blink, but it didn't break her rather stiff reserve. "I have some books and magazines with me. I certainly won't be bored. Thank you, Mister, ah, Cal."

Tucked into the corner of his couch, Brie Quaid looked small, helpless, and fetching, very much like the "Buttercup" nickname Lain bestowed upon her. Yet this woman took guff from no one. That sweet, pretty, and meek exterior hid a gutsiness he couldn't help admiring.

But not too much.

Cal shrugged. "Back to kitchen duty. I'll try to keep the slamming to a minimum."

Brienne Quaid nodded solemnly but gave him a soft smile. "Thanks."

Cal returned to his chores, all too aware of the woman in his parlor. He'd have to work hard at avoiding her for the next two days.

Not exactly the challenge he needed right now.

Five

Was she a witch or an enchantress?

Myles yanked himself away from the brink of the inane musings. Selene Carter was no more witch or enchantress than any other woman he'd ever encountered.

Then she looked up at him with those fey blue eyes.

Was he wrong?

Chapter 4, *Murder, My Love—From the Files of Myles Daemon, P.I.*

* * * *

The arroyo toads took up their nightly ritual mating song— a thousand croaking voices starting and stopping in eerie unison.

An hour ago Cal had been tempted to close the loft window and shut out the familiar racket that he could usually ignore. But even now, well past midnight, the air was stifling, and the small oscillating fan on the floor did nothing but stir the warm, moist air.

He really needed a window air conditioner for nights like this, when monsoon-like weather patterns from the Gulf of Mexico held temperatures and humidity in the arid canyon unusually high after sunset. A "swamp cooler" unit made the downstairs bearable, but the effect didn't reach the loft. So, the screened window stayed wide open to admit a paltry breeze, and the wheeze and chirp of amphibious lust washed into his office-bedroom unabated.

Besides, it wasn't as if the love-starved toads kept him from writing. Had he been suddenly seized by creative insights— which he hadn't been—either of the two e-mail letters he'd just finished reading would have drained him as dry as the canyon in mid-August. The first, from his editor, reminded him again that the deadline for his fourth contracted *Myles Daemon* book loomed. Three weeks ago Cal realized he'd actually gotten used to the knot of anxiety in his gut when he thought about the deadline. He hardly felt it—unless he tried to sit down and write something.

Myles had withheld his stories before. This time, though, the detective took the Fifth in the middle of Chapter Ten, just when the sexual juices between him and the fantasy woman,

Selene, started boiling.

For a brief time, Cal considered removing Selene from the picture. But without her the plot line didn't track. Myles needed this particular *femme fatale* in his life at this moment. Cal just had to convince the cynically intellectual detective, and he was running out of gambits. Even promises to dispatch the sexy, emotionally threatening beauty by story's end hadn't convinced Myles.

But it was the second e-mail, terse and definitive, that completely choked off Cal's creative flow.

Dear Mr. Porter,

We regret to inform you our yearlong investigation into the disappearance of Alicia and Eugenia Porter has yielded nothing to date. In accordance with the terms of our contract, we will suspend further inquiries at the end of the month pending renewal of your contract and receipt of another retainer check. We will send the new contract for your signature by certified mail within the next week. Please return the contract and your payment in the amount of...

In the amount of money Cal could no longer afford after similar contracts with three different investigative agencies. And still not so much as a clue about what had happened to Alicia and Jeanie.

Cal's eyes burned. Thinking he had stared too long at the computer screen, he blinked. Then he felt the wetness behind his lids and realized that after so long the hopeless helplessness could still rip at his insides. Where had Alicia gone that night? Where had she taken Jeanie? And why? Had he really been such an awful husband and father?

The old memories, sodden with guilt and regret, threatened to drown Cal. With practiced mental gymnastics, he jammed those memories into a dark corner of his mind. A couple clicks of his mouse later he had saved the two important messages, then shut down for the night and pushed away from the computer station. Might as well save electricity, since Myles was giving him the silent treatment anyway.

He needed to pace, to think.

He was out of his chair and halfway to the top of the stairs when he remembered Brie Quaid stretched out on the rollaway bed in front of the hearth. After calling a truce about midday, he had ignored her. He'd taken a walk along Milagro Creek, as far as the felled trees and undergrowth would permit. The sound of the water and the hard physical exercise usually calmed his mind.

But not today. He'd come back to the cabin jumpier than ever, fixed a plain but palatable supper with the groceries Lain had sent over, and served it to Brie Quaid on a rickety TV table, while he brought his plate upstairs to work and eat at the same time.

Brie hadn't appeared surprised that he chose dinner in solitude. After the tentative cease-fire agreement between them, she probably didn't want to contend with him any more than he wanted to contend with her.

Now, however, Cal realized with a nasty start that he had to deal with her presence. He was no longer sole resident and master of this humble domain. He couldn't go downstairs and pace without disturbing Brie. He couldn't raid the refrigerator. Miss L.A. had even appropriated the downstairs bathroom, preempting a relaxing midnight shower. The tiny, tiled room smelled like a funeral parlor, with all the scents of flowers and fresh greens. Frou-frou pink and lavender travel bags littered the top of the toilet tank. He'd literally tripped over a bottle of body oil on the shower stall floor.

Cal supposed he should be grateful for the half-bath carved out of the precious loft space. At least he could maintain some sense of personal privacy. Alicia had insisted on the convenience of what she called a "powder room" before she agreed to spend weekends at the cabin home. For some reason he couldn't remember now, he had resisted the demand, though giving in would have spared them both hours of anger and argument. Maybe he resisted simply because it had been her idea, like so many other of her ideas that reminded him he had never been quite good enough for her and her family. Just like it had been her idea to start calling himself "Callan," a name he'd rejected as a child, only because it sounded more polished and professional.

Cal rubbed his eyes with the palms of his hands. Well, at least she'd been right about the powder room. Maybe Alicia had been right about a lot of things.

Blowing out a breath of frustration, Cal turned and took a step toward his bed. Not that hitting the sack wouldn't be frustrating, too. Sleep didn't come most nights before 3:00 A.M. If only those damned toads would stop croaking.

On cue the dissonant mating serenade cut off. For a moment Cal held his breath. And in that moment of pure silence he heard a faint shuffling, something soft and light dragging across wood. He cocked his head. It didn't sound like branches scraping the side of the cabin, or debris shifting across the roof on the light breeze.

It took a moment more to pinpoint the sound. The parlor.

He trekked back to the top of the stairway. "Miss Quaid?" he called in a loud whisper.

No answer. The shuffling continued, but sounded more distant.

"Miss Quaid? Brie?" he called again a little louder.

Still no answer, yet something or someone still moved. Maybe a small animal had scuttled down the chimney or sneaked into the house through an unattended open door during the day. Cal was always careful, but hell, there had been more foot traffic through the cabin in the past twenty-four hours than there had been in the past twenty-four months. Anything was possible.

Swearing under his breath, Cal padded down the first five steps on silent bare feet and leaned over the railing. The lower level lay in pitch-blackness, save for light from a nearly full moon flooding through the cabin windows.

And the open front door!

Cal let out an obscenity and rushed down the remaining eight steps. He pushed off from the landing and bolted for the door. Hadn't he locked up after supper? Had he been that distracted by the upending of his solitary routine?

He reached the door in three bounding strides and was ready to close it when he glimpsed a human form. It shimmered ghostly white in the moon glow halfway down the path that sloped toward Milagro Creek. The figure paused, tried to straighten, then took a hobbling few steps.

"What the hell?" Cal muttered, and then gasped. "Brie?"

How had she moved so quickly on a bum knee? And why was she taking a midnight stroll down by the still-swollen creek that was only marginally less treacherous than it had been the night before?

"Brie!"

Cal's shout cut through the thick night air. She didn't so

much as slow down.

"Brie!" he called again. She had to have heard him. Hell, Lain had probably heard him at the ranch.

Cal bounded across the front porch and down the three rickety steps. Only when the weathered planking scraped the soles of his feet did he think about shoes. But he had momentum now, and if he turned around to pull on his boots she'd get to the creek before he could get to her. Good thing the path was relatively smooth and free of rocks. Now if he didn't run into any lurking wildlife.

"Brie!" he continued to call as he ran to head her off.

Still no response.

Cal barreled down the dirt pathway and started to skid to a halt when he was within arm's length of her. The snowy white sweat suit she wore looked pearlescent in the moonlight. Her disheveled dark hair hung heavy at her shoulders. She didn't turn her head or otherwise acknowledge his existence. Brie Quaid just continued to hobble toward the creek.

Cal grabbed her arm. "Hey! Hey, Brie!" He spun her around and latched onto her other arm. "What's with you?"

Her eyes, milky blue in the moonlight, stared through him. She blinked lazily once and had trouble lifting her eyelids.

Damned, if she didn't look asleep!

Cal gave her gentle shake. She merely grimaced. He shook her again, harder. "Snap out of it!"

Brie shut her eyes tight and frowned. "Here," she whispered in a breathy voice that didn't sound exactly like her, but seemed familiar nevertheless. "It's here." She started to pull away and look back toward the creek. "It's always been here, Callan. Find it. Find me."

Cal yanked her back around. "Wake up!"

This time Brie drew a shuddering breath and grasped Cal's forearms. Her eyes flew open, and for three heartbeats she only stared at him with such confusion he forgot his annoyance.

"Cal?" she breathed, and then shivered. "What are you doing here?" Her eyelids fluttered, and she did a quick look around. "What...what am *I* doing here?"

"I'd guess sleepwalking," he snapped.

But she shook her head. "No, that's not possible. I don't sleepwalk. Ever." And suddenly she crumbled and gasped in agony. "My knee! Ahhhh!"

Only Cal's firm grip on her arms saved Brienne Quaid from

another nasty fall. Reflexively, he pulled her up close and braced her back with both arms while she clung to his shoulders with all her strength. She was light in his arms, almost fragile feeling. But the curves and valleys of her body were all woman. Warning heat flooded Cal. It was a heat he hadn't felt or wanted to feel in a very long time. A heat that told him he still needed a woman's company, if not the painful burden of true intimacy.

Reminding himself Brie Quaid was only passing through on her way to New Mexico, Cal glared down at her. "Then I can't wait to hear you explain why you walked out the front door in the middle of the night on a bad leg."

Planting both feet firmly on the dirt path Cal picked up the confused and frightened woman in the cradle of his arms as if she were a child. "So, let's get you back inside and find out exactly what the hell is going on." He glared down at her. "And what I'm supposed to find in that damned creek."

* * * *

Brie clung to Cal Porter's neck, trying to lose herself in the warm reality of his arms and his clean male scent. His shoulders were solid, his breathing strong and deep as he carried her up the pathway toward the porch. The stubble of his day-old beard brushed her forehead. But she welcomed the chafe. It was real, an honest counterpoint to the terrible shadows that had sent her wandering into the night toward the treacherous creek.

"You're shivering like it's twenty-below," Cal pointed out unnecessarily.

Through muscle-jarring tremors, Brie merely nodded and buried herself deeper into his arms.

"Did you fall?" he interrogated, each word in synch with a sure, hurried footfall. "Did you hurt yourself? You could be in shock."

"I didn't fall," she managed to murmur through chattering teeth. "I...don't think I did. I don't remember." She swallowed a cry of panic. "I'm not even sure how I came out here without my crutches."

His arms tightened around her back. "Shhh," he soothed, his voice marginally gentler. "We'll get you inside and settled down first. Then we'll try to figure out what happened."

Cal Porter wanted the impossible. Brie couldn't explain what had happened, even to herself.

He scaled the porch steps and barreled inside the cabin as if he carried nothing more than a bag of groceries. Some far corner of Brie's mind whispered admiration of his strength. Some deep part of her soul stirred with giddiness at the sudden and somehow deeply satisfying press of his lean, solid body against her body.

And yet the heat rising from his skin didn't ease the chill that enveloped Brie. She couldn't control the trembling that cramped her muscles any more than she could halt the dream-induced dread that seeped into every fiber of her being. No blanket, no heated human touch, could dispel the cold terror of this familiar near-death hallucination.

Cal hit the switch to the overhead kitchenette lights with his elbow, and then kicked the door closed with his foot and headed for the hearth. In short order he tucked her into the corner of the old couch, propped her right leg on a stack of throw pillows, and hunkered down to look her straight in the eyes. "Do you want a blanket?"

His voice sounded so gentle with concern. He hardly seemed the same Cal Porter that half-barked even the simplest of social amenities. Of course, he might just be humoring the psycho Miss L.A.

Even though she hugged her body to ward off the cold, Brie shook her head. She would control this thing. She would not let it control her.

"How about some of that tea you carry along?" he pressed.

She shook her head again. She'd had her daily limit of Sophie's analgesic tea. The results had been evident when Brie went to bed earlier with a much less swollen and painful knee joint. Of course, that was before the unplanned stroll outdoors without the crutches. How much damage had she inflicted this time? If the renewed throbbing was any indication she'd set herself back by a day, at least.

"Maybe a little warm milk?" Her words didn't quiver too much, thank heavens.

Cal Porter looked like he wanted to smile but held back. "That stuff really works without a shot of brandy?"

She nodded and cleared her throat. "Yes."

He set his hands to his thighs, gave a push, and stood. "Okay, warm milk it is. Hope you don't mind skim."

The easy verbal give-and-take helped focus her scattered thoughts. She gave her arms a final brisk rub. "Skim milk is all I drink."

He chuckled as he walked toward the kitchen. "Good.

There's a gallon of the stuff, and it's all yours."

As she closed her eyes and rested her head on the back of the couch, Brie tried to concentrate on the soothing domestic sounds of clinking cups and a microwave hum. Behind her eyes, though, the dream replayed itself in full, horrible detail. The spin, the crash, the overpowering rush of water on all sides sent another violent shake up her spine.

"Hey, are you sure you don't want that blanket?"

He was back already, steaming mug in hand. When Brie blinked in surprise he only shrugged. "Your skim milk has the consistency of water. Heats just as fast. Tell me if it's hot enough."

He handed her the mug. She took it with trembling hands and lifted the mug to her lips. After a sip of the steaming milk she nodded. "Just right. Thanks."

Cal parked himself on the sturdy wooden coffee table in front of the couch. "Here. I found this by the door. It must have dropped off your wrist either going out or coming in tonight."

He held out her moon bracelet by one end. Brie grasped the precious bit of jewelry and held it to her heart. "Thank you!"

"It's special, huh? Looks like you've had it a long time."

With a sigh, she laid the bracelet in her lap and steadied the mug again. "I know it looks like a piece of junk, but it's dear to me. My aunt gave it to me years ago. From the day I went to live with her she called me her 'Moon Child' because my birthday is in July and I landed on her doorstop on the night of a full moon. She found this in a secondhand shop in Albuquerque and gave it to me on my twenty-first birthday. I rarely take it off."

"Better check the clasp," Cal advised. "Meantime, feel like telling me what's going on? Am I going to have to padlock the door? Because I'll tell you, Brie, no one should go wandering around this area at night." He glanced at her dust covered bare feet. "Especially half dressed. I try to keep the brush cleared away from the house, but I've still heard rattlers close in after dark."

The image of tangling with a snake didn't help Brie's already jangled nerves. She clutched the mug between both hands, the only way to keep it steady. "I really don't know what happened. One minute I was drifting off to sleep. The next minute you were standing in front of me outside." She looked up at him in pleading. "Trust me. I don't sleepwalk.

I've never sleepwalked in my entire life!"

He opened his hands as if to ask for calm. "You said something. You said, 'It's here. It's always been here. Find it. Find me.' Then you called me 'Callan' again. What's all this about?"

She shook her head adamantly. "I don't remember saying that. Not tonight, and I've never heard it before in the dream."

"Never in the dream?" he repeated, and narrowed his green eyes. "You mean you were having a recurring dream and it made you want to take a midnight stroll down by the creek, give me instructions to find something, then call me a name I told you not to use?"

Brie no longer heard compassion or even that touch of humor in his voice. The question wasn't exactly cold, but more probing and clinical, even demanding. She didn't fault Cal's curiosity, or disagree with his right to understand. In the aftermath of this latest dream-induced incident she'd carelessly let slip about the irrational shadows that tortured her nights. Fairness suggested Cal deserved some sort of explanation in return for his hospitality, grudging as that had been so far.

Yet she recoiled from telling the terrible dream out loud, or risking having to admit her deepest fears. She'd never even trusted Darien with her secret. And Cal Porter was, after all, a virtual stranger.

A virtual stranger whose touch inexplicably excited her, and whose own dark psyche tugged at her soul.

Self-protection prevailed. Brie withdrew further into the couch and clasped the mug tighter. "I really don't want to talk about it."

Unfortunately, Cal Porter leaned forward as if following her into the corner. "No way you're going to sidestep this. Look, we're stuck together for the next couple of days, at least. I can't be worrying that I'll wake up in the middle of the night and find you've fallen into a gully or gone off and drowned in that creek."

In reflex she winced and shuddered.

Cal leaned closer still. "Is that it? Is that what your dream is about? Drowning?"

His dogged persistence irritated her, but it was obvious he wasn't going to stop pressing her until he got answers. Neither did Brie doubt he'd be content with anything but full disclosure, and he'd somehow know if she held back.

Though she stuck out her chin, Brie felt anything but brave. She felt merely cornered and at the mercy of this stubborn, perplexing man. "It isn't me. I don't drown, even though I feel like I'm underwater in the dream. But someone dies, and I can't figure out who to warn."

Cal went rigid. "Warn? What are you saying? Do you really think you're seeing the future?"

Brie sat up as straight as her throbbing knee would allow. "I know I am!"

When his eyes went wide she caught her breath, and slumped back into the cushion. "I know I am," she said more quietly, and exhaled as if finally saying the truth out loud had lifted a burden. "I have a gift. A gift that's much stronger than mere intuition." She looked up at him. "I'm not a carnival fortuneteller like you described. I'm the real thing. I'm a psychic."

To his credit, Cal Porter didn't laugh outright. In fact, he just peered at her, stone-faced, for a long brace of tense moments. Then finally he dropped his shoulders and blinked. "Uh-huh," he murmured. "So, if you 'know' things, why the hell didn't you know not to turn into this canyon last night?"

The undercurrent of sarcasm and disbelief in his voice cut deep. How many times had she heard strangers ridicule her mother in just this way? Eventually that ridicule ate away at Nancy Quaid's heart and spirit. Brie vowed long ago she wouldn't end up like her mother, a spent shell of a human who was overwhelmed by a talent she didn't want and couldn't handle. Though Brie hadn't wanted the gift any more than her mother, she respected its awful power.

And while she understood and accepted skepticism all too well, she would not let herself fall victim to a skeptic's negativism. "It doesn't work that way," Brie snapped back. "I can't pick lottery numbers or tell my friends if their careers will work out. Or determine if I'm going in the right direction in a rainstorm, damn it! I don't control the substance of images that break through. I can only 'know' raw information."

Cal Porter cocked a brow, but he seemed otherwise unfazed by her burst of anger. "Break through? Like in your dreams?"

Wearily, Brie nodded. "That's how it always starts. Disjointed images when my mind is at rest. I can't help the flow of those images, but I've spent years learning from Aunt Sophie how to control my waking mind. If I couldn't, I'd never be able to work in my profession."

Brie peeled her left hand from around the mug and turned it over to stare at her palm and fingers. "I know this probably sounds like mystical nonsense to you, Cal, but trust me, objects can hold a person's spiritual imprint for years, or decades, or even centuries. The older the piece, the fainter the trace of the long gone previous owners. Still, there is a trace. A vibration of an old soul."

She looked up into Cal Porter's pensive scowl. "That's part of my psychic ability. I can feel those vibrations. If Sophie hadn't taught me to shield myself from the currents of spiritual energy I'd never be able to enter upscale consignment shops, or handle a client's family heirlooms. I'd be inundated with energies of those who had previously owned the pieces." She fisted her hand. "I think I'd go crazy."

From the jump of Cal's brow, she suspected he was already sure she'd gone over the edge. "Is that why you were driving hell-bent for leather to New Mexico? To see if your aunt can perform some sort of psychic exorcism of this nasty dream?"

Blood throbbed in Brie's temples. She lifted her chin. "I wasn't driving recklessly," she retorted. "And I resent your sarcasm in regard to my aunt. She's a kind and wise woman who took me in after both my parents died. You can think what you want about me, but I will not sit here and listen to you belittle her!"

He glanced at her propped right leg. "Just where do you think you'll go?"

Frustration and weariness flooded Brie. She turned her face toward the hearth and shut her eyes tight. "Damn you! Damn this situation! I just want this all to be over."

Brie held her breath to stave off a rush of emotion. When she felt the touch of Cal Porter's hand on her left forearm she jerked around so fast she almost spilled the warm milk out of her mug.

Somehow, without her knowing it, Cal had shifted from his perch on the coffee table to his knees in front of her. Gently he took the mug from her trembling grip and set it on the table. Then he sat back on his heels. "I didn't mean to upset you. The way I talk, it's..." He shook his head. "Old habits, that's all. I didn't intend to insult your aunt, and if it sounded that way, I apologize." He frowned, but now with concern. "You're really spooked, aren't you?"

Brie nodded. "Of course, I am! You'd be, too, if these dreams..." She searched for a word. "Haunted you."

Cal stared at her hard for a few moments, then pushed off the floor and sat back onto the table. He schooled his face into a mask of neutrality. "Okay, tell me about the dream."

That dispassionate voice again. A tone that didn't exactly intimidate but came close enough.

And Brie resented attempts to stampede her into laying bare her soul. Yet waves of intuition she dare not dismiss urged her to try and make him understand. If she were to believe Aunt Sophie's counsel, she was where she had to be. Landing at the bottom of the canyon on Cal's doorstep last night was no accident. Maybe in some way *he* could help her exorcise these mental demons.

Of course, she couldn't tell *him* that.

Cal didn't move. Neither was there the slightest change in his neutral expression. If body language was any clue, he meant to stay put until she talked.

Crossing her arms, Brie sank a little further into the couch. "All right, but no more cracks about Sophie."

In all seriousness, Cal raised his right hand. "I swear."

Brie drew in a breath of fresh air, and gathered her scattered thoughts. "The dreams started a month ago. At first they were just disturbing enough to wake me. After a while, though, they turned into nightmares. Then last week, I was in a client's home, staring at a white wall, and I saw the dream images playing like a movie on a wide screen. That hadn't happened since..."

Old painful memories rose to the forefront of her mind, and she paused a moment to collect herself.

"Since when?" he prodded in a soft, unemotional voice.

She swallowed. "Since right before my parents were killed. I had nightmares then, too. But the images were so vague. Even so, I had this overwhelming sense that death hung over me and there was a car involved."

"The accident?" he coaxed.

She nodded.

"You were psychic as a kid?" he asked.

Again Brie nodded, but with a slow weariness she felt in her bones. "True psychic ability, the kind that can actually be measured, often runs in families, just like eye and hair color. Some powerful intuition turned on in me when I was twelve, but I grew up watching my mother struggle with the gift because she'd never learned how to control the rush of images. When my abilities started to surface, I couldn't go to anyone, even though I was afraid I'd become her."

"What about your aunt?"

"I didn't know Sophie well then. We lived in Oregon, and she already lived in New Mexico. Even though Sophie took me in without question, she was never close to my mother. By that time mom could hardly help herself. She had nothing left to give me. My father was worn out from trying to cope with her problems, and all the while she just kept slipping deeper and deeper inside herself. He grew distant from both of us, especially after he realized psychic ability ran true in me."

Cal frowned, an expression that marked another palpable seepage of darkness from his soul. "Your father should have stood by both of you."

The accusation put Brie on the defensive. "When I was a child I thought that. Now I realize that most of the time he was just as confused and frightened as mom and I were. He couldn't understand what happened to us. How could he? Mom and I didn't understand ourselves."

Brie shut her eyes, but the painful memories flooded in regardless. "I often resented my father unfairly." She sighed. "But I never hated him. Not like I grew to hate my mother."

For a moment, surprise flickered in Cal's eyes. "Hate's a strong word."

"That's the only word that fits how I felt," Brie assured him. "I hated her. I hated the fact that I had to grope through most of my teenage years alone and unaware of what was happening to me. I hated her because she wouldn't take charge of her life for the sake of her family. I had to take charge. I had to be an adult when I just wanted to be a normal kid."

Too late Brie realized that she'd vented old personal complaints even Sophie hadn't heard in years, to a man she'd met only yesterday. A man who remained a cipher even now. She covered her face with both hands for a moment, settled the worst of her emotions, and then faced Cal again. "You didn't need to know that. I'm sorry."

"That's okay. Go on."

She sensed a new attentiveness in him. Perhaps it was only curiosity, but it was sincere curiosity. "The nightmares terrified me, but I couldn't tell anyone. I never told any of my friends about being psychic. I only wanted to be a regular teenaged girl with them. My mother could barely handle herself. I didn't think my dad wanted to know."

Cal leaned forward, bracing his forearms on his thighs. His green eyes bore into her. "How long did this go on?"

Mentally, Brie squirmed under the closer scrutiny, but she pressed ahead. "About two weeks. It got to the point where I wouldn't get into a car. I'd walk in the rain three miles to school before I'd get into the bus. I figured I'd just avoid the circumstances of my dream and cheat death until the nightmares stopped."

"What happened?"

Cold began creeping up her spine again. "The dreams finally stopped suddenly, and I thought I was safe. So, when dad decided we should all drive to Portland for the weekend, the only thing I was worried about was how I could talk him into buying me a couple pairs of new shoes."

Brie wedged herself deeper into the couch, even though she knew any kind of physical warmth would elude her. "We didn't get even five miles away from home. A semi-truck jackknifed in front of us as the driver was trying to brake for another accident up the road. I heard mom scream and dad yell for me to get down in the back seat." She shivered. "Then I woke up a week later in the hospital. My right leg was such a mess the doctors weren't sure I'd ever walk right again. I didn't care. My parents were dead. I thought I was being justly punished because I did nothing to stop the accident."

"You were a kid," Cal pointed out. "You were scared and confused and had nowhere to turn. It wasn't your fault."

Surprised by his defense of her, Brie managed a weak smile as she toyed with the moon disk on the bracelet. "That's what Sophie helped me learn. She doesn't have psychic ability, but she should have because she understands the power and reality so much better than my mother ever did. She helped me work through all the guilt. But sometimes I still wonder."

Cal stiffened his spine. "That's why you're so spooked about this dream. You think you have a responsibility to warn the victim."

Brie shook her head. "I don't know what to believe at this point. All I know is this terrible dream has become a living nightmare. I'm afraid to go to sleep, but I'm afraid to wake up. I meant what I said. The dream haunts me."

Cal Porter just looked at her without discernible judgment.

But the blasé mask didn't fool Brie. His disbelief was as palpable as the incessant ache in her knee.

"You asked for an explanation," she reminded him.

"That I did," he said with a sigh.

"And?"

"Does it matter what I think?" he hedged.

Brie searched her heart. The voice inside that was her true compass answered loud and clear. "Yes," she spoke the answer out loud. "Don't ask me why, but it is important what you think."

"Because your aunt believes in mystical coincidences?" he chided.

"Because she doesn't believe in them. Sophie believes I'm here for a reason." Brie paused, remembering how the darkness in his soul had called out to her at the rain-swollen creek, and how his arms felt right. "So do I," she added with a conviction she rarely felt.

That seemed to surprise him. Cal Porter massaged the stubble of dark beard on his chin and jaw as he peered at Brie. "Okay, you want to know what I think? I think believing in something gives that something power. And I think you believe in all this psychic stuff. Maybe you are sensitive to feelings and emotions. I'm not the person to judge. But I'd be willing to bet money I don't have in the bank that you've just got yourself a damn good case of stress. A handful of powerful tranquilizers and a couple nights uninterrupted sleep would probably get you back on the road to reality."

The lecture stung. "I *am* living reality," she shot back. "I can't medicate the dreams into submission. They won't stop until I know who to warn. Whatever that person does with the knowledge isn't my responsibility. But I do know this thing has me by the throat until I can pass it off."

He was quiet again for a moment. "What are you saying? That I'm connected to these dreams? Is that why you called out my given name?" he finally asked.

She shut her eyes and searched her feelings. "I don't know. Honestly, I didn't care one way or another about guessing your real name. And I don't remember seeing your face, or sensing your presence. There's just this woman, and she's in danger from the water." She slowly opened her eyes and looked up into his stern expression. "Maybe I'm just supposed to warn you that someone else will come down that canyon road, and she won't be as lucky as I was."

Cal let out a long sigh. "Fine," he said as he stood. "I'll consider myself warned. For now, though, are you going to be all right?"

Brie peered up at him. Despite his cynical veneer, there was such sadness about the man. Whatever had buried itself in his soul held him captive as surely as the recurring nightmares imprisoned her. Cal Porter didn't need the burden of her emotional struggle to add to his own.

"Yes, I'll be fine," she answered. "Thanks for the hot milk. And for listening, at least. It's more than I would have expected of a friend, much less a stranger."

He nodded tersely as if he didn't expect the gratitude. "Do you want help back to bed?" He paused. "I mean, if your knee hurts...you know, I can help you get back over there...and comfortable."

Was that embarrassment she noted in the uncomfortable shift of his gaze around the room? Brie held up her hand to stop the babbling before she broke into a grin at his expense. "No, thanks. I think I'll sit up for a while and finish the milk. If you wouldn't mind turning on the table lamp over there, you can switch off the kitchen light."

Cal Porter paused a moment longer, then lifted his hand. "Fine. Good night then."

He turned and headed back to his loft. After a brief stop to turn off the overhead kitchen light he disappeared upstairs.

Brie laid her head on the backrest of the couch and closed her eyes. The room was quiet now, and emptier without Cal Porter's presence. Her heart still hammered and her blood raced. She'd be lucky to get back to sleep at all tonight.

Then the memory of strong arms lifting her, carrying her, gently easing her onto the couch came front and center. She smiled as the fullness of contentment washed over her.

What would Sophie say about this odd, confusing clash of terror and contentment?

The answer lifted immediately from her heart. *This is where you must be, Moon Child, at this place, at this time.*

Six

"You need me, Myles. You need me like you never needed anyone before. I can help you solve this case."

In that moment he realized Selene spoke a many-leveled truth. A truth that could change his life if he allowed.

So he looked away. "I don't need anyone."

Chapter 7, *Murder, My Love—From the Files of Myles Daemon, P.I.*

* * * *

"Good morning, little brother. Wasting half the day in bed again?"

Cal knew he should have followed his instincts and just let the phone ring. Lain's cheerful voice grated on his raw nerves. Incessant sunshine streaming through the loft window made his scratchy eyeballs throb. He pulled the foam stuffed pillow over his head to just above his nose. Damn, he hated it when she had his number. "How I waste my day isn't your problem."

"It's almost noon," his sister retorted. "Why aren't you up fixing that poor little girl breakfast? Make that lunch."

"Brie Quaid has unlimited kitchen privileges. She can make herself some of those frozen waffles you sent over."

"The girl's on crutches, you jerk!"

Cal's brain raced with images of last night, outside, in the dark. "She can get around just fine when she has to," he assured his outraged sister. Then he sniffed the air deeply for the first time. The unfamiliar fragrance of home cooking filled his head and made his mouth water. "In fact, I think she's already helped herself. I'm going to hang up now..."

"No you aren't. Not unless you want me to come over there in person."

"For what?" he growled in a sleep-husky voice.

"To tell you to bring Brie over to the main house for supper. She needs a break after being cooped up with the likes of you for the past two days."

The foam pillow flopped onto the floor as Cal sat straight up in bed. "It's only been a day-and-a-half," he pointed out. "And I'm not bringing her over for supper."

"Then I'm coming to get her," Lain countered.

Cal thrust his hand through the spiky ends of his hair and lowered his voice so if Brie Quaid was in the kitchen she couldn't hear. "I don't think it's a good idea to make the family rounds with her. Trust me."

"Why? Did you do a background search on her with one of those private investigator services and find out she's wanted by the penal system or something?"

Cal let out a breath of air he hoped would express his irritation. "No, but last night she really creeped me out. She got up and walked in her sleep. Outside. Toward the creek."

"Yeah, so, lots of people sleepwalk." Lain seemed completely unfazed.

"It was because of a dream," Cal tried to make her understand. "She says she's had this dream over and over, and it's trying to tell her something. She says she has to warn someone."

"Oh, my God, is she psychic?" Lain asked the question with the breathless awe of someone who had just bumped into a movie star.

Cal blinked hard. "As a matter of fact that's what she claims."

"You don't mean it!" Lain almost squealed. "I just knew there was something special about Buttercup. And she ended up on your doorstep? Cal, you know this isn't a coincidence."

He couldn't believe his ears. Was this his practical, hardheaded, scold of a sister? "I had considered the possibility."

"Cal, you really need to keep an open mind."

So everyone kept reminding him lately. "I like keeping my mind locked down, but thanks anyway for the suggestion. Besides, right now I have a suspicion she's on the emotional edge. I really don't think you want her around the kids."

There was a heartbeat of silence on the other end of the line. "Her? Or you?"

Cal flopped back down on the bed. The springs groaned under his weight, and his heart groaned under Lain's unspoken suspicions. "I know what you're thinking, but it's not true."

"If I wanted a load of B.S. like that I'd take a walk in the barnyard," Lain shot back. "Ever since little Dulcie came to us you've hardly stepped foot in this house."

Lain knew him too well after thirty-eight years. In the eighteen months since she and her husband Gil had adopted a little girl they'd named Dulcie, Cal had made his visits to the main ranch house few and far between. Dulcie was a beautiful two-year-old with bright licorice eyes, silky black hair, and a smile that lit a room. Everyone had fallen in love with her on first sight.

Everyone but Cal. He couldn't let himself give that kind of unquestioning, unconditional love again. He couldn't risk the hurt. And every time he looked at Dulcie he saw his little Jeanie, the way she'd looked and acted and laughed just before she disappeared.

"That's not fair to her, Cal," Lain ranted in his ear. "It's not fair to any of us, especially Eric. He'd like to see his favorite uncle once in a while."

"Eric's fifteen. Last time we were together he ditched me for a trio of very mature looking girls," Cal snarled. "I doubt he misses me much."

"Cal!"

"Don't scream in my ear! I'm not awake yet!"

"No, you've been asleep for too damn long, and it's time you snap out of it!"

Never had Cal been so tempted to slam the phone down in rage. But he couldn't, not when his sister was more than half right. "Leave me alone."

"When you agree to bring Buttercup over for dinner tonight," she wheedled sweetly.

The woman could change moods faster than Milagro Creek flooded its banks.

"All right, all right," he gave in, since it was easier than staying on the phone and arguing. "And don't go giving Brie Quaid nicknames. She's not going to be here long enough for you two to get friendly."

"Too late for that, little brother. See you tonight about six."

The phone went dead. Cal hit the "End" button on the portable handset and tossed it onto the jumble of blankets and sheets at his feet. If only Myles Daemon would yak as much as his sister, he could have a book cranked out every month.

With the clear sense that his world was tilting sideways, Cal dragged himself out of bed and went to refresh himself in the loft half-bath. Ten minutes later, he emerged from the powder room, dressed but still barefoot, and inhaled the aroma of coffee and what smelled suspiciously like savory cooked eggs. He stumbled downstairs and into the kitchenette. To his surprise, Brie Quaid stood at the stove with her back to him, propped on one crutch and working over a pan.

She glanced over her shoulder. "Good morning."

Her soft, lyrical voice soothed his raw nerves like a cool breeze after the hot wind of Lain's scolding. Brie also looked the picture of fresh, summertime wholesomeness. Today she wore one of her signature sundresses, a sleeveless pale green length of lightweight cotton that floated around her body when she moved. Her skin shone with a rosy, just scrubbed blush that was as fetching as her shy smile.

"I'm fixing some breakfast," she explained when Cal did nothing but gawk. "It's the least I can do in exchange for temporary room and board. I heard you up in the bathroom and knew you were awake, so I felt safe heating the pan."

Cal staggered to the electric coffee maker and poured the rich brew into a mug already set out for him. "I don't eat breakfast."

"Okay, then brunch. I guessed since you have eggs and probably do very little scratch baking I was safe making an omelette."

He took a deep whiff of the coffee—mellow, rich, revitalizing, and just strong enough. "Omelette? Yeah, I like omelettes. With salsa."

She tipped her head at the cupboard. "I think I saw a new jar in there. This is almost done. Better hurry."

Did women think he enjoyed being ordered around? Still, and despite his renouncement of breakfast, he knew he'd never be able to resist the delicious smelling egg dish. He retrieved the salsa and parked himself on a stool at the edge of the kitchenette counter.

"What does a career interior decorator know about baking from scratch?" he growled through a yawn.

"How does a quasi-hermit male mystery writer know what 'scratch baking' means?" she parried.

"Writers have to know a little about everything," he replied with strained ennui. In fact, Cal had a hard time not drooling as the aroma of the omelette and coffee mixed to create unfamiliar domestic contentment in his semi-functional kitchenette.

With silent efficiency, Brie Quaid maneuvered around the stove and sink on one crutch as she managed the cooking with her free hand. Obviously she had plenty of practice, as she'd claimed.

"My aunt is an herbalist by profession, and a natural foods fanatic and vegetarian by conviction," she answered while still focused on the omelette. "Sophie tends what most people would consider a medium-sized truck garden. She cans, dries, and preserves everything she eats, bakes her own bread, and even churns butter. I couldn't help picking up a few kitchen skills along the way."

From the smell of the omelette, Cal figured Brie Quaid had picked up more than a few skills. Then he thought of the huge roast sitting in the refrigerator. "Are you a vegetarian, too?"

With a motion Cal could only describe as practical grace, Brie slid the egg dish onto a plate already half covered with orange sections, a branch of green grapes, and three plump strawberries from the stash of "good" food Lain had sent over.

"No," she answered. "My eating habits were formed long before I went to live with Sophie. Both my parents were meat and potatoes type people. I like my steak medium well and my lamb chops broiled medium rare."

She turned, plate in her free hand. Cal started to get up, but her confident smile told him to stay put. With the same practical grace she used at the stove, Brie hobbled to the counter and set the food in front of Cal. "Enjoy."

When she turned away, Cal reached out and grabbed her free forearm. "Hey, what about you?"

She started and seemed to hold her breath. Beneath his fingers her muscles tensed. At the same time her eyes widened with obvious surprise. Cal didn't know what she was thinking. All he knew for certain was that the feel of her cool, silky skin against his palm made prickles run up his hand and through his arm. The odd, electrifying sensation lodged in his chest and intensified with every beat of his heart.

In that moment, his mind blanked to everyone and everything except the woman who stood before him. Myles. Lain. His editor. The gut-wrenching writer's block. Nothing mattered but Brie Quaid, her floaty cotton dress and cornflower blue eyes. Nothing mattered but holding on to her.

How was that possible?

Hard-wired skepticism flooded over the brush with contentment. Cal snapped his hand away and curled his fingers into a fist. The near-euphoria vanished as fast as it had settled on him. But those mere five seconds left him winded and perplexed.

Brie recoiled, too, and took an awkward step backward. Somehow she found her voice before he did. "I ate two hours ago. I...I just assumed you'd prefer to eat alone."

Lain's most recent comments regarding his dismal comportment flitted through his mind. "I'm not completely asocial," he insisted. He even attempted a smile. It almost hurt. "Stay."

She looked uncertain, and scanned the small area. "There isn't another stool."

Cal nodded, stood, and picked up his plate and mug. "I'll eat at the coffee table and you can sit on the couch. Or is that view boring by now?"

She smiled fully this time, and Cal realized he liked the way her soft, full mouth turned up at the corners and her eyes sparkled. "All right."

Cal followed her to the hearth side grouping of frayed and faded furniture. While he spread out his meal on the coffee table and plopped into the horsehair lounger, she nestled delicately into the well-worn couch and propped her right foot up on a battered three-legged footstool that looked as if it had come with the original cabin. Cal didn't realize he'd stared at her shapely legs too long until she draped the hem of her breezy sundress low over her calf.

"Ah, your knee doesn't look as swollen this morning," he commented hastily, and jammed a forkful of food into his mouth.

She reached forward and laid her hand on the joint. "After what happened last night...ah, no it isn't. It doesn't feel as stiff either."

Though Cal wasn't eager to discuss the midnight incident, neither did he want the conversation to dwindle and die. "Omelette's good." Hell it was great.

She grinned, and her creamy skin turned a pretty shade of deep pink. "I'm glad you like it."

For some reason beyond his comprehension, Brie Quaid's unaffected modesty prompted him to smile back. A full smile, too, not some half-baked smirk that passed for amusement these days. Well, at least Lain would be happy to know the city-girl was civilizing him some.

Then he took a sip from his mug. The coffee was the best he'd had in months, probably since the last time he'd visited the ranch. Brie smiled again and nodded her acknowledgment of praise he hadn't shared out loud.

Had she read his expression? Or had she read his mind? She claimed to be psychic. Was she even now interpreting his silent ruminations about the seductive way the flimsy sundress hugged her curves?

Another bite of food went down hard. Cal chased it with a swig of hot coffee and hoped he didn't permanently scar his esophagus. But the ploy kept him from choking over the paranoid thoughts. He didn't even believe in all the hokum, and he had no intention of delving into the subject further. Right? Yes, right.

For her part, Brie just smiled her quiet gratitude at his paltry compliments. No, she hadn't picked up on his lustier thoughts. He was certain.

Relieved, Cal stuck another bit of food in his mouth, chewed, and swallowed. "Did you get some sleep after, ah, your walk?"

She shifted uneasily. The dress pulled tight across her well-rounded breasts. Cal sucked in another mouthful of hot coffee just for diversion.

"I got a few hours sleep," she answered. Then she lifted a hardback book that lay spread-eagle on the cushion next to her. "But first I raided your bookshelf."

Cal almost choked again when he saw the spine: *Murderous Mayhem—From the Files of Myles Daemon, P.I.*

"I thought you didn't read mysteries," he reminded her.

She shrugged, almost too casually. "I don't. But I noticed you had all three of Howard Chastain's books, so I figured as a mystery writer yourself you must appreciate his work. What did one critic call him?"

Brie flipped through the first few pages. "Here it is. 'Chastain is a breakout mystery writer, worthy of every award he refuses to accept in person. His Myles Daemon is the most literate detective in a generation.'" She glanced up at Cal. "Impressive. But I've also heard that Chastain's general treatment of female characters has created controversy. So I was curious to find out for myself. Besides, I figured if nothing else the story would probably bore me and I'd fall asleep faster."

Cal lowered his gaze to the plate and concentrated on cutting off another big chunk of food in an effort to hide the curious disappointment he felt inside. "Did the story sedate you as planned?"

"Unfortunately, no."

Cal glanced up furtively. Brie studied the book jacket as she let the tips of her fingers glide across the slick surface.

"The book didn't bore you?" he asked around a mouthful of food.

She furrowed her brow slightly but didn't look at him. "Actually, it intrigued me. I read to the end, even though I could barely keep my eyes open."

Cal focused on the remaining piece of omelette on his plate and suppressed a self-satisfied grin. "Really."

"You're Howard Chastain, aren't you?"

Glad he had nothing in his mouth to swallow, Cal sucked back some badly needed air and popped his head up.

Brie bit her bottom lip and appeared to keep a laugh inside.

So much for letting down his guard. "Got me again, Miss L.A.," Cal admitted, though his smile felt stiffer and less genuine. "Psychic flash or good guess?"

She ignored the mild sarcasm. "Reasonable deduction from the little I know about you already. Of course, that explains the bagels from New York, too. You must have gotten them while visiting your publisher."

Cal scowled. "I never said those bagels were from New York."

"Lain told me that's where you got them." Brie hid a grin behind her hand. "She also told me your last visit there was three months ago and warned me not to eat them."

"I froze what I didn't eat right away!" Cal claimed in his own defense.

Brie held up her hand for calm. "I mentioned that was probably the case." The grin started to twitch at the corners of her mouth. "Lain implied I should play it safe anyway." She tilted her head, and her expression became soft and serious. "You're Myles Daemon, too."

Cal resisted the urge to get up and pace. Instead, he slumped into the chair and took a leisurely sip of coffee. "Writers can't help creating characters that reflect themselves in some ways. Yeah, I suppose Myles and I are alike. In some ways," he emphasized.

"Were you a private detective?"

He snorted. "Not even close. Daemon is a composite of people I've known over the years. I worked with an investigator who had a lot of the skills I gave to Myles."

"Do you still consult with this investigator?"

Her interest seemed genuine, but the question tripped him

up. "No. We...we parted badly about four years ago
."

Because Jim told me the truth as he saw it, and I was too desperate or stupid or both to give him credit for being a friend.

"But I still admire his methods," Cal said over the voice of conscience. "And his integrity."

She wasn't finished. "What about the lawyer, Jorge Moreno-Diaz? His character is very well drawn. Are you familiar with law?"

Was it the horsehair upholstery that made him itch, or these questions? Either way, Cal couldn't quite meet Brie's unflinching gaze. "I've had some experience with the legal system. A long time ago."

"Is Jorge a composite, too?"

That was easy. "He's the comic relief."

Brie continued to stroke the cover in a way Cal imagined would feel good on his skin. "He came across as an idealist."

That snapped Cal out of the misplaced reverie about Brie Quaid's touch. "Like I said, he's comic relief. Jorge is an idealist and a fool."

Her brow twitched. "Myles Daemon treats everybody as if they're fools."

Restless, Cal leaned forward in the chair. "Daemon's the biggest fool of all. He thinks he can control life. He's sadly mistaken."

Now she frowned. "I think my Aunt Sophie would agree with you there. But Myles treats women with even deeper contempt. I can see why some female readers and reviewers take exception with the books."

"Contempt?" Cal shrugged with a nonchalance he didn't feel. "Don't you think the women Myles meets are deserving of contempt?"

After a moment of thought, Brie nodded slowly. "Yes, they're selfish and manipulative. They use emotional and psychological blackmail to get what they want. But is Myles any better? He uses then discards them and goes his singular way."

Cal chuckled. "That's the pattern of hard-bitten detective stories. Everyone pays for his or her sins."

"Even Myles?"

"Myles most of all," he retorted, a little more sharply than necessary. "He has to go his singular way, as you put it."

"Yes, he did clean everyone out of his life by the end of the story," she agreed with a hint of distaste. "Do the other books end that way, too?"

"Read and find out."

Again that soft brow of hers shot up. Was she offended by his flippant tone, or by the dark psychology of his detective?

"I take it you don't like the ending," he prodded. When she considered her answer for more than a few seconds, he spread his hands in concession. "You've got company. Lain didn't like the ending either."

But Brie didn't jump in to agree. She took a few more moments then said, "The book ended the way it had to end. Myles can't connect with anyone, not even himself, because he doesn't trust anyone or anything."

"A real cynic," Cal agreed.

"A very disillusioned man." She tilted her head. "Are you disillusioned, too?"

Cal almost lifted out of the chair, but restrained himself at the last second. Bad enough he knew Brie Quaid had keyed in on his personal failings. He didn't have to admit as much with his body language. "I do have some imagination," he evaded.

Her appreciative smile sent a niggling of guilt through him. "That's true. You pieced together a great story. Plenty of critics agree. I guess that's why I'm surprised your photo isn't on the book jacket. I should think you'd want to claim credit."

The incessant questioning made him squirm. The last time he'd been on the rump end of an interrogation was during those first bleak months after Alicia disappeared.

Cal shunted the dark memories to an even darker corner of his mind and tried to stay focused on the woman sitting across from him. "Back in the beginning that was partly a marketing decision and partly a personal preference. Let's just say the ploy to make Howard Chastain as much of a mystery as his stories and my personal needs coincided at the time."

"Don't you do book signings or interviews?" she asked in amazement.

"I have a 'no personal appearances' clause in my contracts." Cal chuckled. "Wasn't easy to negotiate that for the first book. But I figured if the editor wanted the acquisition bad enough he'd cave, and he did."

He shook his head when she looked stunned. "Don't get the wrong idea. There was nothing really gusty about that strategy. I wrote *Murderous Mayhem* for mental diversion only. Lain is the one who convinced me to submit the manuscript for publication. I had nothing to lose." He closed his eyes. "Absolutely nothing."

Once again Cal shook off memories of darker days and forced a smile. "Fortunately, I've become successful enough I don't have to do the PR."

Brie's eyes widened. "You must have a good agent."

"I represent myself."

She laughed softly. "A self-reliant man of many talents. You do sound more and more like your detective. The strategy worked, that's for sure. A mystery sells a mystery. I guess, then, few people know who you really are."

"Relatively few." He shrugged again and took the last swig of coffee. "Now you're one of those few. Not that anonymity matters anymore."

From the intensity of her stare, Cal just knew Brie was about to wonder why out loud, and he quickly cut her off. "For a psychic you sure need to ask a lot of questions."

The pretty pink flush crept up her throat again. "I told you, I don't read minds."

"No, you read the 'vibrations' of rooms." He waved his arm in a squirrelly arc. "Then you make magic with *foo young*."

The flush deepened, but Brie grinned. "You mean *feng shui*. You're teasing me, right?"

Cal found himself grinning back at her. "Could be."

Hugging his book to her breast, Brie laughed. "I didn't know you were capable."

Not for a long time, he recalled silently. Not for a damn long time.

He glanced down at his plate, surprised that he'd cleaned it off, fruit and all. He scooped up the dirty dishes. "Thanks for breakfast. Dinner's on Lain. She invited us to the ranch around six. Sound okay?"

Brie lowered the book to her lap. "Sounds wonderful. Ah, Cal?"

"Huh?"

"What I said about your book...please don't take it the wrong way. I didn't mean any of it as criticism. You have a strong talent. And if I drew some wrong impressions about your being Myles..." Her voice trailed off as she grimaced delicately.

Poor Miss L.A. didn't understand that she'd come closer

to the truth about Cal and his *alter ego* than she could possibly imagine. Not that he was about to admit as much to this woman who inexplicably skewed his solitary existence with her sexy innocence and talk of mystical nonsense.

"Everyone's a critic these days," he said, dismissing her apology. "Feel lucky you didn't shell out twenty-five bucks for the privilege. Thanks again for breakfast. I'll do the dishes."

She smiled sweetly. "Fair enough. In that case, I think I'll start another Chastain mystery."

"Whatever passes the day," he teased, and headed to the kitchenette.

He made it to the sink and deposited the dishes there. Then he looked up and stared through the open window at the stark, semiarid beauty of the isolated canyon.

For the first time in years he wanted to be more than some fictional character's literary father. Truth be told, Cal pitied Myles Daemon more than he liked the detective. Is that how he actually felt about himself? Maybe Brie Quaid was on to something. Maybe he was writing himself into the character unconsciously but so clearly that even she, a virtual stranger, could see the similarity.

He didn't want to be the object of pity, his own or anyone else's. What had happened to the Cal Porter who once set out on a far different life course? Suddenly, he yearned to be that man again. An indulgent uncle who could hold little Dulcie without feeling shards of pain and guilt lacerate his heart. A brother who could pull his sister into a long hug, and tell her how much he appreciated and needed her unfailing loyalty and brash but honest love. An honorable person who could call Jim Atwood and admit he'd been a fool, so given over to guilt and self-doubt that he'd let it destroy a solid friendship.

But Cal wasn't that man. He'd sacrificed the essence of nobility long before he gave up on the outward practice.

Long before Alicia had enough and left.

He was empty, heart and soul. Was it this lack of purpose that kept even Myles at bay lately and everyone else at arm's length?

Cal glanced over his shoulder at the couch where Brie Quaid was nestled in for another day alone, reading his books. He didn't believe in psychics, but he did believe that some people had great gut instincts and astute judgment, as he had once. Maybe that's all a psychic really was. Someone with a special gift of cutting through the superficial crap and getting to the heart of a matter. And this woman was special in ways that had nothing to do with her self-proclaimed insightfulness. Her simplest touch made Cal yearn for physical intimacies he hadn't really missed until now. She drew him out of hiding with her forthright intelligence. Cal didn't remember the last time he'd engaged anyone, even Lain, in so much steady conversation, and mostly about himself. She seemed to thaw the frigid corners of his ice-locked soul. Why?

That was the biggest mystery of all.

Cal rinsed the dishes and set them in the sink. He'd tend to them later, along with the unsolved mysteries of his small universe. Right now he had to go back upstairs and try to smoke Myles out of hiding.

But just as his foot hit the first stair something lured his attention back to the hearth, the couch, and the woman who had upended his life. Brie Quaid might be Selene's doppelgänger but she was a person apart from his imaginary sultry siren. She was real and kind and mysterious in her own innocent way.

An impulse, risky yet exciting, struck Cal so fast and furiously he wasn't sure what had triggered it. More amazing, he acted without really thinking and found himself hovering over the couch peering into Brie Quaid's questioning blue eyes without knowing how he got across the room.

"How about this," he said, half-negotiating, half-begging. "You do me a favor and we'll call it square on room and board."

She turned her upper body toward him, pulling the dress tighter across her breasts. "I had a hunch one small omelette wouldn't be enough for a guy your size. Still hungry?"

Yes, he was. But the sort of hunger she ignited in Cal had nothing to do with food. "No, not that," he said more for his benefit than hers. "Though I wouldn't turn down another home cooked meal. I was wondering if you'd like to read a few chapters of my newest manuscript and give me your opinion."

Her brow shot up. "Me? Why? We hardly know each other, and I don't read mysteries. What kind of opinion could I give you?"

"The best kind," he answered. "An honest one."

From the way she groped for words, Cal figured she was startled by the request. "I...I'm flattered, but I don't know..."

"It's important," he rushed to say. "Very important." He swallowed. "Please."

Brie blinked. He sounded desperate, even to his own ears.

Cal got down on his haunches and leaned toward the couch. "Look, the fact of the matter is I'm stuck, and I think I'm too close to the story to dig my way out. I've got a deadline, a nervous editor who's cornered the market on antacids, and a main character who won't talk to me."

She stifled a laugh. "Won't talk to you?"

He chuckled, too. "Yeah, I bet that sounds as nuts to you as your *flim flum* arrangement of furniture sounds to me."

"*Feng shui,*" she slipped in.

"Whatever. The dirty little secret about crafting novels is the characters speak and the writer just takes notes."

She looked even more skeptical. "I'm sure there's more to it than that."

He shook his head. "A little, but not much. And Myles shut down. Can't get a word out of him. I think he skipped town and forgot to tell me."

She giggled at the scenario, and that made Cal smile even wider.

Cocking his head, Cal held her gaze. "I've got to hunt him down. How about giving me a hand?"

After another few moments, she nodded decisively. "All right, I'll read your chapters. But I can't guarantee I'll have any enlightening ideas."

Cal wanted to laugh out loud. An even more dangerous impulse made him want to reach over and give Brie Quaid an exuberant hug. He settled for sticking out his right hand. "Fair enough. I'll get the pages and you can start reading while I take my shower."

She took his hand and gave it a quick shake. "Agreed."

Did he look as eager as he felt? Didn't matter. He was energized. "Be back in a minute."

In less than a couple minutes he'd raced up the stairs and started gathering the scattered sheets of paper. Maybe Lain was right. Maybe there were no coincidences in life. Maybe Brie Quaid had landed on his doorstep for a reason, to help him over this creative hurdle.

Cal stopped himself cold. So where the hell was all this hope coming from? He didn't believe in fate, only man's infinite capacity to screw up a good thing whenever possible. If anything, he was playing the Myles Daemon role to the hilt, using Brie Quaid as a sounding board for the brief time she was in his life. That was all. That was enough.

Wasn't it?

Seven

"Women want lovemaking, not seduction."

Myles smirked, but couldn't hold Jorge's judgmental gaze. "Love? Seduction? What's the difference?"

Jorge sighed his annoyance. "The difference, I'm afraid, is something you cannot comprehend."

Chapter 7, *Murder, My Love—From the Files of Myles Daemon, P.I.*

* * * *

"Then if Selene's the problem maybe I should write her out of the story."

Brie shook her head in frustration. Before she could counter Cal's assumption the ancient Jeep Cherokee hit another rut in the road, the fifth since they started out toward the ranch twenty minutes ago. She gripped the armrest too late to keep from jostling in the bucket seat.

Cal glanced over at her. Though wraparound sunglasses hid the expression in his eyes, his quick grimace spoke a silent apology.

Brie decided not to ask why they hadn't taken the freeway bypass to the ranch instead of what appeared to be little more than a forgotten access road. She figured Cal had his reasons, none of which she was likely to fathom anyway. Besides, she didn't really want to interrupt the flow of their discussion about his current work in progress. She had been both flattered and flustered by his request, but took on the challenge with determination.

With just as much determination, she chose her words carefully when he started a rapid-fire inquisition just before they got ready to leave for dinner at the ranch.

"That's not what I'm saying," she picked up the thread of her critique, raising her voice to be heard over the rattle of the air conditioner. "My sense is Selene's critical to this story. Maybe more critical than even Myles's nemesis because she's changing him."

Cal's jaw tensed. "I don't want him to change."

"Then why did you create a female character who's fully his equal?"

Cal paused only a heartbeat. "I didn't realize I was doing that."

"Did you realize Myles is falling in love with her?"

Cal jerked his head around to Brie for a quick second before he set his eyes back on the rutted road. "You're making some pretty big leaps of logic by the middle of Chapter Ten."

Brie rolled her eyes. "He's in love with her. It was obvious by the beginning of Chapter Two."

The handsome profile tightened into a frown. "I don't remember writing that."

"Trust me," Brie said with a sigh. "You did. Bet you didn't know either that Selene's in love with Myles."

"She's just using him to find her brother's killer," Cal argued.

"That's not why she slept with him," Brie insisted. "Selene is honest and honorable. A woman like that wouldn't make love to a man unless she felt something for him."

Cal gave her a sideways glance. "You think?"

"I know," Brie answered. "I wouldn't."

Even as she made the claim Brie wondered at her bold words. She'd known Cal Porter for a sum total of forty-eight hours, and here she was, claiming to understand one of his characters who had by far and away more sexual experience than she did, fictional or otherwise.

Worse, Brie figured she'd embarrassed not only herself but Cal as well. For once he had no smart comeback.

"I suppose you're going to kill off Selene, like you do your other female characters," she hurried to say in hopes of covering her chagrin.

The worn leatherette of his bucket seat creaked with the shift of his weight. "Well..."

She laughed in spite of the undercurrent of tension between them, and found her stride. "No wonder you don't have a big following among women. I predict if you kill off Selene even Myles will openly rebel. You'll break his heart."

Cal gripped the steering wheel so tightly the skin over his knuckles went taut. "Myles's heart is armor-plated. He doesn't fall in love. He can't. It's not part of who he is."

"News flash, Cal," Brie insisted. "Selene has found a design flaw in his defenses, and she's already gotten in to do damage. Killing her off won't solve the problem, because after she dies Myles won't be, make that *can't be,* the same. He wouldn't ring true. You'll end up disappointing your fans as well as giving your detractors more ammunition."

He chuckled ominously. "My detractors? I already get mail from women who claim, in language not fit for print, that Myles is a good woman's worst nightmare. My editor won't even let me see some of the real flamers. How much worse could it get?"

"A lot worse," Brie assured him.

He gave her a quick glance. "You got all this from ten lousy chapters."

"They weren't lousy," Brie argued. "They were very good. And very revealing."

Brie studied Cal's solidly handsome profile and wondered if he really was similar to his fictional detective. What a shame, if true. Despite the sadness and anger that constantly threatened to overwhelm Brie, Cal hardly repulsed her. Indeed, she knew from the moment they touched there was a decency and goodness at his core that somehow balanced the shadows.

"Are you going to grow the ranks of my detractors by one?"

The question gave her pause. Brie sat taller in the bucket seat. "Not until, and unless, I find out what's in Myles's history that makes him react as he does toward women."

His jaw tightened. "You mean in *my* history."

Challenge came through loud and clear in those few words. He'd detect a lie. "You said writers can't help create characters somewhat like themselves."

Cal let out a slow, steady breath of air. "It's no secret," he replied in an even, but low voice. "There are no happily-ever-afters in my life. Just stories with no endings and none in sight."

Once again Brie felt the onslaught of soul-deep dark emotions. "So you've known the sort of women that populate your books," she dared press.

He said nothing for so long Brie thought she might have overstepped the bounds of simple curiosity and given him reason to shut down. She was surprised when he did finally speak.

"I know the type." It sounded as if Cal dragged each word out with supreme effort. "Beautiful and smart, but spoiled and immature. High maintenance. I..." He paused. "I learned I don't have patience for high maintenance."

That sounded personal. Yet Brie understood Cal Porter enough to know if she pressed him directly he'd shut down. "Selene isn't like most of the women you create," she pointed out, hoping the tack would keep him talking. "Did you know someone like her?"

Cal glanced over again and stared at Brie through his sunglasses for such a long span of moments that she nearly felt compelled to remind him of the road. "That doesn't matter," he finally said in a clipped voice. "The point is she's screwing up my book, not to mention Myles's life."

"I thought you wanted women to screw up Myles's life so he was never tempted to have a serious relationship," Brie reminded him.

"True, but now you say Myles is falling for this new woman. Can't have that."

"Why?"

"Because I kill her off at the end."

"Ah, neat, clean, no mess..."

"No grief." He said it through almost set teeth.

New tension filled the front seat. A tension so thick it seemed to suck the oxygen out of the confined space. Had the air outside not been so warm and humid, Brie would have opened the window.

If she hadn't sensed it before, Brie knew for certain now. Cal Porter had secrets that weighed heavy on his soul and crushed his joy. He desperately needed strokes of compassion and understanding, and she felt a compulsion to reach out with those gifts. But she had no real inkling of what drove him, what saddened him. Where would she begin?

Brie realized, as well, he didn't even accept her as anything but an intrusive blip on his personal radar screen. Cal would likely reject her attempts to understand on an even superficial level...

The Jeep ground to a halt. Brie grasped the armrest, but the seat belt held her in check. "What's wrong? What is it?"

Cal seemed oblivious to her breathy questions as he slowly pushed his sunglasses to the top of his head and leaned over the steering wheel. "Look up the road, about fifteen yards. See it?"

Brie squinted into the glare of late afternoon sunshine. On one side of the dirt road a cactus and brush covered foothill rose directly off a shallow shoulder. On the other side lay open space awash with tall grass, untouched as yet by the worst of the early summer heat. She didn't see the low, tawny body until the creature emerged from the hillside brush.

"A bobcat," Cal whispered, as if the animal might hear.

"Can you see it?"

"Yes," Brie answered, but with a question. "The sun is in my eyes, but I see the cat. Oh, my!"

Cal laid his arm around her shoulder and pulled her gently toward him across the gearshift console. "Better?"

Yes, that was better, even though she had to push against the restraining seat belt. She set her right hand to her hammering heart as the cat sauntered into full view. Small, sleek and wary as it emerged from the bushes, the animal faced fully toward the Jeep and planted itself. It didn't crouch. It didn't bare its teeth. But it waited, assessing and being assessed.

"He's beautiful!" she whispered in awe. "I've never seen a wild cat up this close except in a zoo. Are they common around here?"

"Not as common as they used to be," Cal replied in hushed, almost reverential tones. "As housing developments go up further and further from the cities wildlife is pushed to the edges of the real wilderness. I've been out here seven years, and this is only the third time I've seen a cat like this."

Brie couldn't take her eyes off the beautiful proud beast as he glared back at them. "How sad."

"Sad? It's criminal to push a wild animal to the margins of its habitat," Cal snapped. "People complain about the out of control deer population ruining landscapes and grass, yet they continue to push the deer's natural predators like this cat to the brink of extinction. Humans and animals can coexist as long as they respect each other's territories. Trouble is humans don't remember the animals were here first."

Brie smiled as she watched the cat push completely off the hillside and begin to amble across the road, never letting its gaze stray from the stopped Jeep. "Now you sound like a spokesperson for the Sierra Club."

As she spoke, Brie turned to look up at Cal. Only then did she realize how close he had pulled her to his side. His face was only inches from hers. She could feel his quick, quiet breath on her neck. His clean, male scent brought a queer tremble to the pit of her stomach.

Cal stared back at her as if asking the same questions that unsettled her. *What was happening? Why did neither of them withdraw?*

Then his gaze settled on her mouth. He studied her lips as if seeing them for the first time. Just as the bobcat had assessed their willingness to let him pass unmolested, Cal Porter, consciously or not, assessed her willingness to be kissed.

Brie knew as much, not because of her special psychic gifts. She knew as a woman who wanted this man to kiss her. The barely hidden hunger in his green eyes excited her. The press of his fingers on her upper arm sent out shafts of electricity. Despite the fact that she hardly knew Cal Porter, and understood him less, the circle of his embrace and the heat of his body were all too familiar and beguiling.

A tension unlike any Brie had known before swirled through the front seat of the Jeep. In reflex, she curled her fingers inward. Only then did she realize her left hand and forearm lay on Cal's lean right thigh. She guessed she'd done so to balance herself and steady her injured knee when he'd pulled her across the console. Now her heart needed steadying.

Yet Brie couldn't slow her breathing much less ease the slam of her heart against her ribs. Neither could she harness the runaway impulse that eased her closer to his lips, closer to the kiss they both wanted. This feeling of abandon, of becoming lost in pure sensual bliss, hit Brie with stunning force. Even more stunning, she wanted nothing more than to surrender to the moment.

This wasn't like her. No man before had exerted this power over her senses or her reason. She had never allowed it because opening herself so personally might lead to sacrificing too much control over her psychic sensitivities. If she could feel the presence of people long dead by merely touching objects they had handled, how could she touch a man with such personal need and want and not be overwhelmed by shared desire?

And now, in the middle of a soul-crisis brought on by the nightmares, Brie's grip on her mental and emotional control was tenuous at best. No, she couldn't risk being overwhelmed by Cal Porter's irresistible allure. Not now. Maybe not ever, if opening up and losing control meant sharing even a moment of her mother's fate.

Never that!

Brie snatched her hand from Cal's thigh and snapped her body back into the passenger's bucket seat. Fisting her heated, tingling fingers and jamming them into her lap, she shifted her focus back to the cat, who had already started to disappear into the tall grass.

"Thanks. For stopping that is," she stammered. "That was

a treat." Might he mistake her words? "I mean the bobcat. Don't see something like that every day." She sounded too chipper and felt his stare on her profile. "I mean the bobcat. You sure know how to show a lady a good time. I mean..."

"Yeah, sure," he cut in. "We better get going. Lain will wonder what happened to us."

Lain would wonder? Did Cal hear the irony of his own words?

The Jeep lurched forward. Brie glanced to her left, but Cal had dropped his sunglasses back in place and riveted his attention on the road. Even the ruddiness had started to drain from his face.

"Thanks for the help," he said.

Between the rattle of the air conditioner and the throbbing of blood in her ears Brie wasn't sure she heard him right. "Huh?"

Cal steered the Jeep right, probably to miss a rut. "Thanks for the help. On the manuscript. You gave me a few things to think about."

The manuscript? In the space of ten seconds had he buried that near-kiss in a dusty corner of his mind in deference to more immediate—and most likely more important—considerations?

Feeling a fool, and somehow betrayed by a man who in fact owed her nothing, Brie crossed her arms. "Good," she muttered. "Glad I could help."

With all the ambient noise of the thudding tires and wheezing air conditioning system, she doubted he caught the sarcasm in her voice.

Cal fell silent for the rest of the ten minute ride to the ranch. Brie didn't care. She was too busy exorcising the hurt that had no reason to exist.

* * * *

Cal propped himself against the parlor door frame and scanned the cozy, over-furnished room that tonight, ironically, didn't seem to have enough seats. Gil Sutter lounged in his favorite chair, while Cal's nephew, Eric, sat cross-legged on the floor devouring another piece of apple pie. Two of the family's three mixed-breed dogs roamed freely back and forth between the parlor and newly added sunroom. A third hound, the oldest and, Cal suspected, most hard of hearing, curled his massive black body at Lain's feet as she sat at one end of the couch.

Then there was Brie Quaid. Settled into the other corner of

the couch with little Dulcie snuggled on her lap and surrounded by Cal's nearest kin, she looked more at home in the ranch house parlor than he felt. He had thought to make the dinner a quick in-and-out visit. After all, Brie had been raised an only child in what sounded like insulated environments by both her parents and her aunt. Cal was afraid her sensibilities might clash with the onslaught of his raucous family.

She surprised him royally. Plopped into the middle of baby babble, dog yipping, teenaged braggadocio, and familial give-and-take, Brie drank it all in like a woman parched. At dinner she laughed with genuine appreciation at some of Gil's offhanded bawdiness, all the time blushing her pretty shade of pink. And she treated Eric like a peer. Unless Cal missed his guess, the teenager was half smitten before the main course.

More surprising still, little Dulcie struck up an instant affinity for the unmarried-raised-as-an-only-child-big-city-woman. After dinner, the child made a beeline for Brie, snuggled into her side with a book, and begged for attention with her huge dark eyes.

Brie reacted as if it had been the most natural thing on Earth. She didn't seem to care that Dulcie's fingers were still sticky with supper leavings, or that the little girl crunched the crisp material of Brie's sexy little sundress beneath her diapered bottom. Brie pulled the child into a loose embrace and read a story in hushed tones while the other adults chattered around her. Without embarrassment, Miss L.A. Psychic quacked like a duck, mooed like a cow, and giggled with the little girl.

Of course, he'd heard Brie laugh, chuckle, giggle and chat quite a bit during the evening. What a contrast to those rare times when he'd brought Alicia and Jeanie to dinner with the in-laws. Sometimes, especially after Alicia had been particularly rude, he wondered why Lain bothered to invite him and his family back.

Greta, the middle-aged German chief-cook-housekeeper-sometimes-nanny, suddenly appeared in front of him with a tray of strong coffee. Cal declined with a shake of his head and took a sip of the after-dinner brandy Gil had poured for him. The smooth liquid flowed down his throat like warm silk.

Warm silk. That's how the skin of Brie Quaid's upper arm had felt under his palm when he pulled her close to see the bobcat. She had smelled good, too, like flowers and soap and woman. Cal hadn't been that close to a woman other than Lain for ages. So why should it have been surprising that Brie's feminine charms stirred a healthy dose of lust?

Surprising enough that the mere memory of the brief, unrequited interlude made him catch his breath now, some three hours later. Cal had wanted to kiss her. Hard. And long. She had a mouth made for kissing.

And skin like warm silk.

If she hadn't pulled back...

"Okay, babycakes, time for bed," Lain announced as she reached over to scoop Dulcie from Brie's side.

The little girl hung tight to Brie long enough to get a farewell hug. Then she clung to her mama's neck as Lain carried the child to Gil.

Cal lowered his gaze to the rich brown liquid in the bowl of his brandy snifter. Would the ache ever go away? Would he ever stop envying his brother-in-law's good fortune and happiness?

"Uncle Cal?"

He looked up to find Lain and Dulcie standing no farther than arm's length. No, she wasn't going to make him do this. Not tonight!

Impatient with his panic, Dulcie practically leapt out of Lain's embrace and threw her arms around Cal's neck. He caught the toddler awkwardly but cushioned the impact at the expense of his brandy. The liquid sloshed, and Lain rescued the snifter before he dropped it. Then, however, he had to deal with the choking rush of emotion roused by the brush of baby fine hair against his neck, and the scent of talcum powder.

He glared at his sister. *Why, Lain?* he railed silently.

Yet, some instinct, buried but not dead, made him hold the baby with a father's tender strength. Dear God, how he missed these moments!

Dulcie tolerated the hug for a mere five seconds before she let go and reached for her mother. But those five seconds ripped at the scars on Cal's heart. Lain set the snifter back into Cal's hand, smiled with tender but stern understanding, and proceeded to Eric.

Cal resisted the temptation to throw back the swallow of brandy left in his snifter. Dark memories held that impulse at bay. Numbing emotions with drink was a fool's solution. Hadn't he learned that lesson, too?

He blew out a breath and lifted his gaze...

To find Brie peering at him with concern.

"Want a refill, Cal?"

Gil's question snagged his attention. His brother-in-law looked concerned, too, but in a more sympathetic way. Unwilling to be the object of anyone's pity Cal forced a smile. "No, thanks. Brie still can't drive, so I have to stay relatively sober."

"I can drive you home in our pickup," Eric volunteered.

Glad for the diversion from his dour thoughts, Cal speared the teenager with an almost parental scowl. "And you got your driver's permit when?"

Eric puffed up. "Mom's been giving me lessons."

Since Lain was already upstairs putting Dulcie to bed, Cal turned to his brother-in-law.

Gil shrugged. "Hey, we've got a ranch. Acres and acres of wide-open spaces where the deer and antelope play. If Eric's going to make mistakes what better place to do it?"

"What about the deer and antelope?" Cal asked, trying to hide a grin.

"I've only hit two bucks," Eric whined.

When Cal dropped his jaw the boy broke out in laughter. "Gotcha!"

Cal took a moment to close his mouth and set down his brandy. "Come here, big shot." He beckoned the boy with a crooked finger. "I'll show you gotcha!"

When Eric begged off in mock fear, Cal went after him and put his nephew into a playful headlock.

Lain came sauntering downstairs in time to hear her son "Give!" and shook her head as she went to a serving cart and poured herself a brandy. "Good heavens, boys, settle down. We don't want Brie to think we're completely out of control."

"Too late for that, hon," Gil cooed. "Remember, she met Cal first."

Cal pushed away from Eric, gave the boy good head rub, and cast Lain a snarl which she responded to with an air kiss. As Brie laughed out loud, he ambled back to his place against the wall.

"See, she's having a great time, out of control or not," Gil pointed out.

"Yes, I am," Brie agreed. Laying her hands on her lap, she smiled contentedly. "Dinner was superb, too. I haven't tasted ribs that good in years."

"Greta's recipe from the old country," Lain said.

When Brie started to laugh at the joke, Lain shook her head. "Honest. I didn't ask how or why. I just accepted our good luck that we landed the only German cook and housekeeper in Southern California who could make killer barbecue ribs."

"Well, I'd say Greta is fortunate to be part of this household." Brie looked at both Gil and Lain. "You have a wonderful family. Thanks for letting me share the evening with you."

Gil cricked his neck. "So, how come a pretty young woman like you isn't married with a family of your own?"

Cal could almost hear the air being sucked out of the room. Lain stomped over to her husband and swatted his shoulder. "For heaven's sake, I thought I had the run-on mouth in this family!"

Gil sat tall in defense. "Well, she's good with kids! She had Dulcie eating out of her hand."

"Yeah, you passed the 'Dulcie shakedown,'" Eric said. "All new people have to read her at least one story before she goes to bed. If she doesn't like it, she bleats like a goat."

"Don't sound so put out, mister," Lain chided her son. "Wasn't it yesterday I heard you claim Dulcie was a great chick magnet?"

Eric blushed to the roots of his bristle-cut blond hair. "Mo-om!"

"I think it was the other way around," Brie put in sweetly. "Dulcie had me eating of her hand. She's an absolutely beautiful child."

"Either way," Gil insisted, "you're a natural mom. Am I right, Cal?"

It was an honest appeal, one male under feminine siege appealing to the only other mature male in the room. But Cal's heart wasn't in the warm laughter that surrounded him. He forced a smile and shook his head. "I'm not a good one to judge, Gil. You're on your own in this fight."

"A woman can get by without a man these days, you know," Lain piped up.

Gil actually appeared remorseful as he turned his attention back to Brie. "I didn't mean to pry."

"And I didn't take it as such," Brie assured him. Suddenly, though, she looked squeamish. "In my work I don't come in contact with many eligible men. When I do date it's usually nothing more serious than dinner once or twice."

Cal imagined he looked every bit as surprised as Gil. Brie Quaid was young, pretty and sexy in a wholly innocent way that not more than three hours ago almost had him acting like a rutting idiot. Either she was oblivious to the fact or she was wasting her time with the dolts in Los Angeles.

Then Cal noticed how she clenched her hands as they lay in her lap. There were other emotions at work here, he realized. Something she held back, despite her cavalier handling of Gil's inquisition.

"I really have had a terrific time tonight," Brie repeated, changing the subject with a gracefulness Cal had to admire. "In fact, I was wondering if I could come back when my knee is better and do a walk around the entire place, guest quarters and all. This is a beautifully preserved house, and I'm impressed with the authenticity of your decorating."

"All according to the principles of *fo fum?*" Cal teased.

Brie looked up at him through her lashes with mock impatience. "*Feng shui*. And actually, whether Lain meant to or not, she did incorporate quite a few of the principles."

Lain raised her brandy snifter in a salute. "Spoken like a professional interior decorator." She gave Cal a wicked sideways glance. "Not to mention you put Cal in his place. Sure, Brie, you're welcome anytime. Meanwhile, got any free advice?"

Cal rolled his eyes. Gil snorted. Eric looked as if he wanted to melt into the floor for embarrassment.

Lain glanced around the room at the three of them. "What?"

"Free advice?" Gil said. "Lain, the girl's on R&R. And besides, that's like having Doc Mason over to dinner and then asking him a medical opinion."

"Done that," Lain quipped.

Gil suddenly looked as mortified as Eric. But Brie held up her hand, and Cal could see she was trying hard not to laugh. "It's okay. Free advice is the least I can give in return for inviting me over."

As Lain smiled with a hint of smugness, Brie sat up a little straighter and looked around. "There's really not much I can say. It's obvious you've treated this house with the care and respect its age and history deserve. You've very gently instilled your family pride and love into the original essence of the structure and the furnishings."

Cal felt a tingling in his chest. The way Brie talked about

treating the house with care and respect and the original essence of the place, he just knew she was going into psychic mode whether or not she intended to give herself away. On alert, he held his breath as her gaze landed on the scarred but solid antique sideboard placed just inside the arch between the parlor and dining room.

"That piece came with the place, didn't it?" Though framed as a question, Brie didn't seem to have a doubt.

After glancing briefly at the sideboard, Lain focused her attention on Brie's pensive face. "I noticed earlier you ran your fingers along the door carvings, like you were interested in it."

Brie nodded absently, her whole attention focused on the sideboard.

"The executor of the estate that sold us the house and property didn't want it," Lain explained. "He was just going to sell it for fire wood."

Brie winced, as if distressed by the news.

"That was my reaction," Lain agreed. "It was beat up, but still in good enough shape that Gil and I thought we could use it in the family quarters, at least."

Brie cocked her head, just as she did when she claimed to have heard voices in the cabin. Was she hearing voices now, Cal wondered, and noticed Gil slipped a little forward in his chair as he listened intently.

"The workmanship is magnificent," Brie continued. "But the construction and style of the carvings are unique. My guess is the cabinet was designed and decorated by a very talented amateur craftsman. The work definitely was done with unusual dedication. A labor of love maybe."

Lain's eyes went wide. "That's true. When Gil and I started cleaning it up we found an old letter stuck at the back of one of the bottom drawers. It was from the father of Elsie Matteson, the wife of the original owner of this property. She was from St. Louis. Married the ranch owner and moved out here with him. Her father was a carpenter and made the sideboard as a wedding present."

Brie looked over at Lain. "It belongs back in the guest dining room."

Lain blinked. "Well, that's where we found it, but the piano is there now . . ."

"The sideboard belongs back in the guest dining room," Brie cut in softly. "Put the piano in the guest parlor where the

TV is. Both pieces will be happier in their original locations."

"Happier?" Lain echoed.

Brie caught her breath, and smiled with chagrin, as if she realized suddenly what she had said and how it might have sounded. "I mean, both will conform to the principles of *feng shui* better in those locations."

Lain narrowed her gaze, as if assessing Brie for the first time. "You talk about the furniture as if were alive, Buttercup."

"Well, ah . . ." Brie cleared her throat. "Not alive, exactly, but even inanimate objects have stories to tell in their own way. One just has to listen carefully, you might say."

Lain grinned. "Cal told me you had a special sense about these things."

"He did?" Brie looked over at him with both worry and accusation.

Cal groaned under his breath. At least Lain hadn't used the "p" word. Just to make sure his sister didn't blurt out anything more incriminating, he cast Lain a warning glare.

Lain didn't get the hint. "Okay, he said you were psychic."

Eric popped up on his knees. "No foolin'! Really, Brie? Are you a real psychic? Wow, that's cool!"

Cal was sure he saw pure adoration in the teenager's eyes. Was he the only one who didn't swallow this mystical crap?

"It's just a sense I have about these things," Brie demurred.

"A keen sense, I'd say," Lain said. "Must give you one heck of an edge in your business."

Brie smiled, but with wariness. "On occasion."

"Well," Lain said with a sigh, "we'll just have to get the sideboard and the piano moved to where they'll be happier."

"Hey, mom," Eric piped up, "didn't dad want to keep the piano in the guest parlor all along?"

There was a moment of awkward silence, then Gil let out a loud guffaw. "Guess I'm a natural decorator after all, huh?" he taunted Lain.

Lain sniffed. "You just didn't want to take the trouble to move it when I asked." She then pushed out of her chair, sauntered over to Cal, and smiled with strain. "Got a minute, little brother?"

"Sure thing," he grumbled, and decided he'd take the opportunity to tell his sister once and for all to quit pushing him beyond his self-imposed limits where Dulcie was concerned. Then he'd ask her what the hell she was thinking when she brought up the subject of Brie's so-called psychic abilities.

Leaving Brie to handle the other two males in the parlor, Cal set his drink on the coffee table and followed Lain back through the dining room and into the kitchen.

Greta was nowhere in sight, but the cavernous ranch house kitchen was clean and tidy, without a hint that the cook had prepared a rib dinner for five that evening. He almost ran head on into his sister when Lain turned on her heel in the middle of the room.

A smile quivered at the corner of Lain's mouth as she reached into the right pocket of her slacks and pulled out a sealed white envelope folded over on itself. "Got somethin' for you, Cal." She tucked the envelope into the breast pocket of his shirt and gave the spot a pat. "Wear them proudly."

"Lain, what the..." Cal fished the envelope out of his pocket and held it between his thumb and index finger. Something inside the sealed envelope creaked softly. Then he felt one, no two, no three thick rings. Condoms?

He knew his eyes bugged out. Couldn't help it. "Lain, what's this about?"

She jammed her hands onto her hips. "Come on, little brother. Didn't mom ever have 'The Talk' with you? She did with me. And I quote, 'Keep your skirt down around your knees...'" She winked "In your case, keep your fly zipped. 'But if you *must*,'" Lain continued in singsong, "'be prepared.'" She grinned brightly. "This is your near future, Cal, should you be prepared to accept it."

"My near future what?" he demanded.

"Your near future with Buttercup," she said in a stage whisper. "I got them when I was upstairs with Dulcie. They're from an old stash. Gil and I aren't going to need them anymore, not after last year anyway."

Cal swallowed the worst of his anger at the glancing mention of Lain's own personal trauma of learning she could no longer have the children she desperately wanted. He tried to keep his voice low and level. "What are you thinking? No, maybe you aren't thinking..."

"I know what I see with my own eyes," she cut in. "You and Brie got the hots for each other. End of sentence. Over and out." She snatched the envelope from him and stuck it back in his pocket.

Cal fished them out again. "Are you crazy? I've known the woman for less than two days!"

"Sometimes that's all it takes," Lain answered in an amazingly reasonable tone. "Good Lord, Cal, all night long you stared across the dinner table at Buttercup like she was dessert. When your hands touched over the salt shaker I thought both of you would explode." She cricked her brow. "Now that would have really pissed off Greta. Not to mention the story I would have had to make up for Eric."

It was true. Cal had felt the unmistakable hum of sexual tension all night long. How could he not, after he and Brie had come so close to acting on a sheer—and plainly stupid—impulse on the ride over. "Whatever you're imagining..."

"I'm not 'imagining' anything, little brother," she sassed back. "Brie is pretty. She's nice. The whole family likes her." She tilted her head. "And her perfume is all over you."

In reflex Cal sniffed the shoulder of his shirt. "That's not her perfume," he argued, way too defensively.

"Oh, you've taken to wearing lily-of-the-valley after shave?"

"No...no, it's bath oil."

Lain bit her lower lip to keep a smile from erupting. "Better. Shower together. Conserve water. That's important in these parts."

His blood pressure spiked. "I was *alone* when I tipped over *Brie's* bottle of bath oil in the shower this morning and nearly fell on my ass."

"Then maybe you should shower together for safety's sake."

Cal threw out his arms. "This isn't funny, Lain. Whatever you're thinking, you've got it all wrong."

The playfulness in her eyes disappeared. "No, Cal, you're the one who's wrong. You have been for a long time now. You're stuck somewhere in the past, and you can't get yourself unstuck. This is your opportunity."

"She won't be staying long," Cal reminded Lain. "She's on her way to New Mexico, and she's in a hurry."

"Then slow her down. Divert her."

"I don't pick up strange women, never have, never will," Cal insisted. "And Brie Quaid is about as strange as I've come across in a long time."

"Because she's psychic?" Lain waved off his concerns.

Cal could only shake his head. "You really believe that

stuff?"

"Oh, hell, all women are a little psychic, Cal. Brie's probably just better tuned in than the rest of us." Lain wiggled her brows. "If she's really tuned in then she'll know just what you want."

Cal chose to ignore the salacious innuendo. "Someone as hardheaded and practical as you believes that crap?" he scoffed.

Blood rushed into Lain's cheeks. "Hey, just because I wear cowboy boots and ride a horse every day doesn't mean I'm always 'hardheaded and practical.' I believe there's a lot that can't be explained away by logic or reason. Stuff happens, little brother," she said, and gave him a pointed look that shamed him and angered him all in the same moment. "Sometimes you just have to except it and be thankful. But, damn, I know what I see with my own eyes and hear with my own ears. Psychic or not, you like her. You like her a lot. And she likes you. Go for it."

Cal grabbed Lain's hand and slapped the envelope into her palm. "Not in this century. Even if it were possible, it wouldn't be right."

Lain shook her head, but her eyes were soft with concern. "Right? Damn, boy, I think you've been cooped up so long with your make-believe friends you've forgotten what's real. Are you happy? Do you remember what's *good?* No one would blame you for taking this chance, for the love of common sense! Besides, things weren't dandy between you and Alicia long before she headed for the hills."

"It wasn't all Alicia's fault," he felt the need to say.

"Of course, it wasn't," Lain agreed. "But it was half her fault. You've paid for your sins. You've tried to find the truth. But at some point you have to put all that behind you. You have to accept that the truth may be out there, but you'll never get your hands around it. Good God, even Alicia's son-of-a-bitch father closed down her estate last year."

She jammed the envelope back into his pocket. "You have to get on with life, Cal. Use these damn things or don't. But for heaven's sake, keep them and keep hope alive."

"Hey, mom, is there more pie?"

Cal's hand stalled halfway back to his shirt pocket at the sound of Eric's voice not more than three steps behind him. Too wound up in anger over this latest episode of "My Sister, The Unrepentant Meddler," he hadn't heard the teenager come through the kitchen door.

Lain grinned coyly, patted Cal's shoulder, and breezed past him. "Sure thing, Sweetie. Help yourself. Maybe Uncle Cal would like a piece, too, on his way back out to the parlor."

And she was gone, knowing full well Cal wouldn't have the chance now to offload her "gift" with Eric in tow.

Besides, it wasn't worth the trouble to pursue the matter with Lain. She wanted him to take the damned condoms? Fine. He'd haul them back to the cabin and trash them. Brie Quaid probably would leave by Friday, no worse for her ignorance of this whole, sorry scene, or Lain's grand plan for the two of them.

Still, as far as strategies for getting him "unstuck," as Lain termed it, having a brief affair with someone like Brie Quaid had appeal. She struck a chord of need in Cal, one he'd forgotten existed. Yet even if Brie had hinted she was that kind of woman, which she definitely had not, Cal recoiled from the notion of a one-night stand.

He might have been a washout as a husband, but he'd been an honorable washout.

"Uncle Cal, do you want a piece of pie?"

His head snapped up at Eric's innocent question. "Ah, no, no thanks, Buddy. I've got to be headed home. There's some cleaning out I have to do yet tonight."

He breathed deeply and the paper inside his shirt pocket crinkled.

The envelope would be the first thing in the garbage.

Eight

"Selene. Her name means daughter of the moon," Jorge pointed out as if he were being reasonable. "It's true, Myles. She lights the darkness of your soul. She is your opposite and equal. Let her save you."

"Maybe I don't want to be saved," Myles argued. "If I live in darkness at least I do so of my own free will. I give no one control over my life. Understand?"

Chapter 8, Murder, My Love—From the Files of
Myles Daemon, P.I.

* * * *

Brie didn't get it. After an evening filled with good food, light conversation, and lots of laughter Cal Porter sat behind the steering wheel of the Jeep, stewing in silence. Did nothing relax this tightly wound man?

The dark of night concealed his expression, just as the sunglasses had on the ride over to the ranch. Dashboard lights did little but cast deep shadows on his face. Yet Brie could well imagine the hard set of his jaw and the cool intensity of his green eyes as he watched the road ahead.

Perhaps he had a right to be on guard, Brie decided ruefully. When they drove this back road together before sunset, a moment of shared wonder almost became too intimate for a woman and man who had known each other less than forty-eight hours. Full-blown night encompassed them now, with a natural ambiance of even deeper intimacy. Remembering the incident and how it made her heart kick up a beat, Brie couldn't say she felt entirely blasé either.

Whatever the reason, the tension between them begged for relief. Brie decided to initiate some conversation. "Thanks for driving me over to the ranch for supper. I had a great time."

"Lain deserves the thanks. She did the inviting."

Gracious he was not. She tried again, if for no other reason than to break the oppressive silence in the front seat. "Oh, I intend to. When I get to Aunt Sophie's I'll write Lain and Gil a thank you note. Lain especially has been kind and thoughtful."

"Mmm-hmmm."

A flash of lightning in the southwest sky brought Cal forward over the steering wheel to get a better look at the starless heavens.

Brie counted the seconds until she heard a rumble of thunder. "Do you think we'll make it back to the cabin before the storm breaks?"

"No."

"Oh, good, something to look forward to."

Cal glanced over, but quickly looked back to the road. "Is something wrong? Is it your knee?"

"My knee's just fine," Brie told him, glad the sarcasm finally elicited more than monosyllables out of him. "I think all the moving around actually helped loosen the joint."

"Good."

Good what? That her knee didn't hurt any more? Or that it meant she'd be leaving for New Mexico faster than expected?

Instead of verbalizing the annoyance she felt, Brie smiled, though he wouldn't be able to actually see the effort. "Eric is a nice kid. He hung around you all night. I noticed, too, he barbered his hair to look like yours. A little hero-worship, maybe?"

"Yeah, maybe."

Brie realized she was tapping her left shoe on the floor and stopped it. "Do you have dinner at the ranch often?"

"No."

One more try, Brie thought, and then she'd just burrow into the seat and bear the silence. It would be easier than beating her head against the invisible wall he'd erected. "Dulcie sure is cute."

The leather seat creaked with the shift of Cal's weight. He appeared to sit a little taller, as if his spine had gone stiff. "Yeah, she is."

He agreed, but grudgingly. Brie recalled how he'd gone ashen when Lain had thrust the little girl at him for a good night hug. When Dulcie leaned toward her mother Cal gave up the child with almost palpable relief.

"You seemed a little uneasy around her tonight," Brie ventured.

"Who?"

"Dulcie," she said, reminding him of the current topic of the mostly one-sided discussion. "Your inexperience showed."

"No offense, Brie, but you don't know anything about my experience. Or lack of it," he snapped.

Chastised, Brie bit her lip, and wedged herself between the seat and the passenger door. "You're right. I'm sorry."

So much for trying to carry on a friendly conversation.

Cal let out an exasperated breath. "No, I'm sorry. Lain tells me at least twice a week I act like a cold, insensitive jerk. I usually blow her off, but I've found myself apologizing to you a lot these past two days. Must be something to her complaints."

"I'm sure you don't mean to act like a cold, insensitive jerk," Brie replied. She didn't care at this point whether or not she insulted him. She'd had enough of Cal Porter's temperamental attitude.

He said nothing for a moment and kept his eyes on the narrow dirt road. "No," he finally admitted, "I don't mean it. It's just that for a long time I haven't had anybody but Lain hold up a mirror and force me to look at myself. Guess the reflection isn't pretty."

Pretty? No, pretty wasn't the word for Cal Porter's all-male good looks, Brie thought. And for some reason, the unexplained sadness that radiated from his soul made that physical attractiveness all the more alluring to her.

"I guess I sounded like I was prying," she admitted. "It's really none of my business why..."

Brie clamped her mouth shut. She'd almost done it again; asked why he'd seemed so panicked about holding the little girl.

"Why what?" he prodded. "Why I don't want Lain to force me in directions I don't want to go?"

"I think her intentions are honorable. She cares about you," Brie pointed out.

"Yeah, but I'm a big boy," he snarled. "I don't need a keeper. I don't give Lain my opinion of her life decisions, even when I think she's full of it. I just wish she would return the favor and leave me alone."

The anger radiating off Cal made Brie squirm. "Is that why you hold back with the baby? You don't think the adoption was a good idea?"

He paused a heartbeat, and then his shoulders caved forward. "The adoption was the best stroke of good fortune for everyone involved. Dulcie's a lucky little girl, because Lain and Gil are terrific parents, and Eric makes the best older brother around. I couldn't be happier for all of them."

A wash of relief took Brie by surprise. For some reason it was important to her that Cal accepted Dulcie into his sister's family. She'd sensed a depth of goodness in him, but he covered it so well with an irksome defensiveness that it was hard to tell where his real sympathies lay.

There was something else, too, a wistful longing in Cal's voice that seemed to grow from the sadness that bound his soul. Caught in the backwash of the familiar sadness, Brie found she had to clear her throat of empathetic emotion before she could speak again. "Gil mentioned they might try to adopt another child."

"They always wanted a houseful of kids," Cal replied. "But Lain had a bad time carrying Eric. After he was born she had five miscarriages within seven years. Then last year she had to undergo some surgery that ended any hope she and Gil could have any more children of their own."

"I would never have guessed." Brie shook her head. "Lain looks so..."

"Rugged?" Cal finished when Brie couldn't quite find the right word. "Appearances can deceive. She talks tough and can match physical skills with any one of the ranch hands. But she just wasn't made to have a string of babies. For a while she and Gil did foster care for infants, but the kids were only passing through until they were placed with permanent families. Lain grieved every time she had to part with one of the babies. That's when she and Gil decided to go the adoption route themselves."

He glanced at Brie. "I'm the one who put them in touch with a lawyer friend of mine who handles such cases."

"You did?" Brie heard the shock in her own voice.

He chuckled, low and with a hint of real amusement. "So maybe I'm not a cold, insensitive jerk?"

"Not in this case," she admitted. "And in this case I apologize for misjudging you."

"But all your other judgments stand?" He seemed to be teasing her.

She laughed softly. "For now, until proven otherwise."

"You realize that flies in the face of American jurisprudence?" he lectured. "You're judging me guilty until proven innocent."

"You've made yourself look pretty guilty on occasion, Mr. Porter," she sassed back.

He laughed out loud this time. Brie realized she'd never before heard the full-throated sound of his amusement. She also realized she liked it. A lot.

"I guess as long as we're confessing misjudgments I stand corrected about you, too," Cal offered.

"About what?"

"The Miss L.A. thing."

"Oh, that." Heady with pride that she'd drawn him out of his self-imposed shell even a little, Brie wanted to keep up the light banter. "I guess I'm used to having you call me that now, but I admit at first it was irritating. What, exactly, did you think after one look at me anyway? That I was out with a wild crowd every night, cruising the downtown hot spots, picking up men?"

"You could."

Cal's matter-of-fact statement, devoid of any humor now, took her aback. "Was that a compliment?"

Cal swiveled in the seat as far as he could without letting go of the steering wheel. "Hey, you didn't get huffy when Gil asked you about your social life."

"He didn't ask me if I barhop," Brie reminded him. "Gil asked me why I wasn't married."

He blew out a frustrated breath. "Okay, there's a difference."

"Big difference," Brie emphasized. "For your information there are a lot more women in L.A. like me than not. I don't even live in Los Angeles. I live in Glendale."

"Now I'm supposed to say I'm sorry again?" he grumped.

She waved him off, and stifled a grin. "Never mind. I don't think I could take another one of those sincere apologies."

"Hey, don't get angry because I made the mistake of believing someone like you would be hooking up with guys."

"Someone like me? Oh, do dig that hole deeper, Mr. Porter."

"I *mean* smart, attractive..." He glanced over at her. "Fairly easy to get along with."

Brie wanted to feel good about his assessment, but he'd ticked the attributes off as if reciting a grocery list.

When she said nothing Cal groaned. "That wasn't smooth, was it?"

Brie held up her hand. "No, but I get the point. And please, don't apologize again."

"Fine, I won't," he snapped. "I never claimed to be perfect in the first place." He leaned forward and looked out the windshield toward the sky again. "So, what's wrong with the men in L.A.?"

His question was overly casual. Brie went a little on guard. "Wrong? I never said there was anything wrong. There are lots of terrific guys in Los Angeles. Just, well, not right for me."

"Then terrific isn't good enough for you, huh? Holding out for that perfection most of us males lack?"

There was an edgy undercurrent in his tease that irritated Brie. "Speaking as someone who tried to be a perfect child, let me tell you the concept is overrated. I just don't want to get on that ride. It's... it's a personal preference."

Cal glanced sharply at her for a moment before setting his eyes back on the road. "Whoa, I...I *am* sorry. I...I mean, I'm sorry...damn, talk about misunderstanding," he babbled. "When you talked about dating a guy twice at the most...I assumed...It's okay. I get it now. You don't prefer men."

Brie almost laughed at the leap of logic. "No, you don't get it. I'm definitely a woman who 'prefers men' as you put it."

Then Cal chuckled with what sounded like relief. "Well, that's good. I mean, for a minute there I thought living out here by myself all this time had deadened instincts deeper rooted than my need for civil company." He started to look over at her then snapped his head forward. "That didn't come out right either."

Brie held up her hand. Spewing out one verbal *faux pas* after another certainly made Cal Porter more endearing. But she sensed the conversation would ultimately lead back to earlier this evening when they'd almost kissed. She didn't want to go there, not until she better understood why she felt so inexplicably drawn to this man.

"I'd like to share my life with someone. A male someone," she assured him with a sigh. "The problem is that would mean sharing *all* of my life. *All* of who I really am. And in too many ways, I haven't made peace with the part of my life that sets me apart the most. How can I expect that of someone else?"

"You mean this psychic stuff?" he guessed.

"I know you don't believe in it, but it's real enough to me," she replied.

"I'm learning it's real to a lot of people," he admitted. "Lain and the rest of the family seem to have bought into it."

She winced at his casual sarcasm.

He went on as if he didn't realize how the tone of his comment might have sounded to her. "But you said your aunt taught you to control it."

"Yes," Brie agreed. "And that's part of the problem. I have to control how I connect with the physical world or I become overwhelmed with emotions and impressions. I don't know what would happen if I let down all the shields I've erected over time, or if I lose myself for even a moment in someone else. I don't know if I could ever pull back or separate myself again."

She rubbed her arms. "I think that's what happened to my mother. I think she just got lost and never quite knew where she left off and someone else began. I think it made her crazy, and I don't want to become like her."

"Let me get this straight," Cal recapped. "Are you telling me you've never had..." He paused, with his mouth hanging open.

"Ah, never mind. None of my business."

Brie knew full well what question Cal had almost blurted out. If she hadn't been so chagrined by her lack of sexual experience, she might have smiled at the way he'd almost swallowed his tongue. On the other hand, maybe this was the perfect lead-in to explain her earlier reaction to the near kiss.

"No, I've never had a serious relationship with a man," she admitted with as much discretion as possible.

Her delicate candor seemed to relax him. "Because you're afraid you'll become your mother?" he guessed.

"Or I'd actually *be* a mother to some poor child who inherited this so-called 'gift,'" she added. "I know what it felt like growing up with all the confusion and shame. And I know what I put my aunt through when I first went to live with her after my parents died. I'm surprised she didn't drive me to the desert and let the vultures fight over my scrawny teenaged carcass."

Cal chuckled out loud at that. "You?"

He sounded so incredulous and amused, Brie had to grin despite the memories. "This from a man who derogatorily tagged me Miss L.A. on first sight?"

"First impressions," he reminded her. "Wasn't long before, well, let's say you didn't live down to my expectations."

"Another backhanded compliment, Mr. Porter?"

He shrugged. "So I'm not getting smoother with time and effort I'll work on it. Back to you. Why would your aunt consider turning you into vulture feed?"

Memories flashed through Brie's mind. She was surprised that time and perspective had dampened the emotional angst of that turbulent time and she could actually smile. "To put it kindly I was a challenge. I hit bottom after my parents died. Probably something to do with all the guilt weighing me down. Then there was the pain of my injuries, the physical therapy, the new surroundings, and this woman who was my mother's sister but acted more like some do-gooder fairy godmother. I mean, *I* was the person who was supposed to care for everyone, and here she was daring to care for me. She was stealing my reason for existence!"

Cal laughed at the melodrama. Brie decided she did indeed enjoy the mellow, lighthearted sound.

"I was a mouthy little brat," she admitted plainly. "When I finally started back to high school I made a mess of that, too. I cut classes, failed at least three subjects, and wouldn't make friends. I had to take my junior year over again. Sophie understood what was going on, and she kept trying to teach me how to control and use the psychic gift. I finally gave in, but only if she promised to show me just how to hold back the images. I didn't want the responsibility of having to do something with the information I received."

Brie sighed. "She agreed, but she's always been uneasy about the bargain. She warned there would come a time when I'd have a psychic breakthrough, like a clogged drain becoming unstuck."

"Not a pretty image," Cal put in.

"You should have it floating around in your consciousness for half a day or more," Brie told him. She shook her head. "No, I'm not sure I'd want to pass along that part of myself to an innocent child. As far as marriage is concerned..." Brie took a second to tamp down the welling of old resentments. "I saw what happened to my mother and father."

"You think most guys couldn't take it?" Cal pressed.

"It's hard for anyone to accept the reality of this 'gift' I carry around," Brie insisted. "Much less accept it as the basic make up of someone you want to share your life. Didn't you compare me to a carnival fortuneteller?" she asked quietly.

"I feel another apology coming on."

But Brie shook her head. "Don't bother. You're part of the vast majority. People say they keep an open mind, but there's so much stigma attached to the pretenders..."

"That the real things, like you, don't get respect," he finished.

She nodded. "I haven't even told my best friend, Darien."

"The *fie foo* master?"

"*Feng shui*," she corrected absently.

"*Boyfriend* potential?"

The subtle tease edged his words again. Brie grinned. "Darien already has a domestic partner named Owen." She glanced over at him in the dark. "And no cracks about L.A., all right?"

He held up his hand, palm out. "Fine. But you know, Brie, if a Darien, or anyone else for that matter, wants your company bad enough he'll accept you. *All* of you."

"That's just it," she said. "I could never give all of myself. I'd always have to hold part of myself back, because if I let go too much..." She shivered at the very notion of that unknown peril.

"You might lose yourself like your mother did?" Cal guessed.

"Exactly. And I'm just not ready to risk spilling my heart to anyone yet," she insisted.

"You spilled it to me."

She almost laughed. "That wasn't hard. I have nothing to lose. You aren't even my friend."

He said nothing for several heartbeats. In Brie's experience that meant he agreed, but she didn't want to be so rude as to say so.

"Speaking of spilling," he finally muttered, "and at the risk of finding myself apologizing again, I hope the conversation about the furniture didn't make you feel too uncomfortable. Lain has a way of getting information out of me that I don't even know I'm willing to give up. But I wish she hadn't put you on the spot like that tonight. It's just like her to push an issue if she wants to find out something."

"Like if I'm really a psychic?" Brie grinned with rare contentment. "Actually, it's okay your family knows about me. I mean, I felt really awkward at first, and scared that maybe I'd get rushed out of the house. But everyone was so accepting. Even Eric. That was nice."

"Lain's a believer," Cal assured her with what sounded like resignation. "I didn't get a chance to talk much to Gil afterward, but he probably is, too. As for Eric." Cal glanced over at her. In the dark she couldn't read his expression, but his voice had a hint of a tease in it. "You had him in your corner the minute you walked in the front door. The boy's got a crush on you."

Brie laughed with embarrassment, but also with a lightness that had eluded her for so much of her life, and felt herself blushing. She even felt a bit of unexpected pride that Cal Porter, in her presence, seemed to be relearning some social graces and finding a teasing sense of humor.

But then he lapsed back into silence, leaving her feeling suddenly alone and small, out under this big, cloud-laden sky with a man who merely tolerated her presence.

Lightning streaked across the sky. Rolling thunder sent vibrations through the front seat of the Jeep.

Or was the vibration inside her, a jump in her heart rate triggered by this uncomfortable conversation?

She laid her hand at her throat and felt the uneven jump of her pulse. Perhaps it was time to extricate herself from this flow of thought. She tried to laugh, but it sounded as hollow as the forced brightness of her words. "So it appears if I ever want a man in my life, which I haven't decided," she stressed, "I have my work cut out for me. I'll have to find someone who's so irresistible that even fears and misgivings won't be enough to make me run for cover."

Then she cast what was meant to be a throwaway glance at Cal Porter's shadowed profile. Instead, Brie caught and held her breath at the sudden flash of blinding insight. Hadn't Cal's soul called to her soul before she so much as glimpsed his features? Didn't his touch feel too familiar and unreasonably exciting given she'd met him barely two days ago? Had she not felt that "irresistible" pull of desire and need earlier when they stopped to admire the bobcat?

Brie turned her face to the passenger's window. Nothing lit the landscape but flashes of lightning. The darkness seemed as impenetrable as the questions that chased each other around the corners of her mind. *Why, indeed, had she found herself sidetracked on that canyon road? If getting lost was no mere twist of fate how could Cal Porter possibly be linked to the terrifying dreams? Maybe he wasn't linked to the dream at all, but she needed to be here anyway. So just why was she here, on this dark road, with this man who was far too young to be a practicing curmudgeon? Was she merely supposed to teach him how to find his good manners? Or maybe he was supposed to teach her patience and humility.*

Enough, Brie told herself, and stashed the questions away for later consideration. In the few moments she'd been questioning the whims of the Universe, the air had grown heavier. The storm felt imminent. "How far are we from the cabin?" she asked.

"About ten minutes," he muttered. "Here comes the rain."

Brie turned forward in time to see the first drops splat against the windshield.

"The road won't get too bad before we get back to the house," Cal said, as if she'd spoken her concerns out loud. "It's running up to the porch without getting soaked that worries me. Seems you and I are fated to get caught together in thunderstorms."

Fated? Sophie preferred the term "synchronicity." Brie could almost hear her aunt lecture gently, *"The Universe doesn't deal in coincidences, Moon Child."*

The downpour came without warning. Sheets of rain hit the hood of the Jeep so hard the droplets bounced upward. The headlights strained to push past the double curtain of rain. Cal leaned forward until his chin was almost level with the upper rim of the steering wheel.

He was driving on instinct, certainly not by what he could actually see. Brie could tell as much from his fixed gaze and taut jawline. Twice they hit deep ruts. The Jeep bounced, and Cal muttered something, but didn't take his attention from the road.

Brie grabbed the armrest. Cal must have seen the movement out of the corner of his eyes. "I know this road. I could drive it with my eyes closed. We'll get home safe."

Brie stared at his profile, and her heart agreed. "Yes, I know we will."

"Yeah, right," he murmured, "you just know. You trust me completely. Any predictions about whether or not my electricity will still be on?"

The sourness in his voice jolted her. At his urging, Brie had just spent the better part of the last twenty minutes sharing her deepest personal fears. And now he seemed to be ridiculing her instinctive trust in him.

She opened her mouth to fire off a retort, but a crack of thunder cut her off. The wind picked up, too, and the downpour slashed the Jeep sideways. Despite her confidence in Cal, Brie expelled a grateful breath of pent up air as the headlights shone on the rail fence that marked the entrance to the back of the cabin.

Cal maneuvered past Brie's car, parked on the side of the house, and pulled up as close to the front porch as possible. He shut down the windshield wipers and headlights, and then turned off the ignition. In the pitch dark, with only lightning giving his face any definition, he turned to her. "Do you want to wait it out?"

What a choice. Hobble up to the porch in a drenching rain, or sit in the dark for who knew how long with a man who had trouble holding his own in a civil conversation for more than five minutes.

"I can always dry off," she decided, and unfastened her seat belt.

"You won't be able to use your crutches in all this muck," he warned.

She calculated the distance from the Jeep to the first step of the porch, a matter of four feet. "My knee's much better. I can get as far as the handrail on my own."

Cal groaned. "Yeah, and slip again in the mud. Wait here."

Before she could stop him, or even figure out what he was doing, Cal had thrown open his door, leaped out, and was halfway around the front of the Jeep. In the next moment, he yanked her door open and pulled on her arm. "Come on, Miss L.A. This is one ride you can't pass up right now."

She thought he meant only to guide her up the slope to the first step of the porch. Instead Cal scooped her into his arms and lifted her chest high. Brie gasped, but threw her arms around his neck. She didn't dare put him off balance by struggling.

The rain pelted her face so hard she closed her eyes. But Cal's body warmed her chilled, rain-slicked arms even though he, too, was drenched by the run around the Jeep. His scent lifted from his neck, his clothing. In his arms she felt the oddly familiar strength and promise of protection as he slogged through the muck and stomped up the three steps.

Though she did none of the physical work, Brie was breathless by the time Cal scooted them under the porch roof. The wind-driven rain no longer pelted her skin, yet she didn't open her eyes. She wanted to hold this moment of all-encompassing security. She wanted to hold tight to the man who made the moment possible. How ridiculous was that? She held her breath and waited for him to lower her feet to the porch floor.

"Brie?"

Had she heard Cal whisper her name? With the background rumble of thunder and the steady drum of rain on the porch roof she couldn't be sure. One thing for certain, he still held her aloft. Maybe that was the problem. After all, she clutched at his neck as if he were a life preserver.

Brie lifted her eyelids. Cal's face hovered only inches from hers. She felt his gaze more than she actually saw it in the shadows. If his features reflected the tension in his body she imagined his brows drawn together in a frown, and his mouth an uncompromising slash.

Her next breath brought with it his scent, a rich blend of clean skin, rain water, and male earthiness. Brie's heart picked up speed until she felt the pulse in her neck flutter. It was happening again, just as it had earlier on the way to the ranch for dinner. She was slipping under the spell of Cal Porter's vital presence. His soul might be in agony, but physically he hummed with life. Never had Brie felt such conflicting energies roll off a man. But never had she been so lured by a man's essence that she allowed those energies to touch her in return.

The words she thought he wanted to hear came hard and sounded thick with the reluctance she felt. "Thanks. I think I can stand now."

Slowly, gently, he released her legs. Cal eased her down the length of his body, a graceful sensual slide, until her toes and heels touched the planks. Brie loosened her arms from around his neck and brought both hands to rest on the ridge of his shoulders.

Cal didn't move. Neither did he withdraw his right arm from around her waist. In fact, he eased a half-step closer until his thighs pressed to her thighs. Even if Brie wanted to back away, her spine already nudged a rough-hewn support post.

But she didn't want to back away. She didn't want to move from the sensual pressure of his solid body or the whisper of his breath on her cheek. She didn't want to stop the erotic magic that seemed to be swirling around them with the wind-driven rain.

Brie's insides quivered with an eagerness so wanton she didn't recognize herself. She was losing precious control. For a half-second that gave her pause. "Cal," she murmured, "what's going on here?"

Cal leaned closer, pinning her gently to the post with his solid body. His mouth, warm and scented with the residue of brandy, hovered over Brie's lips. "Beats the hell out of me."

Brie could hardly take more than quick, shaky gulps of the heavy, humid air. "I...I think you're going to kiss me."

Nine

"All things change. And Selene has already changed you. Why can't you just accept it?"

Myles shot Jorge a murderous glare. "I never asked to be changed. And I'll thank you to shut up."

Chapter 9, *Murder, My Love—From the Files of Myles Daemon, P.I.*

* * * *

"Good guess, Madame Psychic. Are you going to stop me?"

Stop him? She should, if for no other reason than his typical mocking of her intuition. Ironically, this time her "knowing" had nothing to do with psychic ability. She knew because she was a woman who felt the sudden, overwhelming power of mutual physical need.

As both a woman and a psychic, she was also aware of the imminent danger of this moment. Hadn't she explained as much to Cal just minutes ago?

Perhaps he did understand. His question betrayed uncertainty. If he asked for guidance, for permission, he was asking the wrong person. Brie wasn't quite sure how to answer. She should push him away until they both had time to reconsider.

There were other, better, reasons to deny both him and herself. After knowing Cal Porter a mere forty-eight hours Brie's heart beat too fast with wanting as she stood in his demanding embrace. Reckless abandon was not part of her nature. And if the rushing need to act out of character wasn't warning enough, the darkness that still welled up from his soul should have sent her fleeing in panic before she was overcome with empathic pain and sorrow.

Yet Brie found that her fingers sank more deeply into Cal's arms. Her lungs ached for air, but she couldn't find the wit to breathe. After years of denying herself the intimate caress of any man for fear that she'd lose too much of her precious control, Brie now desired nothing more than to open herself to this moment, to this man.

Stop him? Not a chance. Brie had never wanted something so much in her life. Still, she was confused.

"But...but you don't even like me," she argued weakly.

He cut her off with a brush of his lips that made her body

sizzle like the storm-electrified air. "That's how much you 'know,' Brie Quaid. I like you." He pressed his mouth briefly to hers, and then pulled back as if he'd been burned. "I like you way too much."

The admission came hard, but honestly. Cal understood no more than she did. His needy innocence seduced her, and snapped loose the last anchor of Brie's resistance. The leaden weight careened around her soul, shattering her carefully guarded control into a million pieces. Beyond reason and past worry she wanted only one thing, and she fitted her lips to Cal's mouth to have it.

Suddenly there was no storm, no rain or thunder or wind. The post no longer edged into her spine. The past and future had no meaning. There was nothing but the urgent pressure of Cal's mouth on her mouth, and the glorious chaos it wreaked on her will.

Vaguely Brie realized that he'd taken her inside both arms and held her as close to his body as physically possible. Hip to hip, Brie felt the evidence of his arousal. For a moment the sensation shocked her. She'd caused this explosion of unexpected passion. Why? How? Is this what it meant to lose oneself in another?

None of that mattered. This moment simply existed. *She* simply existed in the erotic haze, and she opened her heart as she'd never before dared. Cal was there to meet her. His essence surrounded Brie's soul as his arms coiled around her body.

Trembling with the onslaught, Brie fought back currents of fear even as she let herself be drawn in deeper.

And then it happened, preceded by a sizzle of warning like the hair rising on skin just before a lightning strike. The bright and wild abandon of passion gave way to something dark and heavy and riddled with pain. Brie recognized the signature of Cal Porter's soul-deep sadness. She felt the defensive wall descending even as he still threaded his fingers through her sodden hair and circled the inside of her lips with his tongue.

So when he suddenly came up for air, Brie cried out a silent protest at the loss of a treasure just found and the overwhelming sense of wrenching loneliness.

Without warning Cal released her and took a stumbling step backward. Brie collapsed against the post and gasped for air as panic, and then anger, swirled between them. Bemused and afraid, she snatched the sleeve of his shirt. "Cal, what is it?"

He yanked away and quickly stood a moment as lightning illuminated the planes of his stricken face. Then he turned to the turbulent night and ran both hands through his drenched hair. "Damn, damn, damn," he yelled over the storm. "This can't happen!"

For a moment longer he just stood there, less than an arm's length from Brie but somehow well beyond her reach. "It *did* happen, Cal!" she shouted back. "I don't know why or how, but it felt good! And right!"

So right! her heart echoed.

He whipped around to look at her. "No, it's *not* right! Damn!"

Cal jammed his hand into the pocket of his jeans, retrieved a key, and headed for the front door. Brie could only watch and wonder at his frantic motion. Her mind and body and soul had not yet reintegrated from the shattering impact of the shared passion. Her skin still hummed with sensual tension and her arms ached to hold him again. Brie's thoughts raced, even as she stood paralyzed.

When Cal finally got the front door open he reached around and grabbed her arm. Though her knee sent out a warning ache, Brie pushed away from the post and let him haul her inside. Just over the threshold Cal steered her to an old cane chair and left her seated there as he stomped toward the kitchenette.

In the near total darkness, Brie huddled against the wall, seized by an all-encompassing cold. Rain dripped down her face and arms. Thunder still shook the cabin. She wasn't sure if the vibration she felt was the explosion of the storm or the echo of her heart reverberating with erotic anticipation cut short. A moment later, the warm yellow glow of electric lamplight made her blink.

Suddenly Cal stood in front of her again, but at least three feet away. Brie peered up at him through wet lashes. He frowned and held himself awkwardly, legs apart and arms half extended. She almost felt sorry for him. And then there was the smothering sadness, so thick it felt even heavier than the sticky warm air.

"Brie, you said you trusted me," he said. "You said you 'know' I won't hurt you."

The pleading in his voice made her wince. "Cal, I can't explain what just happened." She choked on the words and had to swallow. "All I do know is that if I didn't trust you, I wouldn't have allowed it. But you didn't hurt me."

"Oh, yes, I did," he said, cutting her off. His frown deepened to a scowl. "I hurt both of us. But it won't happen again. It can't happen again."

Brie put out her hand to beckon him forward. "Cal, I don't understand. There's something between us..."

He flinched and shuffled backward. "You got that right. There is something between us, but not what you think. This 'something' is going to keep us apart from here on out." He took a shallow breath and exhaled his next words. "I'm married."

Married?

Brie knew she mouthed the word, but didn't hear it for the buzz in her ears. How could this be? There had been no outward sign that he was spoken for—no ring or mention that he shared his life with another. And the brief passion they shared felt good, and right, and somehow fated.

How could her intuition have steered her so wrong? Cal Porter was married. The warmth and security of his arms belonged to another woman. The electric kiss they shared was nothing but an "Oops, sorry" moment, triggered by runaway hormones and the opportunity of the moment.

A crack of thunder roused Brie from self-pity. Inhaling sharply she stiffened her back and scrambled to regain control. "I knew I sensed a woman when I first stepped foot in this cabin," she recalled, and met his pleading gaze with a glare. "You acted like I was crazy!"

He shook his head and started to hold out his hand, but he dropped it to his side. "Brie..."

She swiped the air with her arm and cut him off. "Where is she, Cal? Why didn't you tell me? Why didn't Lain?" Her anger ratcheted with every question. "I...I shouldn't be here." She started to stand. "I can't be here. I have to leave."

At that point Cal lunged forward and set his hands on her shoulders to keep her down. "And go where? Up the canyon road? Back to the ranch?"

Reason kept her on the chair. But unable to suffer his touch Brie batted away his hands.

Cal retreated as if the effort pained him. "I don't know what you thought you heard Monday night, Brie, but it wasn't my wife." He drew in a breath. "Alicia hasn't been here for...for a long time. She left me. Not that she didn't have cause, and not that I ever expect her to come back. But I don't know where she is. And until I do know..."

His voice cracked and his features twisted with the sorrow that marred his soul. "I have to know what happened to her. It's important."

Alicia. Cal's wife. A woman with a beautiful, lyrical name. Gone without a forwarding address. So that was the source of the still fresh pain.

Anger and empathy warred inside Brie. She glanced to the closed front door and tried to keep the hurt and sarcasm out of her voice. "So what happened on the porch, Cal? In the dark, in the rain, in the loneliness of the moment, did you just mistake me for Alicia?"

"No."

The tender anguish in that one word brought Brie around.

Cal stared at her without blinking. "That was the problem. For one moment I had no history with Alicia. I didn't need to find her. I forgot she existed. You made me forget. But I can't forget her and still hold on to..."

Cal closed his mouth. Brie felt his withdrawal even though he didn't move. "Hold on to what?" she pressed.

"Hope," he ground out. "I have to hope." He shook his head when she opened her mouth to press him further. "I didn't mean for any of this to happen. I'm sorry. And don't be angry with Lain. In her mind Alicia gave up the right to be called my wife when she took off."

Brie searched his face, every crevice every line of worry and pain. "But that's not how you feel," she whispered in resignation.

"What I feel isn't important," he countered. "It's what I have to believe. There's still too much at stake." Again he clamped his mouth shut, took a deep breath, and made a sudden lurch toward the door. "I'll go out and get your crutches."

He needed to escape, even if it meant going back into the storm. Brie needed to let him escape so she could cope with the storm inside her soul.

The front door slammed behind him. His boots pounded on the plank porch deck, and then she heard nothing but the pelt of rain on the windows and the whimpering of her bruised heart. Good heavens, what was happening to her? First, the horrible dream that drove her to distraction and finally to run like a coward back to Sophie. Then the wrong turn into wilderness hell and a rendezvous with a man who should have repelled her with every word and deed, even as he lured her closer.

Now this. The first time in her adult life she'd let down her practiced defenses and followed her heart she'd met with emotional disaster. What good was her "gift" if she couldn't foresee something like this?

Or maybe she'd just gotten so good at ignoring her deepest intuition that she'd allowed herself to be blindsided by the flow of events.

Either way she'd been a fool. She let Cal Porter touch her soul, touch her body, touch her heart. Willingly she'd given him a little piece of each, a gift he couldn't return.

Because he was married.

The front door burst open. Cal blew in on a gust of humid air. Holding both crutches in one hand, he slammed the door closed with the other. Then he shook off the worst of the rainwater.

A strange calm descended over Brie as she stared up at Cal. Perhaps it was the emotional equivalent of going into shock. Without warning she'd been shaken, battered, and betrayed by her own instincts. Now she was merely numb. The feelings would come back, but later, when she could deal with them without shattering.

Brie didn't wait for Cal to hold out the crutches. Slowly she rose from the chair, feeling the pull of her strained joint with every inch of height, and stood with her hand out. "Thank you. I can take it from here."

He frowned. "Are you sure? I can help you to the couch."

Accepting his offer would have been a wise course. Her knee throbbed, probably from the dampness and overuse this evening. But she didn't want to risk touching him or being close to him. She needed distance. "Don't bother," she said, and wrested the crutches from his hands. "I can manage on my own."

Without further comment Cal stood back. Brie fitted the wet implements under her arms, tested the rubber foot grips to make sure they wouldn't slip too much, and took off across the room toward the hearth without looking back. When she got to the couch she flipped on a low wattage lamp on the end table before letting herself down slowly onto the worn, familiar cushion.

"Can I get you anything?" Cal asked as he waited by the front door. "If you're chilled, I can start a fire."

Unwilling and unable to look at him, Brie set the crutches on the floor next to the couch with deliberate care. "Start a fire?" she repeated. "Too late for that."

She heard him take two steps toward her and then stop. "Brie, I'm sorry."

She held up her hand. "Like I said, too late for that."

He must have considered her words a dismissal. The kitchenette light went out, leaving her in the muted lamplight. A moment later Cal pounded up the stairs double-time. The cabin went deathly quiet.

Brie lolled her head onto the couch's backrest and opened her eyes to the beamed ceiling that lay in shadow. *More bad feng shui, and hanging right over your head,* Darien would have counseled. For a moment she made herself focus on her right knee. The joint hurt, but the pain wasn't debilitating. Still, she didn't have enough flex to drive safely all the way to New Mexico. With luck, a little judicious exercise tomorrow, and regular doses of Sophie's analgesic tea she could spring herself from this loony bin no later than Friday morning.

Out of the corner of her eye she spotted the deer head. Pale lamplight sparked life into the poor creature's soulful eyes. "What are you staring at?" she whispered at the head. "I didn't put you there!"

But the deer's eyes seemed to express less blame than pity. That was even worse.

Despite the throb in her knee, she levered herself off the couch and hobbled to her bag on the floor by the rollaway bed. She rummaged through the contents until she found the washed-out, ratty pink cotton cardigan, a piece of "comfort clothing" she carried along with her on every trip away from home. Perfect.

Expertly, she balanced most of her weight on her left leg, aimed, and tossed the sweater at the head. As she'd hoped, the sweater caught on the tines of the antlers and draped over the animal's morose face. "Sweet dreams."

Job completed, Brie shuffled backward until her legs hit the rim of the bed, and she lowered herself onto the thin mattress. Weariness flooded her body while her mind hummed. Even with privacy from the deer's pitying stare she realized she'd sleep little. What she needed was a cup of Sophie's tea laced with something that would deaden her senses. Unfortunately she wasn't certain she had enough energy to change for bed, much less prepare a cup of hot water.

So once again she reached into her roll bag and felt for the white sweats. As she searched for the suit Brie's fingers skimmed the cracked face of the doll she'd bought for Sophie. Without much thought, except that the pretty piece made her feel closer to her aunt, she eased the doll from between the protective folds of clothing.

Again she marveled at the finely crafted piece, despite the damaged face. The taffeta skirt felt cool and somehow refreshing on her overly warm skin. Brie smoothed back a delicate lock of the doll's hair, made of fine gauge, funky blue-green twisted thread. For a moment, Brie imagined the doll grinned with real amusement. An odd perception, since one side of her mouth was etched with the disfiguring spider web crack.

In spite of the turmoil that still churned her insides, Brie smiled weakly back at the doll. Aunt Sophie would love this little fairy. Or angel. Or whatever the sprite-like figure was. Once again, as had happened often since she found the doll a month ago, Brie wished she could keep it for herself. If only she hadn't promised Sophie.

At least she had this moment to admire and touch the toy that irrationally stirred her longing. Brie folded the doll into her arms as she'd done with her stuffed animals as a child. Ruminations of a time more innocent and less burdened with the realities of life helped still the clash and conflict of more recent, frenzied memories. Lethargy stole over Brie until she almost dozed sitting up. She didn't dare disrupt this rare moment of inner peace.

Her bedtime rituals could wait. So could changing into the sweat suit. The quiet of the moment called to her. Holding fast to the doll, Brie eased her legs onto the rollaway bed, lay down on her side, and let her eyes flutter shut. The roll of thunder became distant, as did the patter of rain on the roof and windows. Bliss cocooned her, suspended her far above temporal cares.

Her thoughts drifted and took her ocean side on a cloudless summer day. She smiled, or at least imagined smiling, as the sun warmed her skin and a breeze swept the hair back from her face. Frothy waves tumbled to shore, smoothed the beach of footprints. She could sit for hours and watch the tide come in...

A brilliant flash made her gasp and yanked her out of the reverie. For a split second Brie imagined lightning had hit the house or somewhere very close at least. But there was no sizzle in the air. No immediate deafening clap.

More curious still, Brie realized that her eyes were closed, and no matter how she tried she couldn't force them open. That's when the rush of images and scenes began playing out like a series of still photos run through a slide projector. *A stunning woman. Strawberry blond hair and topaz eyes, wearing a red- and white-striped swimsuit cut low to expose lots of full cleavage. She was at the ocean, on the same beach as Brie. An oversized green umbrella was anchored in the sand nearby. The woman laughed as she held on to a giggling little girl, her daughter, Brie sensed. The two danced with barefoot abandon in the sand. Then a shadow fell, like an eclipse of the sun. The woman shouted angrily. Then there was rain. So much rain. Blinding rain that slashed from all sides. Screams. Pitch and roll. Sickening unending roll...And darkness.*

Brie gasped again and opened her eyes to nothing but pale lamplight, the smell of cured wood, and the solid floor beneath her feet. Somehow she had sat up on the rollaway bed, but she labored for air, as if she'd run around the small room a dozen times. She had to squelch an urge to cry out in terror. Her chest hurt with each breath. Her skin tingled, and her body trembled. She felt hot and cold in the same instant, and she couldn't swallow for the dryness in her throat.

A full-fledged panic attack, Brie realized. She realized, too, that she gripped the doll with both hands so tightly that the taffeta skirt squeezed out between her fingers in wrinkled wads.

As if it were a talisman, Brie clutched the doll to her breast until her breathing slowed to normal. She could do nothing, however, about the race of her mind. She must have drifted off to sleep and had another nightmare. Though different from the one that sent her running off to Sophie, the series of images was no less confusing and ultimately terrifying. Who was the woman? And the child. A girl child, no older than three. Were they tied to the first dream? Good heavens, were they the victims of the disaster her dream foretold?

A chill coursed up her spine. Brie held the doll in a death grip and shivered as if she'd been plunged into a cold bath. Sophie would say she had to accept the dream and somehow pass along the message to someone who could make sense of it. Perhaps that meant she had to track down the beautiful woman and her little girl.

Brie hunched her shoulders and curled inward. A dry sob bubbled up her throat, but she didn't vent it. No use running the risk of alerting Cal Porter to this latest psychic drama. He didn't believe anyway. And truth be told, these past days in his company had tautened her already stretched nerves and had probably strengthened the urgency of the dreams.

What did *that* mean?

Should she risk the drive to New Mexico in spite of her strained knee?

No!

The answer came so fast inside her head Brie felt a moment of pain. She had to trust, despite the intensity of these visions, that the meaning would unfold gradually, as Sophie promised.

Regardless, this burden was crushing her.

What was the mantra Sophie taught her? *Feeling great? Meditate. Feeling down? Move around.*

Brie scooted to the edge of the rollaway bed and retrieved the crutches from the floor. This was definitely one of those "move around" moments.

Ten

"All right, Myles, I'll leave and stay away. You give me no choice." Selene picked up her coat from the back of the overstuffed leather chair and started for the door. Then she stopped, and looked over her shoulder. "But with or without you, I'll find the person who killed my brother."

She left, closing the door behind her.

"Good riddance," Myles ground out.

But her scent lingered in the air, and the office was suddenly too quiet.

Selene Carter was a menace. She didn't know when to give up. Her interference with this investigation could get him killed. Could get her killed.

So what? She wasn't his responsibility.

"Damn!" Myles shot out of his chair and charged after her.

Chapter 10, *Murder, My Love—From the Files of Myles Daemon, P.I.*

* * * *

Lain's laughter jarred Cal awake. He hoped he was just having an unpleasant dream.

Another loud chuckle dispelled that wish. He groaned and got up on one elbow. The grit behind his eyes told him he wasn't yet slept out even though the digital alarm clock read 9:00 a.m. Part of him wanted to wrap the pillow around his head, shut out the sunlight and laughter, and go back to sleep. Part of him wanted to follow the aroma of fresh-brewed coffee downstairs, despite the conclave of female trouble that lay in wait. And this time he didn't have either Gil or Eric to run interference.

What kind of a coward was he, anyway? A stiff, grumpy coward who craved a shot of caffeine, he decided as he threw his legs over the side of the bed and ran his fingers through wayward hair. A stiff, grumpy coward who wasn't ready for another verbal go-around with Lain, especially if she probed about whether he and Brie did "The Nasty" last night.

"Not quite, big sister, but too damn close," he grumbled, as he retrieved his shirt from the floor and gave it a hard shake to bring the left sleeve right side out.

Plop, plop, plop. The three condom packets Lain had stuffed in his pocket dropped to the plank floor. In his groggy state Cal imagined the packets sounded like heavy footfalls to the women below.

Paranoia of the guilt-ridden, he guessed. Guilt that he'd so much as walked off the ranch with Lain's "gift." Guilt that the little packets rubbing against his chest on the drive home had fired all sorts of degenerate notions about Miss Brienne Quaid. Guilt that he'd almost played out one of those notions on the front porch before even deeper guilt grabbed him by the throat and shook some sense back into him.

It was Lain's fault, he decided, scooping up the packets and tucking them under his mattress for safekeeping until he could dispose of them. His sister had accepted Brie, Miss L.A. psychic, the instant they met. Lain had decided, without consulting him, a woman he'd known for less than three days might be "the one" to save his sorry soul and lift him out of his comfortable isolation. She planted all those ideas in his head when she planted the condoms in his pocket.

Cal hung his head. No, that was denial in the first degree. He didn't need Lain's urging to find Brie Quaid desirable. Her uncanny resemblance to Selene, the ideal woman of his youthful fantasies right down to her dark hair and cornflower blue eyes, probably explained some of his immediate attraction to her. More than that, however, there was an understated, unaffected loveliness about Brie that heightened her aura of innocence. While she carried herself with simple grace, dignity, and competency, she appeared vulnerable. And he'd always been a sucker for vulnerable women.

But the attraction went deeper than physical or emotional appearances. Despite her questionable claims about possessing psychic abilities Brie Quaid had wit, poise, and intelligence, qualities he admired in both men *and* women. More importantly, she anchored her decisions with a strong sense of ethics. When he pronounced himself married after kissing the daylights out of her, she'd looked at him as if he'd confessed to murder.

He'd literally been accused of that and worse. Still, while time and trial had taught him not to care about what other people thought, he'd never felt the shame he had last night, no doubt because last night he really was guilty of gross misconduct.

Cal realized he didn't want Brie to be afraid of him. Against all reason, he felt the need to help her. She was a woman in crisis, someone who needed to work through recurring nightmares. Unfortunately, his conduct last night couldn't have deepened her trust in him, and it rocked Cal's belief in his own judgment. Despite what Lain, Jim Atwood, and even Alicia's father believed, he wasn't free. Not in his heart. Not until he knew for certain...

He punched his arms blindly into his shirtsleeves, buttoned up, then rounded up his jeans and socks. Yawning, he made for the steps.

As he got further downstairs the women's words became clearer. Lain's voice boomed as she chatted about Eric and little Dulcie. When Cal reached the landing he started to turn right into the parlor. Then he heard Brie respond in the calm, quiet tone that sent little shock waves up his spine.

All those feelings that had left him restless last night, unable to work or sleep, hit him between the eyes. How could he face Brie this morning when the memory of her passionate kiss was so fresh it made his knees watery?

He changed direction and started for the kitchen. Maybe coffee first...

"Hey, Cal, hope we didn't wake you up." Lain sounded amused.

Cal figured he looked pretty amusing. He probably should have checked himself in the mirror first. But that would have been consciously admitting he cared how he looked in front of Brie. He did, but...ah, hell, he was busted. Might as well just surrender.

He heaved a heavy sigh and did an about face. Immediately he honed in on Brie who was seated at her usual place on the couch. Once again she wore the yellow sundress, the one that floated around her shapely legs when she walked, even with crutches. He could almost smell the clean of her still damp, newly washed hair from across the room. Her shoulders were relaxed as she concentrated on sipping from her coffee mug.

The prim, proper, and pretty picture made Cal want to smile. He would have, except she wouldn't turn to acknowledge he'd entered the room. Not that he blamed her. He hadn't been the most congenial—or gentlemanly—host this side of the Continental Divide.

"The proper greeting is 'Good morning, ladies.'" Lain drew the words out as if teaching a child.

Cal shifted his attention to the fireplace where Lain stood. Out of the corner of his eyes he sensed something amiss, and diverted his gaze to the brickwork above the hearth. "What's hanging on the deer?"

Lain laughed. "Nice touch, isn't it? I love what Brie's done to the place. I'm thinking a red silk scarf over the coyote. The fox would be lovely in blue cashmere."

When Brie laughed softly Cal shifted his gaze to the couch. She put her fingers over her lips to stifle her amusement. Cal remembered all too well the way he'd tasted and savored those lips less than twelve hours before.

"Cal, are you fully in charge of your faculties this morning?"

Lain's question shook him once again, this time before Brie could see him acting like an idiot.

"Depends. Are you here for a reason, other than to torment me?" he grouched at his sister.

After a quick series of glances back and forth between him and Brie, Lain sauntered toward Cal. "As a matter of fact, I didn't come to see you. I came to drop off a cane for Buttercup. Last night she seemed to do pretty well without the crutches for short stretches of time, so I thought she could graduate to something simpler. I was right."

Lain halted just before she stood toe-to-toe with Cal, and looked him up and down with obvious disapproval. "I was thinking of taking her into town for the day. Lord knows she could use the change of scenery. You missed a button, little brother."

Cal swatted halfheartedly at Lain's hand when she tried to flick the placket of his shirt. "Town? Saratoga Springs isn't a town. It's a wide spot in the two-lane highway less than a block long. Don't oversell it."

"Hey, there's a fine general store that even sells lottery tickets," Lain pointed out. "And Rojo Steak House sells the best rib eye sandwich in a hundred mile radius, so we can have lunch there. Oh, there's plenty to keep us gals busy." She glanced over at the couch. "But you look a little peaked, Brie. Did Cal keep you up too late last night?"

Cal opened his mouth right away to deny what Lain was imagining.

Brie, however, rose from the couch with the help of her newly acquired cane before he got the chance. "No, no, I'm great this morning," she hurried to say, though Cal noted the weariness that tugged at her eyes. "A drive into town sounds wonderful."

Despite her newfound perkiness Brie still wouldn't look directly at him. She let her gaze dart around the room, anywhere but in his direction.

"Great," Lain said with a grin. "Wow, I feel just like the Saratoga Springs Chamber of Commerce."

"Saratoga Springs doesn't have a Chamber of Commerce," Cal growled. "It hardly has any commerce, period."

Lain ignored him. "You know what? We might even have time to walk through the Lost Mines Museum," she suggested, as she honed in on Cal again.

"Sounds fascinating," Brie agreed, and lifted her small purse from the end table.

Brie slipped the shoulder strap over her head so the purse lay diagonally across her body. A neat trick to foil purse-snatchers in the big city, he knew. But the shoulder strap also pulled across her bodice in such a way that it outlined Brie's curves.

Uh-uh, no way! Cal stuck out his hand. "Now wait a minute, Lain. That 'museum' is nothing more than the backroom of the tavern. Don't you go taking Brie in there."

Brie limped past him as she headed toward the front door. Cal noted she did quite well with the help of the simple cane. "Why not? I'm well over twenty-one."

Now wide awake, Cal held up his index finger as if lecturing both women, as he might a teen like Eric. "Because it's no place for a lady! I almost got decked in that bar!"

"You weren't wearing a skirt, hobbling on a cane, and generally looking pretty and a mite helpless," Lain pointed out as she strode to Brie's side.

He bobbed his head frantically. "That's asking for bigger trouble!"

Brie forced a sweet smile that Cal didn't believe for one minute, but at least she now looked right at him. "It's kind of you to be concerned about my safety. But, as you're fond of reminding me, I'm from Los Angeles. I can handle whatever comes my way."

She was throwing his own sarcasm back in his face!

Lain waved off his objection as she and Brie strode out the front door and onto the porch. "It's not like it's Friday night, Cal."

"No, it's almost Thursday afternoon, when all the trouble rolls into town on motorcycles for the long weekend," Cal called after them.

Lain shrugged. "We'll be back by mid-afternoon."

Cal took after them. "Lain, I still don't think this is a good idea."

"It's a great idea," Brie answered in her calm, sweet, rational voice as she slipped on her sunglasses. "Just think, today you'll have the entire cabin to yourself again. No distraction. Imagine all the work you'll get done on that new manuscript."

Cal *was* imagining, and it didn't add up to much if he worried that Lain would lead Brie Quaid into a backcountry adventure for which she wasn't prepared. "What...what about your knee?" he scratched for excuses. "Maybe you shouldn't walk so much, especially with just a cane."

Brie already had the door of Lain's pickup truck open. "My

knee feels great this morning. Walking will be good therapy to keep my joint from stiffening up." Without help, Brie hoisted herself into the Sutter family pickup truck and slammed the door.

Cal watched helplessly from the bottom step of the porch. "Mid-afternoon," he yelled out as Lain started the engine. "That's three o'clock."

Lain waved absently, so Cal wasn't sure she even heard him. The truck lurched into drive, kicked up clots of dirt still wet from last night's rain, and headed for town.

And for the first time in a very long time Cal felt alone.

* * * *

The cabin disappeared in the passenger's side rearview mirror. Cal's tall, unkempt image diminished by the second as Lain slowly negotiated the road up and out of the canyon. Settling back in the bucket seat, Brie closed her eyes behind the sunglasses.

Despite Lain's promises of fun and fresh air, about the last thing Brie wanted to do this morning was walk the streets of a small town. Between the memory of Cal's soul-jostling kiss, the unnerving news he was a married man, and the strange addendum to the old nightmare, she'd hardly slept a wink. She drifted off to sleep only to start awake minutes later, breathless and trembling. Even Lain's bright monologue might not be stimulating enough to keep her awake right now.

Propping her elbow on the window rim Brie leaned her cheek against her hand. As the road sloped upward the roadside brush thinned. The landscape floated by...

Until suddenly the shoulder dropped away and Brie opened her eyes wide to a new perspective that sapped her breath. The truck had climbed to what must have been the crest of the canyon wall. There was no more than a half-yard clearance on the passenger's side of the road. Then a steep drop-off plunged at least twenty yards before the sheer rock walls disappeared in a dense tangle of dry underbrush, flat-headed cactus, and tall yellow grass.

Every nerve in Brie's body screeched, as if someone had dragged a scouring pad across her skin. Despite the heat of morning sun magnified by the windshield and side windows, she went cold to the bone. Her stomach lashed side to side, and she sat up straighter to keep her meager breakfast of toast and tea from rising in her throat. Frantically she rolled down the window for air.

"Something wrong?"

Lain's question registered in the back of her mind. Brie sucked in more air to counter a wave of vertigo. "I...I didn't realize the road was so narrow," she breathed.

"Nasty view, isn't it," Lain agreed. "Especially if you get spooked by heights."

Despite the moment of panic, Brie couldn't take her eyes from the spiraling descent. "I'm not afraid of heights...is this the road I came down?"

"Sure is," Lain answered. "You missed the turn to the main highway just another half-mile further up. Happens to folks who aren't familiar with these back roads. The intersections aren't well marked, and there's a couple of winding curves. We've had some pretty bad accidents because of the confusion over the years." She smiled with reassurance. "You were lucky you stayed close to the canyon face when you came down in that rainstorm."

Brie folded herself inward and rubbed the gooseflesh from her upper arms. "How deep does the canyon wall run?"

"Ever hear the term 'dead drop?'" Lain quipped. "That sums it up good as anything. If you took a dive down that wall and managed to survive you'd end up in a remote branch of Milagro Creek. It's a nasty place in itself. Thick with years of undergrowth. A natural haven for the canyon's wildlife, probably because it's so inaccessible. Once every couple of years the county has to send a rescue squad in there because some inexperienced hiker gets lost or injured. The locals know enough to leave that little corner of nature alone."

A cold, as deep as it was painful, enveloped Brie. Her head whirled with so much force she had to close her eyes behind the sunglasses to keep from pitching into the dashboard. But closing her eyes helped, and gradually the dizziness went away.

By the time she regained full balance Lain had made a gentle left turn onto a paved, two-lane highway. Brie's inner world no longer seemed upended and poised on the brink of oblivion. "Why isn't there a guardrail?" she managed to croak.

"The road is used mostly by locals." Lain cast her a worried glance. "You don't get car sick, do you?"

Brie shook her head as she concentrated on the cool air streaming from the vent right in front of her face. "No."

"You sure?" Lain didn't sound convinced. "You're way too pale, even for a city girl. I can turn around. I mean, good lord, Buttercup, you look like you've seen a ghost." She caught a breath and gave Brie a careful sideways glance. "Did you?"

Brie blinked and tried to focus on Lain's question. "Did I what?"

Uncertainly, Lain grimaced. "Well, see a ghost. Being special like you are, and all."

"Special?" Brie replied with a weak laugh, though she realized she liked being called "special" by this kind and honest woman.

"Yeah, you know, psychic?"

Brie's vertigo eased a bit more, and she tried to smile reassuringly. "I don't see ghosts, Lain. I feel impressions of people by touching objects they've handled."

"Well, isn't that kinda like seeing ghosts?"

Brie had never thought of it that way, and considered Lain's comment. "I suppose, a little."

"All the same," Lain hurried to say, "if you don't feel well, or you're having some kind of psychic attack and want to turn around, I will."

Less enthusiastic about spending the afternoon alone with a brooding married man who kissed like a rogue than she was about exploring Saratoga Springs, Brie forced another smile. "I'm fine. I think I just now realized what a close call I had. For the first time, I understand why Cal was so upset when I first told him how I'd gotten down to the cabin."

"And speaking of the ogre, what kind of burr did Cal have under his saddle this morning?" Lain demanded out of the blue. "He was nine times snakier than usual. Did you and he have words last night?"

Brie sat up straighter. Even though her sunglasses would have hidden any hint of guilt in her eyes she didn't dare glance at Lain. "We...talked for a while. I, ah, think I asked too many questions. He doesn't give up much of himself, does he?"

Except when he plants those kisses.

Brie clasped her hands in her lap, as if the physical tension could somehow lessen the thrill of those guilt-ridden erotic memories. She'd kissed a married man. Passionately. Had she committed mental adultery?

"Yeah, he can be tight-lipped as hell," Lain agreed. "Wasn't always that way. Back home, in Salinas, he wasn't just the smartest kid in the whole high school, he was the most outspoken. Captain of the debate team. Senior class president. Always ready with an edgy remark, or an opinion about changing things for the better. Even made the teachers stop and think sometimes." She sighed. "And you should have seen him go off at the mouth in court."

"Court?" Brie turned toward Lain. "If you don't mind my asking, what was he arrested for?"

Lain frowned, then laughed and shook her head. "He wasn't arrested." She kept her eyes on the road, but smiled with affection and pride. "That kid was not only the youngest, but the most successful assistant prosecutor in Santa Barbara County. He had more convictions than any other three lawyers in the office put together."

Brie opened her mouth to voice surprise, but nothing came out. Cal was a lawyer. That explained much, from the depth of knowledge poured into his writing to his method of asking questions which seemed more like a hostile interrogation.

"Something else he didn't tell you?" Lain wondered, and didn't give Brie time to answer. "Sounds like Cal. No wonder he's a good mystery writer. He can misdirect by choosing the right words."

Lain nodded. "Yeah, the kid was a lawyer. A hell-bent-for-leather prosecutor," she repeated. "Great instincts. Lots of confidence. Way back, when he was still practicing law, Cal used his position to become a crusader against domestic violence. A gender-bending Joan of Arc. He even made a run at politics." Lain's jaw hardened. "But that didn't work out worth diddly."

Brie leaned closer. "Why not?"

Lain sighed. "He lost the election." She worked her jaw muscles the same way Cal did. "Actually he lost everything. That's when he gave up on law and started writing. I wish you could have known him back then, before all that loss. He actually had a sense of humor." She grinned coyly. "Since you blew in with that storm, though, I see flashes of the old Cal. I've been waiting to see a sign like that for a long time. You're good for him."

Uneasiness pricked Brie's skin. "I, well, I wouldn't know about that."

"Your cheeks are candy apple red, Buttercup," Lain pointed out. "You like him. I can tell. And I know he likes you."

Brie held up her hand. "I think you may be reading something into this situation..."

"What I'm reading should be rated 'M,' for mature audiences," Lain interrupted playfully. "Brienne, there's so much sizzle and spark between you and Cal that if this was the dry season I'd have the local authorities declare that cabin a Fire Hazard Zone."

"No, really, Lain," Brie tried to beg off. "It isn't like that. I'm just passing through."

Lain slid her a look that held no hint of amusement. "Sure you want to do that?"

What was happening here? Lain didn't seem like the sort of woman who would intentionally play innocent. Nor did she seem like someone who would bait another for pure sport. Bemused, Brie held down both her voice and her temper. "Yes, I'm sure. Considering he's a married man, Lain, I think that's the right decision."

Lain jerked her head around and stared at Brie. "What did you say? Married? Cal?"

The fists in Brie's lap drew tighter. "That was my reaction when he told me last night. Oh, sure, he told me his wife walked out on him, and that he didn't expect her to return. He didn't get into specifics..."

"Back up, Buttercup," Lain cut in. "Cal really told you he's married?"

"I'm glad somebody did!" Brie felt control over her emotions start to slip. "I mean, I don't want to sound like I'm complaining because you've been so kind to me, but maybe *you* should have said something. My staying at the cabin alone with Cal could have led to an embarrassing situation at best, and at worst something scandalous for him and your family!"

Brie massaged a dull pain over her right eye. "The point is, Lain, whatever you see, or think you see, or want to see between me and Cal isn't going to happen. I know you want him to be happy. But even if I was interested—" She held up a cautionary finger. "—and I'm not admitting I am, I don't keep company with married men."

Lain's jaw worked harder. "I'll give you the benefit of the doubt on this one, Brie, because you don't know me very well. But for the record, don't even imagine I'd condone infidelity on *any* level, no matter how unhappy Cal is, or how worried I am about it."

That gave Brie and her anger pause. "Then why..." The insight took her breath away. "What are you telling me? Cal isn't married? He...he lied to me?"

Now Lain looked uneasy. "It isn't a lie if you believe it's so, I guess." She hit the steering wheel with the flat of her hand. "Damn, little brother, what's it going to take? A smack upside the head with a two-by-four?" She drew a deep breath while Brie held hers. "Okay, yes, Cal was married, the operative word being 'was.'" She gripped the steering wheel hard. "Alicia walked out on him eight years ago."

"Eight years!" The air left Brie's lungs in a rush.

"Eight years ago next week, to be exact," Lain assured her. "She just disappeared, without a trace. Her own father stopped hoping she'd reappear and settled her estate last year. She's officially dead."

As Lain interrupted her story to concentrate on a right turn, Brie scrunched into the seat. Though relieved she'd lost her senses while kissing a man who was technically a widower and not a would-be adulterer, Brie understood some part of Cal still held on to Alicia. What had he said about hope? "He must have loved her very much if he won't let go," she muttered, more to herself than Lain.

"Cal just needs answers," Lain countered. "He won't let go because he hasn't found out what happened to her or why. I always knew he needed to somehow or another close the books on Alicia. He's plowed nearly every penny of his royalties into investigations, trying to find out what happened that night. He lost a friend over the first try, Jim Atwood, a pal from college, who flat out told Cal he was wasting his time and money. Jim suspected the worst after a year with no leads."

So Cal used to have a close friend who was an investigator. And he was himself an idealistic lawyer like the fictional Jorge Moreno-Diaz. How much else of the Howard Chastain novels were semi-autobiographical?

"As for love," Lain went on. "There wasn't much of that in their marriage for a while before Alicia disappeared. Everyone knew it, except maybe Cal. That's what made it so bad when..." Lain cut off the stream of thoughts and drew in a deep breath of the artificially cooled air. "Let's just say when Alicia took off she stripped Cal of every good thing that had ever happened in his life, whether she meant to or not."

Lain's voice cracked and she bit her lip. Brie leaned across the console and touched her arm. "What do you mean? There's something more you're not telling me, isn't there?"

But Lain composed her features and shook her head. "There's a lot more, but it isn't my right to tell the rest. For once I'm keeping my big mouth shut. Gil says I always make messes by meddling where I don't belong. I don't want to mess this up."

She glanced over at Brie. "I don't need your special gift to guess how much you like Cal."

Brie looked over at Lain and started to open her mouth to protest. Lain only smiled sweetly. "You do like him don't you, Buttercup?"

How could she lie to someone as open, honest, and accepting as Lain Sutter? "There are plenty of reasons I shouldn't," Brie said, dodging the truth.

Lain chuckled. "There are times I don't like him much myself. He can be stubborn, ornery, opinionated, and silent as a tomb." Her smile flattened. "Of course I could just as easily say he's single-minded, strong-willed, loyal, and discreet. Qualities that made him a great lawyer." She glanced at Brie again. "Qualities that make him a fine man. You've got a special gift of knowing, Buttercup. Use it to look into your heart, and you'll know what I'm saying about him is the truth."

Lain didn't have to defend her brother. Yes, Brie knew as much about Cal Porter She'd touched the goodness along with the darkness in Cal Porter's soul that first stormy night by Milagro Creek. She'd trusted him from that moment, based on nothing but strong intuition. And last night, Cal had proved that goodness. He could have taken advantage of the sudden sexual fire that ignited between them. He didn't. He couldn't. For some reason he still considered himself a married man.

"If it's important for you to know the rest, Buttercup, you ask Cal yourself," Lain advised. "And if it's important enough for him to tell you, he will."

So, that was the heart of the matter. Trust.

"Cal had a chance to tell me everything last night, but he told me only part of the truth," Brie argued. "Do you really think he'll want to want to dredge up a painful past for a perfect stranger?"

"Cal doesn't have to dredge up a damn thing," Lain told her. "The past isn't *in* the past. It haunts him."

Just like my dreams haunt me.

"And," Lain cut into Brie's dour reverie, "Cal doesn't look at you like you're a stranger."

He didn't kiss me that way, either, Brie reminded herself.

Something deeper than physical attraction connected the two of them. As Sophie was fond of saying there are no coincidences, only opportunities presented by a generous Universe.

So be it, Brie decided. She could no more force him to be open with her, to share his heart and deepest pain, than she could stop the gut-wrenching nightmares. The next move was up to him. What happens happens.

But would that be enough?

Eleven

"Ask what you need of me, Myles. Only ask, and I'll give it."

Selene's blue eyes bored into his soul and he felt himself weaken.

Myles Daemon begs for nothing, he reminded himself.

Chapter 11, *Murder, My Love—From the Files of Myles Daemon, P.I.*

* * * *

The late afternoon sun beat down on Cal's head. Though he shaded his eyes with both hands he still had to squint as he stood in the middle of the porch and stared up the road. The only thing that moved besides the tall yellow grass in the warm breeze was the solid, rapid thump of Cal's heart.

His watch read five o'clock. Brie and Lain should have been back long before now. A full-scale, Chamber of Commerce-style tour of Saratoga Springs might have taken a couple of hours this morning. That is it would take that long if the two women strolled leisurely through each one of the town's three major retail attractions—Joe's General Store, the Tack and Feed Supply Company, and Santiago's Service Station.

Okay, so throw in a tour of the Lost Mines Museum and chew up another thirty minutes. Early lunch. Ride home. Cal figured they should have been back no later than two o'clock.

He rubbed his burning eyes, then cupped his hands over his forehead again and set his gaze back on the canyon road, as if wishing he'd see Lain's forest green pickup truck would make it appear out of the heat shimmer. Could the truck have broken down or gotten a flat tire? In that case, Lain would have called for assistance on her cell phone.

As if prodded by his mental turbulence, the phone inside the cabin jangled. Cal's pounding heart jumped into his throat as he raced through the front door, made a sharp right and almost skidded on a throw rug before reaching the handset. "Hello?"

"Hi, Cal. Is mom over there?" His nephew sounded royally pissed.

The panicked rhythm and pace of Cal's heart kicked up a notch. "No, ah, haven't seen her since this morning when she picked up Brie on the way into town. Why?"

Eric let out a breath of teenaged disgruntlement. "She was supposed to take me driving at four-thirty. I can't hang around much longer. Jason and Rob are picking me up at six."

That wasn't like "responsible mom" Lain. At the very least she'd have left a message on the answering machine at the ranch if she got held up in town. "Did you call her cell phone?"

"She let me borrow it Tuesday and I left it at Rob's house. He's bringing it over tonight."

"Damn!"

"Cal, is everything all right?"

He couldn't let Eric sense his worry. If, indeed, there was reason to worry. "Yeah, everything's fine. Look, your mom and Brie probably just started having fun in town and forgot about the time."

"Fun? Doing what?"

Cal wondered that, too. "Well, whatever women do for fun. Talk?"

"Shoot, Cal, even mom can't talk *that* much."

"Okay, really, everything's fine," Cal told himself as much as he told Eric. "I'll drive to town, and see what's keeping them. I'll probably pass them along the way. And if you hear anything in the meantime, call my cell phone number."

"Got it. Thanks, Cal."

Cal slammed down the handset, grabbed his keys from the kitchen counter and flew outside. "Everything's fine. Everything's fine. Everything's fine," he muttered as he propelled himself behind the wheel of his Jeep.

But part of him didn't believe the mantra. Fear, the sort he hadn't felt in nearly eight long years, squeezed his stomach as he made a sharp U-turn and tore up the road.

* * * *

Lain's green pickup truck was parked alongside two cars in front of the Saratoga Springs' general store. Cal swerved into a slot next to it, and turned off the engine. As he started to catapult himself out of the driver's seat Lain emerged from the store chatting with the tall, weathered store proprietor, Joe Harvey, who helped her manage four bags stuffed with groceries. Cal noticed right away that Brie was nowhere in sight.

Joe looked up and spotted him first. The usually gregarious shopkeeper lost his smile. "Mr. Porter," he greeted with a curt nod. "Haven't seen you in town for a while. Things okay out at the cabin?"

Cal tried not to wince at Joe's stiff formality. Lain had warned him time and time again that his penchant for solitude and lack of congeniality in general were speculative grist for the small but active Saratoga Springs rumor mill. Joe Harvey probably had cause to assess him with wariness.

Doing his best imitation of a friendly non-stressed smile, Cal relieved Joe of the bags. "Everything's great."

At worst that was a lie. At best a social exaggeration. In cold hard truth, everything felt like it was coming apart at the seams.

Then Cal sent a glare Lain's way. She actually looked surprised and worried, something that didn't happen often.

Joe wiped his forehead with the back of his hand and nodded again. "Good to hear." Then he turned to Lain. "You say hi to Gil and the kids, now. See you next week." And he ambled back into his store.

Lain hardly let Joe get inside the store before she turned on Cal with controlled panic. "What are you doing here? Did something happen at the ranch?"

Cal set the grocery bag down in the truck bed a bit too hard. "Fact is I wondered that about *you.* Eric called because you were supposed to take him driving and he didn't know where you were. I lit out when I realized I didn't know, either."

Lain set her hands on her hips. "Darn it all! I talked to Gil about four. He said he'd leave a note for Eric on the kitchen bulletin board." Then she noticed that Cal waited impatiently. "Brie and I were having such a good time we didn't watch the clock."

Cal spread his arms wide. "What the hell is there to do around here for seven hours?" He craned his head and scouted the immediate area. "Where's Brie? Still inside?"

Lain set her hands on her hips. "Lower your voice, Cal, or all you'll get out of me is specific directions where to go. And it won't be somewhere cool and breezy!"

Cal slammed the tailgate shut. "Cut the big sister crap, Lain, and spill!"

Amazingly, Lain cracked a smile, crossed her arms, and leaned against the truck's dusty fender. "Okay, since I guess that's as much courtesy as I can expect from you today. After I showed Brie the sites in town we had lunch at the Rojo. I talked up how beautiful this area was, and she asked me to drive her around. Girl's got curiosity a mile wide and just as deep," Lain commented with approval. "Wanted to see everything. So I showed her. Took her for a long ride into the canyon conservancy area."

She gave a nonchalant shrug. "When we got back to town it

was almost three-thirty. I still had to pick up a few things at Joe's, and I knew I'd never make it home for Eric's lesson so I called Gil. I figured Brie wouldn't want to stand around while I picked out disposable diapers and lettuce, so I stashed her over at the museum lounge."

Cal went cold. "You didn't!"

"I did, and she liked it," Lain retorted. "Introduced her to Fred. Right off she told him his place had a unique ambiance. Had Fred strutting around like he was head rooster. You can bet he made Brie feel more than welcome after that."

Cal couldn't believe what he'd heard. "You left her alone in that tavern?"

"Don't be ridiculous," Lain scoffed, and then smiled coyly. "Before I left, Fred made a point of introducing us to a couple of guys who had stopped in earlier for a meal on their way through town. When I left Brie was having a great time. I don't think she even realized I was gone."

Cal's chest constricted. "Two guys?"

Lain nodded. "Interesting pair. Wish I could have stayed. At least Brie was having fun. Heaven knows the poor girl's probably starved for social exchange after boarding with you."

He stifled an urge to give his sister a shake. "What were you thinking? Damn, Lain, I know what kind of 'interesting' guys hang out at the tavern!"

Lain held up her hand. "No, really, Cal, these guys aren't that kind of 'interesting.'"

"That's it. I'm going in after her." Cal pushed past her on his way to the Jeep. "You can leave. I'll take Brie back home."

"Home?" Lain called after him. "That cabin isn't a home, Cal Porter! It's your hidey-hole!"

The accusation made Cal pull up and spin around. But as he faced his sister, he realized she only spoke the truth as she saw it. And she was right. The cabin had been nothing more than shelter from the elements, a place to brood and nurse the pain of loss and uncertainty. When had it become his home?

The answer wasn't as much of a shock as it was a revelation. The change arrived with Brienne Quaid, when she blew in with the storm, dripping rainwater on his floor and leaving her scent throughout the stuffy cabin. She took over the bathroom with her bottles of powders, shampoos, and fragrant body oils. She draped her clothes over the dead animal heads that he'd barely noticed until she took umbrage at them. The mug from which she drank her special tea sat next to the one he used for his coffee on the kitchen counter. Since she came he'd eaten breakfast twice, a meal he usually skipped and later regretted doing so. Dishes no longer piled up in the sink until he ran out of spoons and plates.

Brie Quaid had made the cabin a home. Not intentionally. Not because she meant to stay. But because she was Brie Quaid. And in that moment of revelation, Cal realized that he liked what had happened. He liked it a lot.

Shaken by the moment of truth, Cal only lifted his arm as if to wave off Lain's comment, then yanked open the door of his Jeep.

"Would you slow down, little brother!" Lain yelled. "You go off half-cocked now and you're going to make a fool of yourself."

Cal paused only a moment to look over his shoulder and cast her a glare.

Lain threw up her arms. "Ah, hell, you always did take yourself too seriously. Maybe it's about time you played a fool."

Cal ignored her, vaulted into the front seat and slammed the door. Two minutes later he turned the corner at the only stop sign in town and ground the Jeep to a halt across the street from the erstwhile Lost Mines Museum.

Brie didn't make it hard for him to find her. She leaned against a rough-hewn wooden rail that separated the boardwalk in front of the tavern from the street. She looked cheery as sunshine in her yellow dress and a new floppy-brimmed straw hat decorated with bright orange and light blue ribbons. On either side of her stood two men dressed in black jeans, t-shirts, and riding boots. One of the men towered over Brie. The other was shorter but built like a bull.

Two leather jackets were draped over the rail close to Brie's arm. It didn't take much of a leap of logic to figure the jackets and a pair of Harleys parked nearby belonged to the men who were turned toward Brie, as if she were the center of the universe.

On a gut level Cal understood why. She looked beautiful just then, as the breeze tossed her dark hair and rippled the hem of her yellow dress across her slender legs. She'd draped the strap of her tiny purse diagonally across her chest again, shoulder to waist. And again the press of the strap on the bodice of her dress outlined those perfect breasts.

And she laughed. Even from across the street, Cal could see pure pleasure light her face. She'd never laughed with such abandon when she was alone with him. But then, Cal realized dourly, he'd given her no reason. When she raised a brown beer bottle to her lips and took a long swig, his heart froze. If those two guys were getting her drunk...

Cal leapt out of the Jeep and slammed the door. That got the trio's attention. As he marched to the storefront, Cal noticed out of the corner of his eye that the tall guy on the right took a step forward, beer in hand. On guard in case the biker decided to swing the bottle his way, Cal nevertheless riveted his full attention on Brie.

Her eyes grew wide with surprise as she pushed away from the rail and stood without benefit of her cane. Cal planted himself in front of her and jerked his head toward the Jeep. "Come on. Let's go."

Brie blinked. "Go where?"

The tall guy took a half step toward Cal. "Excuse me, we haven't met."

The man's deep but gentle voice and polite formality distracted Cal for a moment. When he glanced over he realized the well-modulated words came with a cool, penetrating stare. Cal's hackles went up. "No, we haven't." He turned back to Brie and held out his hand. "Come on."

She shook her head. "Lain said she'd pick me up after she was finished at the general store."

"Plan's been changed," Cal announced in a low, commanding voice. "You're coming home with me."

"Home?" she echoed, and chuckled softly. "You mean 'back to the cabin?'"

No, he meant home, dammit, a place where she'd be safe from the likes of these two motorcycle brutes. And where he could explain a thing or two about making nice with bikers passing through Saratoga Springs. Where were her city survival skills, for crying out loud?

"Whatever," Cal said abruptly. "Let's go. It's getting late."

She held her ground. "It's not even six."

The other guy set his beer on the ground. "I think Miss Quaid wants to stay a while longer."

Cal directed his glare at the man on the left who had the face of a choirboy and the shoulders of a linebacker. "Miss Quaid's coming with me."

The linebacker spread his biker-booted feet in attack stance. "Not if she objects."

That's when Brie put up her hand and spiked Cal with a furious scowl. "All right, fine. I'll come."

The guy on the right caught her arm gently. "Brie, are you

sure you want to go with this guy?"

Cal opened his mouth to tell the guy where to go and what to do once he got there. But Brie smiled her prettiest smile at the man and shook her head. "It's okay, Neil. This is Lain's brother. He's putting me up until I can drive again. He's safe enough." She brought her eyes back to Cal. "He's married."

The gist of her pronouncement hit Cal like a sucker punch. Safe. Married. Deliberately or not, she'd mocked him with his own words and pared him down to inconsequential size in front of the two substantial men. He felt like a blathering fool.

Well, hadn't Lain warned him?

To add insult to injury, Brie looked back at Neil, took his hand inside hers and gave it a gentle shake. "I shouldn't keep you standing here talking anyway. You have to get on the road before dusk so you can make your next stop. It was so nice meeting you." She turned to the other man. "And you, Hank. I can't think of a more pleasurable way of spending a warm, lazy afternoon than talking with you two."

Images of much better ways to spend a warm, lazy afternoon with Brie Quaid flitted through Cal's mind. And they all had to do with cool sheets and soft feather mattresses. So much for safe, Ms. L.A.

If his face betrayed those unbidden lusty notions Brie didn't notice. She was too busy bidding fond farewell to her new friends.

"Neil" held on to her hand a moment too long and eyed Cal suspiciously. "Are you *sure* you want to go with this guy?"

She grinned. "Don't worry. His bark is worse than his bite."

Another solid verbal blow. It seemed sweet Brie Quaid could have given his Selene a run for her money any day, all at the expense of the male ego.

"Hank, Neil, safe journey," she said as she started to move past Cal toward the parked Jeep. "You have my address now, so be sure to write and tell me how the rest of your trip goes."

Cal almost missed a step. Had he heard right? Had she given those two bikers her home address?

"And I'm easy to find, so when you pass through Los Angeles stop by!"

"Sure thing, Brie."

"You take care, Brie."

They sounded fawning. Then Cal caught sight of the bikes and ground his teeth.

He wanted to grab her by her narrow waist and speed her along. Instead he walked with his arm just touching hers and waited until they were out of earshot before he started whispering. "Are you out of your mind? I thought you were a Big City woman? What's with giving those two guys your address?"

"I wanted to keep in touch with them," she replied through set teeth. "Neil and Hank are..."

"Probably wanted men!" Cal finished furiously.

She turned to him in abject surprise. "Just because they ride motorcycles..."

"Big motorcycles," Cal emphasized.

"And are a little unkempt because they've been on the road..."

"I'd guess they haven't showered in about three days."

"A lot you know, Cal Porter," she fired back under her breath as they reached the Jeep. "You might try expanding that narrow mind of yours once in a while."

Cal flung open the door. "My mind is expanded enough, thanks. My patience, though, is shrinking. And give me that bottle. No open beer in my car."

"You supreme idiot!" she breathed, and stuck the bottle under his nose. "It's *root* beer! We were all having a bottle of *root beer!*"

Cal didn't have to take a big whiff of the sweet liquid to realize he'd made a slight mistake. "Yeah, okay, so I jumped to a conclusion."

"Just one?" she seethed. "The only reason I let you drag me away from that porch is so I wouldn't have to stand there and watch you make a pathetic fool of yourself any longer. Really, Cal, what is your problem?"

"My problem is you were standing there with two bikers like you were at a Sunday picnic at the beach."

"Give me a little credit! I have instincts about people, remember? I'm psychic."

"More like psycho if you trust your instincts about those guys."

She breathed in disgust. "*Those guys* are Dr. Hank Fitzgerald from Chicago, and Father Neil Patterson from Des Moines, Iowa. They're college buddies who finally got together for a dream cross-country biking trip. They're going to go up and down the California coast to try to visit every historical mission. Thanks, Cal. You rescued me from a neurosurgeon and a priest!"

Taken aback by the revelation Cal nevertheless paused only a moment. "Yeah, that's what *they* say!"

"That's what I *know!*" she fired back almost before he got all the words out.

Yeah, she did know, Cal realized. Whether it was true psychic ability or just a well-honed skill didn't matter. Brie Quaid could peg people. Lots better, it seemed, than he could.

Having punched a hole in his righteous indignation with her twin pickaxes of confidence and reason, Brie tossed the cane into the back seat and scrambled into the Jeep without help. Winded by embarrassment, Cal only watched as she slammed the door behind her, strapped on her seat belt, and stared ahead with her arms crossed.

What had he done? Made a flaming ass of himself in front of two strangers—harmless strangers—and the woman he'd set out to save.

Why? Good question. Brie Quaid was nothing to him. She was passing through his life as she ran from her own problems. Heaven knew he had problems of his own without worrying about a self-proclaimed "psychic" who walked in her sleep and turned his life upside down from the minute she practically rammed through his front door.

Yet even now, as she tore the straw hat from her head and refused to meet his eyes, Brie Quaid exuded an alluring air of innocence and wholesomeness that brought him to his knees. She was warm and giving and passionate. All those things he missed in life and now suddenly craved again. Yet he'd done everything in his power to push all that goodness away. Keep it away. Because he was so afraid to let honest emotion touch him again.

Yes, he was a fool. Had been for years. Brie claimed nothing in life happened by coincidence. Maybe it was true she had entered his life for a purpose, and he'd been too self-involved with ancient grief to accept this gift offered by fate.

And now it was probably too late.

Or maybe not.

Cal rounded the front of the Jeep, opened his door, and noticed the two bikers—that is the doctor and the priest—were still eyeing him with ill-concealed suspicion. Then Brie looked out her window and waved. The two men returned the gesture with smiles all around and began their own preparation for hitting the highway. A spasm of jealousy took Cal by complete surprise.

He hefted himself into the front seat and turned on the ignition. But before he shifted into drive he looked over at Brie's frozen angry profile. "Look, I'm sorry."

"Direct your apologies to Neil and Hank," she suggested tartly, and turned to glare at him. "Then start figuring out a way to get out more often so you can rid yourself of this annoying habit of stereotyping people at first sight."

Since he'd been clearly in the wrong, Cal fought back a burst of temper and revved the engine. "I said I'm sorry. But I was worried. And I've had a history with that tavern."

"What gives you the right to be worried about me to the point where you practically yank me off the street?" she railed.

Cal jammed the Jeep into gear, stepped on the gas and did a screeching one-eighty turn. "I didn't yank you off the street," he countered. "I politely asked you to come with me."

"You *demanded* I come with you."

He was finding it harder to keep his temper in check. "I thought it was in your best interest at the time."

"My best interest is not your concern. You're no longer some crusading lawyer, Cal Porter. And I'm not a victim."

He jerked he head around. "Lawyer? Who told you...Lain!"

She tapped her foot on the floor. "Yes, she told me. Like it should have been some state secret! 'I've had some experience with the legal system,'" she mimicked his exact words from a few days back. "The way I hear it from Lain you could have destroyed Perry Mason!"

"Lain exaggerated," Cal tried to defend himself.

But Brie wouldn't give him a chance. "Don't give me that. Lain said you were the master of understatement." She turned her beautiful cornflower blue eyes on him, but there was nothing soft or sympathetic about the way she glared at him now. "Of course, I realized that myself when she mentioned your wife disappeared eight years ago."

Cal almost blew through the stop sign. He slammed on the brakes moments before he broadsided a tanker truck pulling out of Santiago's Service Station. While the truck lumbered past them and the driver gave him the universal one-finger salute of contempt, he stared ahead and waited for a tongue-lashing.

When Brie said nothing more, Cal snuck a sideways glance at the passenger's seat. She was still there, still staring at him, but now seemed to be waiting.

He drew a breath, screwed up his courage and turned to face her. "All right, what do you want me to say?"

She lifted her eyes to the roof for a moment. "Oh, I don't know, Counselor." Those blue eyes honed in on him again. "How about the truth, the whole truth, and nothing but the truth?"

He turned forward. "I told you the truth."

"I said the whole truth. Your wife's been missing for almost a decade and declared dead for a year."

He snorted. "You and Lain had quite a talk."

"It wasn't as comprehensive as you imagine," Brie snapped. "For some reason she believes the details should come from you."

"Well, that's a refreshing change," he muttered.

"Will they?"

In reflex, Cal glanced back to Brie. "Huh?"

Anger no longer tautened her face. Brie Quaid peered at him as if pleading. "Will the details come from you? Damn it, Cal, if you were embarrassed by what happened last night between us, or if it was just a moment that got away from you, then fine. But don't use a marriage that's been over and done with for years as an excuse to put me off. Be honest."

Be honest? Did she know what she asked? Did she really want to know how close she came to ending up in his bed last night? She'd leap out of the Jeep and run back to her biker buddies. And did she really want him to share all the darkness of his past? Did she really believe that would set him free?

Some things were better left unsaid and unexplained.

Cal's heart thrummed so hard he felt the pulse in his throat. "If you want, I'll take you back to the general store and you can ride home with Lain."

Her shoulders sagged forward. Brie blinked a few times then eased face forward. "Just take me back to the cabin, please."

The quiet resignation in her voice pricked Cal's conscience, but he stepped on the gas. "Okay."

Brie sank back into the bucket seat, folded her arms, and said nothing for the rest of the ride. Maybe she just needed some time and space, and then she would understand he didn't want to be pushed and prodded into giving up parts of himself he had kept closely guarded for so long. He didn't want to take out that part of his life and examine it again. He didn't want to rehash the mistakes, and open up that pain. As long as he kept it in the background of his life he could keep hope alive.

And once they were back at the cabin he'd try another apology. She had a right to her anger and frustration. He'd admit that out loud. Yeah, he'd get it right. He'd make her understand.

But Cal no more than pulled up in front of the cabin and shifted into park than Brie reached behind her for the cane and let herself out the door. She was halfway to the front porch before he fumbled out of his seat belt and scrambled after her.

She hobbled up the steps amazingly fast and pushed through the front door, which Cal had forgot to lock in his haste to get into town. He followed at a distance, since hovering had been disastrous. When she went straight for the bathroom he breathed a sigh of relief. She probably just wanted to splash some cold water on her face, compose herself a little, and then they'd talk. Rather, he'd apologize—again—in the most abject terms.

To his surprise, Brie emerged from the bathroom in less than two minutes, carrying the waterproof case that held her toiletries. With purpose she marched to the foot of the neatly made up rollaway bed, and unzipped her soft-sided suitcase.

Cal edged toward the hearth. "What are you doing?"

She glanced up briefly and gave him a "don't be a dolt" look, then went about her business. "I'm giving you back your solitude," Brie replied, in a voice that sounded less strident than her actions appeared. "I'll drive over to the ranch and see if Lain will put me up for the night. Tomorrow, I'll head out for New Mexico. Thanks for letting me stay these past few days."

For a moment, her words didn't track. "What? You're leaving?" As his thoughts raced, Cal took another step forward. "You...you can't leave now."

"Why not?" she asked without looking up.

She was still angry, Cal rationalized. She was acting out of pique. He couldn't let her leave like this. "In the first place, I've got more food in the refrigerator than I know what to do with," he blurted out.

Brie headed back for the bathroom. "Have Lain and the family over for dinner sometime. It'll be a nice change for them."

He followed her to the bathroom door and watched as she scooped up some loose bottles. "But you...you still need the cane to walk!" he sputtered. "How can you be sure you can drive all that distance?"

Though he fairly blocked the door Brie edged her way past without so much as brushing him. She shuffled back to the roll bag and stashed the bottles. "I'll get by. I have before."

Cal had gotten by, too, for eight years. Now, watching Brie Quaid pack up to leave, he wasn't sure exactly how he'd managed it.

She glanced around the room and noticed the sweater still hanging from the antlers of the deer trophy. "Cal, will you please get that down for me?"

He took an automatic step toward the fireplace to oblige the request, but then stopped himself. "No." The word just slipped out.

Slowly, guarding her right knee, Brie turned in place. "No?"

What was he doing? Isn't this what he'd wanted since

Monday night?

Maybe then, but not now. Cal shook his head.

Brie screwed her mouth into a frown. "Look, tossing that sweater up there was one thing. I can't get it down without your help. Now please..."

"No."

She pursed her lips. "It's the only sweater I packed. I need it."

"And I need you to stay. Don't go."

Again the words just came, unbidden, surprising Cal as much as they obviously surprised Brie.

"What?" she gasped. "Don't be ridiculous!"

Cal drew a shuddering breath and took a step toward her. "I don't want you to go."

Her arms dangled at her sides. She appeared helpless and confused, much like Cal felt.

"I want you to stay." He took another two steps. She was within arm's reach.

Brie didn't move. Her cornflower blue eyes softened. "Why?"

What should he say? That the thought of being alone now terrified him? That he no longer wanted to share this rickety cabin with nothing but wildlife long dead and memories that should have been buried years ago?

"I...I guess I've gotten used to you, to your company." He had reached her now, and he slowly raised his hand to touch her cheek. Such a lovely cheek, so smooth and glowing rose with emotion. But he held back. "I'd miss walking downstairs in the morning and seeing you on the couch in that yellow dress."

She stood taller, and though she didn't move back, she somehow withdrew. "My dress? Fine. I'll go change. You can have it. Run it up a flagpole and salute it at sunrise."

He flinched at the desperate sarcasm in her voice, but dared touch her cheek with the tips of his fingers. "Brie, I've never begged for anything in my life. I'm begging you now. Stay."

"Why?" she whispered, trembling as he caressed her warm skin with his cool fingers.

Or was that his trembling?

He set his other hand beside her face and tipped her head up. Her eyes were so wide and beautiful in their innocence. "I don't know," he confessed. "But I do know this. If you leave now I'll be more alone than I ever have in my life. More alone than I've been in these past eight years." He shook his head. "I don't want to be alone any more."

"You aren't alone," she argued. "You have Lain and her family."

"Not enough," he answered, and the truth surprised him. "Not any more. Maybe it never was."

For a very long moment she only peered into his eyes, mirroring the confusion that constricted his chest. Then she placed her hand over his. "Don't you see, Cal? I could stay another day, another ten days, or a year, and you'd still be alone. You can't just take from me. You have to give something back. You have to trust me."

Instinctively he pulled away, cut himself off from Brie's warmth. "Don't push," he warned.

She jerked up her chin. "You mean 'don't push back.' No, sorry, Cal, this isn't a courtroom where you can browbeat a witness into giving the answer you want to hear. You're asking for a relationship. Mind to mind. Soul to soul. That means *quid pro quo*. Remember that term from your law school days?"

She was slipping away. He could actually feel her anger creating distance. And yet the old pain and fear held him in check. "Brie, I don't know if I can..."

She didn't let him finish before she turned and set her attention on the roll bag. "Forget the sweater. I'll borrow one from Sophie when I get to New Mexico." Brie zipped up the bag, set the strap on her shoulder, and leaned over to grab her new straw hat from the coffee table. "Good-bye, Cal."

He let her get two steps. "No!"

His plea didn't slow her down.

He had a choice. Let go of his fear or let go of this woman.

Cal shut down his brain and listened to his heart. Lurching forward he threw himself in her path.

Brie pulled up just before colliding with his body. Her eyes narrowed with new anger. When he calmly began divesting her of the roll bag, she started to sputter, "What...what do you think..."

"Come with me," he said, wresting control of the bag and letting it drop to the floor.

She shook her head. "I thought I made myself clear..."

Cal grasped her hand, and held tight until she looked up at him. "You did. And I heard. Come with me." He held his breath. "I'll tell you what you want to know."

Twelve

He could take a woman and make her body sing. But he could not—would not—touch a woman's soul.

Yet when this woman's soul called out to him Myles had to answer.

Chapter 12, Murder, My Love—From the Files of Myles Daemon, P.I.

* * * *

When Cal had grasped her hand and pleaded with his eyes to follow him, Brie listened to her heart and took a leap of faith, letting him load her back into his Jeep.

Now, fifteen minutes later, she sat on the bench of a dilapidated picnic table, in a grove of massive live oak trees that looked as old as the northern California redwoods, and waited for her faith to be rewarded. From the lay of the land behind her, the sizable branch of Milagro Creek in front of her, and the canyon face rising on the opposite creek bank, Brie guessed this place was part of the conservancy area she'd toured with Lain.

She also calculated this wasn't far from the place where the canyon road did a "dead drop" into no-man's lands.

Yet, despite the memories of Monday night and the debilitating vertigo that seized her as she wound up the canyon road with Lain earlier in the day, Brie felt no residual terror. And the reason stood with his back to her, arms at his side, feet apart not more than a couple yards away on the creek bank. Cal Porter. She trusted him. He wouldn't let her come to harm. She'd known that from the moment he'd touched her Monday night while the storm raged around them. She trusted him still, even though part of him remained inscrutable.

Would he trust her enough to let down his guard, even a little?

As the minutes ticked by she started to wonder if her faith had been misplaced.

Brie took off her sunglasses and set them alongside the new straw hat on the plank table behind her. Though dusk was still more than an hour away the canyon face blocked the setting sun. A cool breeze stirred the live oak leaves overhead. The dry rustle played background accompaniment to birdsong and the rush of creek water.

"This is a beautiful place, Cal," she finally said, at the risk of appearing impatient.

He nodded and looked partway around to her, but didn't meet her eyes. "It never changes much. That picnic table has looked like that for fifteen years." He smiled, a brief and rather sad expression, and then heaved a sigh. "Maybe that's what I like about this place. It has a timeless quality in spite of how everything else changes. I used to come here quite a lot."

"With Alicia," Brie guessed, and hoped her voice didn't betray a niggle of jealousy that lodged in the pit of her stomach.

To her surprise Cal shook his head. "No, not Alicia. She hated it out here. She hated the cabin, and the isolation, and the dust, and heat. But once in a while I got her to compromise and she came with me."

His wife hated this place? Then perhaps the feminine essence that still echoed in the cabin didn't belong to Alicia...

Immediately Brie's intuition told her otherwise. The essence belonged to Cal's missing wife. But that would mean he couldn't let go of Alicia's memory. He kept it trapped in this space and time. Why?

Cal fell silent again, a silence that snapped Brie's fraying patience. "Why did you bring me here?"

He pivoted then, a slow almost hesitant move. "I...I'm not sure. It seemed like a good idea at the time."

Brie pressed her lips tightly and tamped down her anger at the weak jest. "No more hide and seek, Cal."

He only shook his head. "I don't know where to start."

His confusion took the edge off Brie's anger. She didn't know where to start either. She'd asked for the truth. No, she'd demanded the truth. But now that the moment was upon her she wondered if she wanted to risk hearing Cal still loved his wife, wanted her back after eight years, and would keep wanting her in the face of circumstantial evidence that she wasn't even alive.

Still it was better to understand Cal Porter's motivations now before she lost her heart to him.

Brie flinched inwardly. How could she expect him to honor the truth if she didn't do the same? Somehow, some way, she'd already lost her heart to Cal Porter—lawyer, writer, junior curmudgeon—whoever he was deep down inside. His soul had called to her soul. She never expected this flame of physical attraction to spark and grow between them. But there was no denying that either. She couldn't go back. No matter how dangerous, she had to go forward.

But slowly. Gently, for his sake as well as hers.

"I can think of a half-dozen starting points," she prodded. "Let's begin at the beginning. Why didn't you tell me you were a lawyer? Why all the misdirection?"

Cal peered at the featureless, dusty earth for a moment, then ambled to one of the live oaks and sat down on a rise of gnarled roots. Leaning forward and bracing his weight on one raised knee, he looked back to the creek. "I didn't mean to deceive you. Fact is I haven't been a practicing lawyer for almost eight years. After what happened to me at the hands of the law, I don't think I want to practice ever again."

"Are you telling me you were disbarred?" she pressed.

"No," he said slowly. "Not disbarred. Just disbelieved, disgraced, and disabused of the highhanded notion I could change the world and hold a failing marriage together at the same time." He snorted. "Blew up in my face big time."

Reliving these memories was painful for him. Brie sensed the terrible constriction of his soul at the same moment she saw the anguish clouding Cal's eyes. But she needed answers. She had to protect herself, as well.

"Lain told me you championed the rights of abused women and children," she encouraged gently.

"Championed?" He allowed a wisp of a smile. "A kind word for something I felt compelled to do." Cal turned his gaze on Brie. "Did Lain tell you why?"

When Brie shook her head, Cal drew a deep breath. "It was my father."

"You took up his cause?" she guessed.

"Hardly. I wanted to prove I wasn't like Callan Porter, Senior." His eyes narrowed with barely suppressed rage. "I hated being named after him, almost as much as I hated him. He wouldn't call me anything else unless it was something derogatory or obscene. That's why I've always called myself Cal."

He sighed as if expelling long pent up air. "My father was a mean son-of-a-bitch, Brie. He'd get drunk and strike out at anyone within reach." Though he still looked at her, his focus seemed far away. "One Saturday morning when I was eight he started to beat up my mom. Lain usually got me upstairs and out of the way when he started looking for a punching bag, but that day she wasn't home. So for the first time I had to stand there and watch."

Brie's stomach clenched with empathetic rage. "Oh, Cal, that must have been terrible."

"I don't remember what I felt," he answered. "I just reacted.

I rushed him, the way I saw football players do on TV. This skinny little kid thinking he could drop a guy three times his size."

Cal shook his head. "I hit his thigh with my shoulder. He was either way drunk and unbalanced, or just taken off guard. Maybe both. Anyway, he went down hard on the kitchen floor. My neck and arm hurt like hell, and I jammed my face against his knee so my nose started to bleed. But I stood over him with my fists clenched and screamed at him to stop beating on mom, now and forever, amen. I expected him to haul his ass off the floor and whale on me, too."

Brie set her hand to her throat where emotion lodged so tight she couldn't talk for a moment.

"I guess dad was embarrassed he'd been decked by a third-grader," Cal went on. "He staggered to his feet, stumbled out the door and was gone for three days. When he finally did show up again, he packed a bag, left, and never came back."

Brie flinched at the zombie-like monotone of Cal's voice that contrasted so sharply with the active pain in his eyes. "For someone so young you acted bravely."

He ignored the compliment. "Even though we were better off as a family without him, we struggled financially. For months I had it in the back of my mind I was responsible for making him abandon us. Lain tried to set me straight." He smiled faintly. "Some things never change. Finally, mom got us all into counseling and we moved past it."

"But you held on to the cause," Brie put in.

Cal faced her now, and his eyes were hard with anger. "Ever hear that saying, 'No good deed goes unpunished?' It was the one thing my dad may have been right about. Yeah, I took up the cause against domestic violence. I ran with it. Made a career of it." He clenched his fist. "Made a mockery of it, more like. I pimped it for all it was worth and that arrogance came back to haunt me."

"That's not what Lain said," she told him. "She called you a gender-bending Joan of Arc. She said you even ran for political office because of your convictions."

Cal lowered his gaze to the dusty ground. "That's not exactly true. The truth is I started believing my own press. I listened to my ego instead of my brains. Everyone told me I was some kind of hotshot lawyer. That I could really make a difference by running for elective office. I had the right 'star-quality.' The tough luck background, scholarship sponsored education, take-no-prisoners attitude." He paused and leaned back against the trunk of the live oak. "And a beautiful wife from a wealthy, connected family in San Francisco who came to the marriage with an unlimited trust fund."

"Alicia," Brie whispered.

"Alicia," he repeated, though she wasn't sure if Cal really heard her or if his memories had just started to carry him along. "She was the only other person who insisted on calling me Callan. She said that 'Cal' sounded like a cowboy. That it was unsuitable for a young man on his way up. I gave in." He shrugged. "She had class and breeding that I didn't, so I figured she had to be right. But I never wore the name very well. I think it made me resent her, too, because I felt like I had to give in, even though it was going against my better instincts."

Cal drew in a deep breath. "Anyway, we met our senior year at Stanford. She was intelligent, well-traveled, sophisticated, and yet basically a fragile person." He rolled his eyes. "Must have appealed to my protective instincts, I guess. And I think she wanted someone who could stand up to her control-freak father. I was a common sense, ambitious country boy who really didn't give a flying care that her daddy was one of the ten richest men in the country. He was still a jerk, and I told him as much in private the day I signed a prenuptial agreement at his insistence. See, he didn't want me getting my greedy, dirt-poor hands on her money."

He rested his head against the tree trunk. "Neither Alicia nor her father understood I didn't care about her money. I guess that should have been just one of the red flags we were headed for eventual trouble." He inhaled deeply. "Alicia and I tried to make it work, but maybe her father had it right all along. Maybe he understood, from the vantage of someone who had been divorced three times, the differences that looked so appealing when we were in college would eventually get between us. The ambition Alicia admired got me ahead. She enjoyed the backwash of fame. I think she enjoyed proving her father wrong about me, too."

Cal narrowed his gaze, as if trying to see beyond the beautifully stark landscape. "But she didn't like my absences, or the way I focused on my job at her expense. The fragility that appealed to my vanity turned into pathetic neediness. We fought over everything. I lost track of how many times in those first years I thought about divorce. But then I remembered my father leaving. And while it wasn't the same situation I didn't want to be anything like him. I didn't want to be a quitter. I thought I could just gut it out and make it better through persistence. So I hung on."

Sadness began leaching from his soul again.. "And then Alicia got pregnant. We had a little girl. Jeanie." He whispered the name like a prayer. "She'd be almost twelve now."

For a moment, Brie couldn't quite get her arms around the new revelation. A child? So Cal's reaction to Dulcie wasn't disapproval or inexperience. It was the reaction of a father separated for eight years from his daughter. Holding Dulcie, feeling her petal-soft skin and breathing in her baby-scent had surely been torture for him.

Cal must have glimpsed her stunned reaction. "Lain didn't tell you that?"

"No," she breathed out, her voice trembling.

As she grieved for Cal's loss a more rational part of Brie realized she'd felt a woman's presence in the cabin, but not that of a child.

"Yeah, well, the announcement surprised me, too," he admitted. "We wanted kids, but we kept putting it off." He held up his index finger. "Strike that. I kept putting it off because I wasn't sure our marriage would last. Alicia decided otherwise. At first I was angry because she'd taken it upon herself to make this major change in our lives. But the pregnancy made such a difference in her. She loved every moment of it, the planning, the attention. Maybe she thought a child could give her the companionship and purpose that I couldn't."

He shrugged. "Whatever her motive I went along because life was easier and happier." He smiled wryly. "We had only one major argument during those months, and that was over the baby's name. I wanted Jean for a girl, after my mother. But Alicia said that was too common. She said she'd go along with Jean or Jeanie as a nickname, but insisted on Eugenia for the birth certificate. I let her win the battle of the names again." His smile sagged. "But I always called our little girl Jeanie. Maybe it was my way of finally standing up for both of us."

The bittersweet memories brought tears to Brie's eyes.

Cal didn't notice. He'd focused on that distant imaginary spot again. "For a while before and just after Jeanie was born it seemed, to me anyway, we were on the road to happily-ever-after. That lasted until I started my political campaign. I was gone more than ever. The mutual anger and resentment got deeper. Worse, I wouldn't ask her to dip into her trust fund for campaign money, so Alicia had no way to control me except for tantrums. Then one night she pulled out all the stops and threatened to take Jeanie and leave. I blew off the threats and went to a fund-raiser because I knew she was too dependent on me to follow through."

Suddenly he pushed off the ground and stalked past Brie to another live oak that bordered the grove. Hands in his pockets, face to the sky, his profile tight with tension, he ground out the rest. "I guess she'd had enough. When I got back later that night, she and Jeanie were gone. They just disappeared into thin air. The police found a couple of gas receipts that made it appear she'd headed north, toward San Francisco and her father. But she never made it that far. Alicia's father claimed he never saw or heard from her. That was eight years ago next week."

"Oh, Cal," Brie said on a sigh. "I'm so sorry."

He swung around. "Save your sympathy, Brie. I don't deserve it. I lost my marriage and my daughter because I felt such contempt for Alicia that I didn't take her seriously. I was too wrapped up in the rightness of my cause, and too angry that she didn't understand how important all this was to me that I failed to try and understand her. I drove her away." He raked his hair with both hands. "Believe it or not that was just the beginning of the nightmare."

How much more pain could there be, Brie wondered, as he started pacing back and forth in front of the picnic table.

"I thought the horror of losing my wife and child would blot out everything else," Cal went on. "I learned otherwise. First the police investigated me. As a prosecutor I expected that. But it was also common knowledge I'd experienced abuse as a child, and that made me a higher than normal risk for repeating the cycle."

"You're kidding!" she blurted out.

"I would have considered the possibility," he said. "But I wouldn't have floated unsubstantiated rumors and gossip. Within a couple days of Alicia's disappearance word got back to my campaign manager that there were whispers she'd left because she had been a battered wife and I might have had something to do with the disappearance. Her father said nothing to the contrary, even though the police came up with no evidence that I should even be considered a suspect. He started his own investigation on the premise he didn't trust my 'friends' in Santa Barbara law enforcement."

Cal smirked. "He always thought I was a fortune hunter out to make his little girl a trophy wife and get my hands on her money. Having been a father, even for a short time, part of me understands. But my political opponent jumped on the bandwagon for mercenary reasons. She was behind in the polls and wanted to make damn sure I didn't get a sympathy vote."

"She conducted a smear campaign?" Brie croaked.

"She didn't smear me, she buried me," Cal muttered. "I didn't care about losing the election, not when I'd already lost so much more. But her attacks robbed me of my reputation and my credibility in the community, and because of all that, eventually my job. I was a tainted prosecutor. A hypocrite. My convictions of abusers were called into question. I was asked, politely but in no uncertain terms, to resign."

"That must have been awful," Brie sympathized. "To be accused of what you fought against your entire life."

"It was hell for everyone I knew and loved," he told her. "The media camped out on my mother's doorstep up in Salinas, and even tracked down Lain at the ranch. Gil hired his own security guards to cordon off the property, but he lost months of business anyway."

He stopped in his tracks and squeezed his eyes shut. "Damn, I was angry. But mostly at myself." Cal shook off the emotion and purposely loosened his arms and shoulders. "I came back here to the cabin, holed up, and tried to forget what had happened while I hung on to the hope Alicia and Jeanie would someday come walking through the front door."

A faint smile stretched his mouth. "Lain was the one who got me to start writing. She told me I was building tragedy on tragedy by brooding my life away. In language I won't repeat she suggested I do something constructive with my time before my brain rotted. I started writing the Myles Daemon mysteries just to shut her up."

"Your plan failed," Brie observed. "She still won't leave you alone."

Cal nodded, and his features went soft for a moment. "Yeah, but her plan worked. I didn't rot. Not completely anyway. And I earned enough money with my writing to keep looking for Alicia and Jeanie, even when my father-in-law gave up his search. But I still kept everyone at a distance. Even Lain and her family. I burned a lot of bridges."

"Lain mentioned what happened between you and your friend, the private detective."

He nodded. "Jim Atwood. He's a stand-up guy. His mistake was telling me something I didn't want to hear. Maybe I still don't want to hear it. Or believe it. Parents have disappeared with children and stayed 'lost' for years before something inconsequential blows their cover. Alicia had lots of her own money, and connections through her father."

"Do you think her father may have helped hide them?" Brie asked incredulously.

"It's crossed my mind more than once," he admitted. "But she could have done it on her own. And if her father ever did know anything, he sure as hell wouldn't tell me."

Cal pinned her with pleading eyes. "Brie, I have to know what happened to Alicia and Jeannie. Part of me has to hope they're still alive, even if it means holding on to a marriage that was over before Jeanie was born. I want Alicia back so I can have answers. I have to know if Jeanie's..."

He couldn't say it out loud. He couldn't admit there was a good chance his little girl might be dead, along with her mother who had already been declared so.

Brie saw him struggle with his emotions as he looked out at the creek. "Jeanie and I used to come here alone. She loved to run around the trees. The last time we were here she was about to turn three, and she brought along her backpack that was like the 'big kids' carried."

Cal smiled at the memory, and for that moment his face was transformed with utter joy. "Jeanie surprised the hell out me that day. She reached into the backpack and pulled out a doll that was some fancy showpiece Alicia bought for display. Jeanie didn't care about fancy. She just had taken a liking to the doll and wanted to play with it. But since her mom wouldn't even let her touch it at home Jeanie decided to smuggle it out of our house for a little R&R. As her daddy I knew I should reprimand her. But she looked up at me with these big brown eyes and I laughed instead. That got her laughing, and she tossed the doll at me."

Brie grinned at the mental image, a child and father getting their kicks by doing something forbidden together in a place nature seemed to have carved out just for them.

"We got a pretty good game of peewee football going," Cal remembered. "For a three-year-old Jeanie had a good arm. But on one throw I tossed the doll at her too fast, before she had time to set herself. It fell on the rocks and broke in a way that made hiding our sins impossible. When Alicia saw the damage we both caught nine kinds of hell. She did something with the doll, I don't know what. Probably tossed it because it was no longer perfect and had lost monetary value. A week later there was a new showpiece to replace it."

Deep loneliness emanated from him again. Only this time, Brie felt surrounded by a softer, shimmering awareness. Unable to focus on the awareness and Cal at the same time, she couldn't capture its essence long enough to determine if she recognized it.

Cal picked up his narrative, and the awareness dissipated as quickly as it had appeared. "I've replayed that scene in my mind every day for the past eight years, Brie. It was the last time I got to play with my daughter. I know it sounds stupid, but I wish I had fought Alicia for the doll. At least I'd have something to hold on to besides memories and this ridiculous belief I'll find Jeanie. Dear God, I miss her!"

His soul cried out to her again. Brie pushed off the bench, limped the few steps to where he stood, slipped her arms around him, and pulled him close. It took three heartbeats but slowly, uncertainly, Cal encircled her body with his arms. As she buried her face against his neck and breathed in his now familiar scent, Brie felt his loneliness dissipate.

"What's this for?" he murmured into her ear.

"Comfort," she whispered.

He pulled back enough to look down at her. "I'm not sure I deserve it. I made my own hell."

"We all do to a certain extent," she answered with a trembling smile. "But you've suffered enough. Lain knows that, too. She's offered you her version of comfort far longer than I have."

He searched her face. "I like your style better than hers." Cal brought his right hand to her face and slid his fingers over her cheek, across her lips, and down her neck. "And I haven't opened up to her this way in the past eight years. Did you work some sort of psychic mojo on me, Miss L.A.?"

Brie forced a wobbly grin, but shook her head. "No magic. It was time. You needed to open your heart. I was here."

"Yeah, you were," he muttered. "Maybe it's true what your aunt said. Maybe you are exactly where you're supposed to be. For the first time in a long time I'm not just chasing after hope. I'm feeling it. There's still the uncertainty, but I don't feel so empty."

Cal tightened his embrace. "I need you, Brie. On so many levels I can't even sort out which is most important. I...I'm drawn to you. I feel this attraction to you that I haven't felt in years. I don't understand it. Maybe I need..."

Brie held her breath. In his eyes she saw passion flare, felt his desire to kiss her again.

But should she allow it to happen? By his own admission Cal Porter was still a man haunted by the unanswered questions of the past that bonded him to a lost wife and child. He might be thankful to Brie, and even desire her on some elemental level. But his heart and soul were not free to give.

And Brie understood, even as she cherished this moment in his arms and the way he seduced her with his green eyes, she needed far more from Cal Porter than his humble gratitude or raw passion. His soul's identity had left its imprint on her. His kiss ignited emotions held in check by fear that no longer existed. She'd used a gift that until now she'd resented and avoided to bring a measure of comfort in another person's life. But somehow, and despite Cal's every attempt to keep her at bay, she'd fallen in love with him.

Yet he was not free to fall in love with her.

She wanted the truth. Here it was. Plain. Unvarnished. Heartrending because of what had been spoken and what had been left unsaid.

"Stay," he murmured, then brushed his mouth against hers. "Brie, I never begged Alicia to stay, and now I'm begging you."

Brie closed her eyes and gathered those few seconds of bliss into her open heart. Cal Porter knew who she was, what she was, and still wanted her. He didn't look at her with dread and disgust the way her father secretly looked at her mother. He might not believe in her gift, but he believed in her. And now Brie believed in herself.

Dear heavens, he wanted her to stay! He was a man of honor. He wouldn't take her love and simply cut her loose. But he was also a man waking from the sleep of isolation, loneliness, and guilt. Opening his eyes to the light after dwelling in such a dark place disoriented him. Last night in the rain he'd reached out to her in desperation, as one person seeking to connect with another. Perhaps he'd confused his need for simple compassion and companionship with physical needs too long denied.

In that case maybe she had served her purpose to the Universe at large by being here, by stirring up the *status quo* of Cal Porter's life. Falling in love with him had been her invention.

"Brie," he whispered, with his lips parted only by a breath from hers. "Stay. Please."

Suddenly, instead of contentment and peace Brie winced at the sharp pang of grief. She knew what she had to do. For both of them. Before it was too late.

Gently, she laid her hands against his shoulders and pressed until he let her go. The fear of loss in his eyes nearly broke her already bruised heart. "I can't."

Thirteen

Myles forced himself to look into Selene Carter's fey blue eyes and give her fair warning before she shared his bed. "I believe only what I can see, hear, taste, smell, and touch."

"Do you believe in loyalty? Compassion? Trust?" Selene paused and seemed to hold her breath. "Or love?"

He slipped his fingers into her thick, dark hair. "None of the above."

Chapter 13, *Murder, My Love—*
From the Files of Myles Daemon, P.I.

* * * *

The losses in Cal's life had been many and harsh. Yet his feelings obviously weren't calloused. Brie's rejection brought him up breathless, hurting, and angry.

For reasons beyond his mental grasp, and against all common sense, he'd let a woman he met barely four days ago into his life, something he allowed few other people to do. And like too many other people in his life she was leaving, walking away, abandoning him just when he began to emerge from loneliness and self-doubt.

He took a step back, though he wanted to hold on to her with all his strength. "Didn't you hear me?" he demanded, letting anger override the pain. "I want you to stay. I begged you to stay. I need you, Brie. I don't know why..."

"And that's why I think I should go," she cut in softly. "There are too many emotions in play right now, Cal. I feel the same attraction to you that you feel toward me. But what is it? Gratitude that we've managed to fill up each other's lives for a while?" She shook her head. "That's not enough for me."

He grabbed her arm when she started to turn away. "But it's a start," he countered.

Brie looked up at him with sad, cornflower blue eyes. "Maybe it's an end," she argued gently. "Maybe helping you find your way back to real hope is the reason I ended up at the bottom of the canyon Monday night. But right now I'm in danger of getting lost again, only this time I can't just take off up the road to find my way home. Aunt Sophie would say..."

"To hell with what Aunt Sophie would say!" Cal interrupted. "What do you say? What do you feel?"

Brie's chin trembled. He hadn't meant to upset her, but at least he had her full attention. "What do I feel?" she repeated in a shaky voice. "I feel it doesn't matter if I take off now or in a few days. Either way I'm going to leave a big piece of my heart here with you. And the way things stand now you can't give me back what I need to make my heart whole again." She lifted her quivering chin. "Can you?"

"I'm not sure what you're asking of me," he admitted.

Brie nodded before the last word left his mouth. "That's what I mean. You have no idea that I'm more than a little in love with you, Cal Porter."

The news hit him harder than the pain and anger. "How? Why? Brie, this is too fast. How can you trust what you feel?"

"Because I trust you," she answered without pause. "Because I trusted you the moment you first touched me out by the creek on Monday night. Yes, this is fast. So fast my mind spins at the notion. But this is what my intuition is telling me. And my intuition is never wrong. I've come to trust that much about myself."

Panic twisted his gut. Cal wanted to say the right thing, but he didn't want to lie. "You're asking a lot right now. You aren't being fair."

Brie shook her head. "No, it's not fair to either of us. I can't stay just to be your emotional crutch and run the risk you'll give me up some day when you can make it on your own again. And until you air your heart and soul completely, there will never be enough room for me in there next to the memories of Alicia and Jeanie."

"I can't let them go, Brie. Not yet."

"I don't expect you to let them go. Ever. They were part of your life. They helped shape the man you are today. The man..." She swallowed. "The man I can care about." She shook her head again. "But you're still so confused and afraid."

Brie touched her heart. "I feel what you feel, remember? You still carry such sadness and guilt. I don't want whatever you could possibly feel for me to be touched by sadness and guilt and fear. That destroyed my parents long before they died. I can't..." She grimaced. "I won't love under that same burden."

Cal took both her arms and tried not to sound as desperate as he felt. "I do care for you, Brie. You've made me feel part of the real world again."

"Then maybe I've served my purpose, and that's all there is to it," she answered with resignation.

"I won't accept that," he claimed through set teeth.

"And I won't accept less than what I need," she answered softly, and then shifted her gaze to the Jeep. "I should finish packing so I can get on the road before it gets too dark."

Brie wiggled her arms against his grip. Reluctantly Cal took the hint and let go, but he wasn't ready to give up. "Don't even think about taking off tonight."

Brie swung her head back around. Her usually gentle gaze was hard as steel.

Cal knew he'd sounded like a drill sergeant and held up both hands. "Do it for my peace of mind," he explained. "I'd feel better if you got a fresh start in the morning."

Her shoulders relaxed. "I'll consider it." She turned and walked away.

Cal stood in place and watched until Brie nearly reached the Jeep. He'd bought some time. Maybe. She'd consider his request, at least. Good enough. He'd find a way to keep her in his life, even for a short time. And perhaps, in that short time, he could find a way to give back to her what she needed.

But love? Yes, he cared about Brie. It was as if she'd brought sunshine into the gray existence that had settled on him in a decade of self-contained brooding and soul searching. He was grateful she'd shaken up his complacent world. But she was right. Gratitude wasn't enough to shape a relationship.

Did he even want a relationship? He definitely wanted Brie, with her warm sensuality and hungry, innocent kisses. But that wasn't enough. Not for her.

Cal listened to his heart and realized it wasn't enough for him, either.

The wind stirred the leaves of the live oak trees that shaded the picnic area. The breeze had turned cooler. Dusk would descend quickly on this, the sheltered side of the canyon. Though he was familiar with the road back home it was still safer to drive while there was some light left.

By the time he trudged to the Jeep Brie was already strapped into place. As he rounded the hood, opened the door and dropped into the seat next to her, she averted her gaze from him to the stand of trees. Though he wanted to press her about staying another night, he decided it was better to give her some time and space to think.

However, the silent fifteen-minute drive back to the cabin took all the patience he could muster. When he pulled up to the front porch, Brie was halfway out the door before he turned off the ignition. Not a good sign. Had she decided to leave tonight in spite of his plea?

Without saying a word he followed her up the porch stairs, unlocked the front door, and waved her inside. While he lingered by the kitchenette Brie went to the hearth and started gathering her belongings. Cal noted, as well, she walked without the cane and hardly limped. There really was no reason for her to stay.

Except that he'd begged her to stay.

Obviously he hadn't pleaded his case well enough to this jury of one, stubborn woman.

When she looked up at the sweater draped over the deer head Cal winced as a sense of impending loss washed over him. He could be gracious in defeat and rescue the sweater for her. Or he could make a last stand, refuse to help, and reopen the debate.

The jangle of the telephone startled Cal, but gave him a stay from making an imminent decision. He snatched the handset off the wall but kept his eyes on Brie as she made a half-turn toward him.

"Hello?" he growled.

"Cal! Where the hell have you been? I've been ringing you for the past half-hour!"

Lain sounded breathless and agitated, not at all like his big sister. Cal's heart picked up rhythm. "What's wrong?"

"It's Gil," she hurried to say. "He was out riding with three of our guests when a rattler spooked his horse. He got thrown and went down hard. He's hurt."

Cal clutched the phone tighter. "How bad?"

Brie turned fully toward him, her eyes wide with apprehension. Cal held up his hand to her as he listened to his sister.

"Bad enough," Lain said. "He was out cold for a couple of minutes. By the time we got the paramedics here he was doing his He-Man imitation and swore he didn't want to go to the hospital. But since he was flat and I was standing over him I got my way. The ambulance just pulled out. He probably has a mild concussion and a couple broken ribs."

She paused. "Cal, I need you to come over. I want to follow the ambulance and be with Gil. But Eric's out with his friends, and it's Greta's night off. I'd rather not take Dulcie with me. It's pushing her bedtime, and the last thing I need is to have to walk the emergency room floor with a cranky baby. I know I'm asking a lot..."

"Hold tight. I'll be right there," Cal said without thought.

"Maybe you can bring Buttercup," Lain suggested. "She got along good with Dulcie."

Cal looked into Brie's wide, worried eyes and realized he might never see Miss L.A. again if he walked out the door. But Lain needed him. Now. "Give me twenty minutes," he answered.

"Thanks, Cal." Lain's voice trembled, and she hung up.

Cal jammed the handset back into its cradle and looked over to Brie. She'd advanced a few feet toward him, obviously hoping for an explanation.

"Gil took a fall off his horse," he said in clipped tones. "There's no one around to watch Dulcie while Lain goes to the hospital." His heart squeezed when he realized he might actually have to hold and cuddle the little girl for hours before Lain returned home. Already sweat broke out on his forehead. "She needs a baby-sitter."

Brie peered at him for a handful of seconds, her face lined with thought and concern. Then she pulled herself tall, nodded, and walked toward the door. "Okay, let's go."

He did a double take and caught her arm as she passed by. "I thought..." Cal glanced to the hearth then back at her. "You don't have to do this."

She smiled shyly. "It never hurts to have backup."

Had she read him so easily again? Did she "feel" his apprehension about Dulcie? Probably. Yet she was kind to his ego and offered help without mentioning he probably looked pale as death.

That gesture of kindness and understanding brought a new lightness to his heart. Brie Quaid was a good woman to have at his side in a pinch. A very good woman. How could he let her go?

How could he make her want to stay?

Cal exhaled and dredged up courage. "If you still want to stay at the ranch tonight I'll take your bag to the car and you can follow me over."

Brie shook her head. "The last thing Lain will need tonight is an uninvited guest. No, I'll come back here."

Despite the fact that he faced a long evening with a toddler he'd taken great pains to avoid, Cal wanted to vent the relief he felt with a big laugh. However, he contained the emotion and merely grinned. "Okay, Miss L.A., let's go."

* * * *

Dulcie went into "I-may-be-a-toddler-but-I-know-something's-wrong" mode the minute Lain walked out the door about seven o'clock. The sweet little girl disappeared and the whiney baby emerged. By seven-fifteen Cal started to miss the quiet cabin.

Both Cal and Brie tried every trick in the book to entertain Dulcie, and finally resorted to some tried-and-true baby-sitting standbys. Cookie bribery worked for a while. When the little girl had her limit of snacks she agreed to a round of hide-and-seek, with Uncle Cal doing most of the hiding. He tried to fit his body into closets and under furniture. It wasn't really much of challenge to find him, which was probably why the charm of that game wore off fast.

While Cal worked hard to entertain the little girl he realized he hadn't forgotten a desperate parent's inventiveness. And even though he let Brie handle the snuggling and cuddling duty, he found he was having fun making himself look ridiculous.

Brie didn't seem to mind the trade-off. The toddler, however cranky, gave into hugs easily, and Brie appeared delighted to have the little girl's pudgy arms circling her neck.

Cal envied her the ability to open so easily to a child's unconditional love without feeling the anguish of remembered loss. Yes, Brie was right. He still had far to go, and so much grief to put behind him before he could risk reaching out again. She was right, too, in deciding to protect her own heart and walk away.

The notion, however reasonable, didn't make him happy.

By nine-thirty Cal lounged in an easy chair, and Brie sat in the corner of the plaid sofa that dominated the family quarter's living room with the little girl planted on her lap. It was well past Dulcie's bedtime, and she had grown quieter during the course of the last two stories Brie read to her. From his vantage, Cal noticed a couple times when Dulcie let her eyelids droop and stay closed for a few seconds, before she forced them back open. Mr. Sandman was definitely close by.

By now he should have been counting the minutes until either Lain walked through the front door, or Dulcie gave in to sleep. Instead, an inner quiet had taken hold of him sometime during the course of the evening. He was still on guard, but he was hardly on the verge of panic as he'd been when Lain thrust Dulcie into his arms after dinner Tuesday evening. Having Brie as backup helped, and he appreciated her sacrifice. Cal knew she wanted to be on her way to New Mexico, and yet she had set aside her needs to stay and help.

He smiled to himself. In spite of what she thought she needed, Brie Quaid looked as if this were exactly where she belonged. At least for now.

Dulcie finally nodded off. Brie waited a minute to close the storybook and set it aside on the sofa. Carefully, she looked around to Cal and mouthed, "Dulcie's asleep. I'll take her upstairs."

Something inside Cal shifted. Maybe it was seeing Brie worn out at the end of a long day. Maybe it was the sense that as the toddler's closest kin he needed to share more of the workload.

Or maybe it had something to do with the burst of will that shot through him. Whatever the reason, Cal pushed out of the chair and went to the sofa. "Sit for a while," he whispered, and lifted the little girl carefully from Brie's lap. "I'll put her to bed."

Brie looked shocked. She had cause. Cal didn't understand this change of heart either, but grinned with self-deprecation as he stood and let Dulcie snuggle against his shoulder. "It's been a long time, but I remember how to do this."

Brie just sat there with her mouth dropped open as Cal turned and walked slowly to the stairs. Dulcie squirmed in his arms, and her eyes fluttered open. When she let out a weak squeal of protest Cal rubbed her back and murmured soft nonsense words in her ear.

Cal measured his footsteps down the long hall to the baby's room. Amazingly, he felt right at home in a room festooned with frilly pink curtains, "ABC" wallpaper, and overflowing toy boxes, even though he'd never before had the inner fortitude to set foot across this threshold. It was all coming back to him, the skill of holding a baby snug and safe. At first his heart clenched at the memory, but then the tension faded. He wasn't holding Jeanie but he could still feel the joy and contentment of being needed.

Dulcie squirmed and sputtered a small cry. Spying a rocker near the window Cal eased into the padded seat and set up an easy back-and-forth rhythm as he cradled the little girl. Words of a lullaby wandered into his mind, and he started singing softly in a voice husky with disuse.

He rocked the chair steadily, slowly, expertly. Dulcie went limp in minutes. Yet even when there was no longer any practical purpose for Cal to hold the child, he didn't want to let go of the moment.

Why had he resisted this? Better question still, why did he resign himself now?

The answer came like a ray of sunshine after a storm. Brienne Quaid. Miss L.A. Madame Psychic.

The woman who claimed to be in love with him.

Whispers behind him cut short Cal's soul-searching reverie. He glanced over his shoulder and found both Brie and Lain peeking around the doorframe.

"Dear Lord, Brie," Lain gasped in a loud whisper, "what did you do with my little brother, and who's this stranger you left in his place?"

But instead of feeling embarrassed that he'd been caught playing surrogate daddy, Cal sent the two women a parental scowl and mimed for them to shush. Then he carefully rose from the rocker, ambled to the crib and laid Dulcie on the mattress. Tenderly, he covered the child with a satin quilt and tiptoed to the hallway.

He ignored the obvious question in the two sets of female eyes and honed in on Lain. "Is Gil okay?"

Though she looked tired, Lain cocked her head with typical aplomb but kept her voice a whisper. "He's taped from armpits to bellybutton and has to stay overnight in the hospital for observation. But he'll recover to fall off his horse another day, thank God. Forget him though. I'm the one who's going to have a heart attack. What happened to you, Cal Porter? This room is the last place in the house I expected to find you. *Alone* with my daughter!"

Cal shifted his gaze to Brie. Her blue eyes seemed to shimmer a little more than usual in the muted hallway light. "I guess I got a wake-up call." He turned back to Lain. "And that's all you need to know."

Lain blinked at the undercurrent of command in his voice, then nodded. "Yeah, sure."

More gently, Cal laid his hand on Lain's shoulder. "Are you going to be okay?"

In an instant, Lain recovered her composure. "I'm fine. Would you two like some coffee before you head out?"

Cal immediately shook his head. "We should go if you don't need us." Then he set his eyes on Brie, and the familiar sense of loss returned. "Brie needs to get a good night's sleep. She's leaving early tomorrow morning."

For the second time in less than two minutes Lain looked shocked. "You're leaving us, Buttercup?"

Brie seemed taken off guard. "Well...I..."

"She's had to stay three days longer than she anticipated," Cal interjected reasonably. "Her Aunt Sophie's waiting out in New Mexico. We can't be selfish and keep her forever, can we?"

Could he? Forever sounded amazingly good right now.

"No, I guess not," Lain said with a sigh, and pulled Brie into a tight hug. "I'll miss you, Buttercup. Maybe you can stop and visit on your way back to L.A."

"Sure," Brie muttered. "I'll miss you, too, Lain. I'll miss you all. You've been so kind. Thanks for everything." She closed her eyes and tightened her embrace. "I want you to know something that I felt the first time I held Dulcie. She's so happy to be your daughter. In her way, she loves you, and Gil, and Eric very much."

Lain whispered something Cal couldn't hear. But when his sister backed away from Brie she swiped at tears and forced a brave smile. As Brie blinked away her own unshed tears Cal made the rest of the good-byes and hustled her outside to the Jeep.

There was no use trying to put off the inevitable. Brie might be staying another night at the cabin, but it was her last night. Time wouldn't stand still, no matter how much Cal wished it.

Fourteen

Myles spun the chamber of the revolver, snapped it shut and shoved the weapon into his pocket. "Don't tell me what I need, Jorge. I don't want entanglements. I lead a dangerous life."

"Selene is the only real danger in your life," Jorge retorted. "She made you fall in love with her."

Chapter 14, *Murder, My Love—From the Files of Myles Daemon, P.I.*

* * * *

As they bumped and jostled along the back road, Brie stared into the night, suddenly dreading the coming of the next day. She was going to leave. Cal had accepted it. She was certain he'd no longer try to convince her to stay. Aunt Sophie waited in New Mexico and could, hopefully, help her solve the riddle of the sleep-stealing nightmares.

So why did she feel so suddenly empty? Wasn't she getting what she wanted? What she needed?

Brie stole a glance at Cal's profile. Even in the eerie green reflection of the dashboard lights his features appeared composed, almost serene. She envied him.

"Cal?" she called out softly.

He turned to her and waited.

"What exactly did happen with Dulcie back there?" she asked.

He set his eyes to the road. "I'm not sure," he admitted, and sounded truly perplexed. "Maybe I realized I had to find the courage to get on with life instead of just backing into it like a coward. I guess there's some of the bulldog prosecutor left in me."

But then he shook his head. "No, that's not it. Prosecutor Cal Porter wanted to control everything so he wouldn't be hurt. I think it finally hit me I can't control anything. Alicia's gone. Jeanie's gone with her, wherever that is. I can't force the words to write my book." He paused. "And I can't make you stay. So what else is there, Brie? I can't change what happened. I can't predict the future. I had to start living again, with real hope, not some lead weight of emotion that anchored me to the past and kept me from living the present. Dulcie was just the first step."

He chuckled. "It wasn't as hard as I thought it would be."

For the first time Brie heard lightness, almost amusement in his voice.

Peering at him in the semidarkness Brie realized waves of sadness no longer emanated from his soul. Cal Porter had let go of more than control. He'd let go of the past and let down the emotional barriers that set him apart from life.

And that's when Brie realized she had a new decision to make, one that shook her to the core. Just hours before she'd claimed to have fallen in love with Cal. But then she knew he had no room in his heart to receive that love. That was no longer the case. He had changed, almost in the blink of an eye. How or why she wasn't quite sure.

Now, though, Brie had a chance to give these new feelings free rein. All she had to do was stay and risk opening her heart and soul to a man in a way that could overwhelm her psyche.

Or would she once again choose to walk away and be safe?

Earlier, when she confronted Cal with the truths of his heart, she'd been so confident. Now, as he pulled up at the front porch and came around to open her door, she trembled under the weight of uncertainty. Would he even still want her to stay?

The overhead light popped on as Cal yanked back her door and held out his hand to ease her down from the bucket seat. Once her feet hit the ground, he let go and hurried up the porch steps to unlock the front door.

Had he mentally let her go, too, along with the rest of his past?

The question nagged her as she climbed the steps and walked past him into the cabin. He flipped on the overhead kitchenette light and shut the door behind them. Brie's gaze locked on her sweater, still dangling from the deer antlers.

If she asked him to pull her sweater down again would he oblige, or refuse in another desperate and nonsensical gambit to hold her here?

Heedless of her tender knee, Brie turned in place. "Cal?"

Only a couple steps behind her Cal stopped dead in his tracks. He started to ask something, probably why the heck she almost caused a rear-end collision. Then he glanced at the floor between them, bent down, and brought up her moon bracelet.

Tenderly he rolled the worn leather band between his fingers. "Next time this thing flies off your wrist you may not have someone trailing behind you to pick it up."

Cal slowly lifted his gaze to hers. There was resignation in his eyes. "I keep some tools upstairs for when I have to dig around inside my computer. I should have a pair of small pliers." He tucked the bracelet into the right front pocket of his jeans. "I'll tighten the clasp and have it ready before you leave in the morning."

Brie lurched forward and grasped his forearms. "No!"

He blinked. "You don't want me to fix it?"

"No," she repeated, and then grimaced. "I mean, yes, fix it. But no..." Her brain locked up.

Cal waited a few seconds. "No, what?" he finally prodded.

Brie's heart beat so fast she was sure Cal could see it jump beneath the bodice of her sundress.

Frowning now, Cal placed his hands beneath her forearms. "Brie, you're shaking. Are you all right?"

"Yes, I'm all right," she murmured. "I shouldn't be, but I am."

He tilted his head. "Huh?"

Restraining a smile that he might misunderstand, Brie let out a long breath of air. "I should be scared to death," she explained. "Literally. I'm about to take a leap of faith that defies every rule I've lived by for half my life. But..." She searched his confused expression, and then did smile. "This *feels* right."

He shook his head. "What?"

"I want to stay," she blurted out. "Cal, ask me stay."

The old tension narrowed his eyes to slits. "You don't kick a man when he's down and half dead," he said, his voice low with anger.

She set her right hand over his heart. "You're not down, Cal. And you've never been dead. Just asleep."

Lifting her hand to his face, Brie smiled up into his confusion. He didn't flinch at the touch of her cool fingers against his warm cheek, yet he watched her warily. She palmed his chin and moved a step closer. "I think we've both been asleep, but not any more. Please, ask me to stay."

He eyed her skeptically. "Is that what you want?"

"Yes," she said without thinking.

The muscles in his forearm bunched. "I can't promise forever," he warned. "Not yet. Maybe not ever."

She lifted her chin higher. "You can promise now. That's all life can ever guarantee. That's all I have the right to ask."

His green eyes went soft, but he still frowned. "Is that enough?"

In answer, Brie slipped both arms around his shoulders, slid her hand up the back of his neck, and gently guided his head forward. She met his lips with her lips, a soft but sure kiss.

Cal's muscles tautened under her hands, but his mouth didn't move against hers.

Brie parted her lips and tentatively pressed them against his. He didn't respond.

Had he lost his need for her when he finally made that first, precipitous break with his past?

Brie closed her eyes to keep anxious, embarrassed tears at bay. "Am I too late?"

She swallowed the rest of her words when Cal clamped his hands over her shoulders and pushed her back another few inches. She gazed up at him, holding her breath.

"Make very sure this is what you want, Brie," he warned, his voice thick and his green eyes more intense than ever. "I don't know what I can feel for you."

Blinking away the unshed tears, Brie tried to smile. "Cal, it's all right..."

He cut her off with a gentle shake. "No, it isn't. I've hurt enough people in my life. No matter what happens or doesn't happen between us tonight, I'm afraid I'm going to hurt you, too."

Lifting his right hand to her cheek, Cal winced. "Brie, I don't know if I'll ever be capable of loving you the way you deserve to be loved. I..." He closed his eyes briefly and clenched his jaw before he could look down at her again. "You as much as admitted you've never made love before. I'm not the man for that honor."

Where had all the arrogance gone? Where had this endearing humility come from? Brie blinked away the last of her tears and laughed softly before she turned her face inside the cup of Cal's hand and kissed his palm.

"Cal Porter," she whispered, "you're the *only* man for that honor. I trust my intuition." She lifted on her toes and brushed his lips again with her mouth. "And I've always trusted you."

"Yeah, because I'm safe," he growled.

"I was wrong about that," she admitted in a moment of insight that surprised her. "You aren't safe. Risk is what I've always avoided, and it's what I need right now. Maybe that's why I came here, so you can show me how to trust and risk at the same time."

"Aren't you afraid of losing yourself, like you mother did?" he countered.

"Afraid?" she repeated. "I'm tired of being afraid. I've spent most of my life being afraid. Didn't you say earlier you don't want to just back into life anymore, but face it with courage? So do I." She skimmed her hand over his cheek and down his neck. "Now, Cal. With you."

A moment passed. And another in which Cal steadily peered

down at her. As Brie stood in the protective circle of his arms, she sensed the conflict in his soul, saw it in his frown.

When he suddenly drew her close, so close there wasn't room for a breeze between them, she gasped in surprise. "Yes, I want you," he murmured.

Her heart pounded with joy as she pressed her body against his. "I know."

Sighing, Cal ran a trail of kisses across her face and over her mouth. "I need you," he breathed in her ear.

Brie sank into his embrace. "I know that, too."

"Of course, you do, Madame Psychic."

Her head whirling with desire, Brie inhaled Cal's scent. "I told you, it doesn't work that way."

"Oh, yeah?" he teased, running his hands up Brie's spine, rippling the material of her sundress against her skin in a way that made her shiver with anticipation. "Bet you know what I'm thinking now."

"Yes," she agreed. "It's what I'm thinking. Make love to me."

The words barely left her mouth before Cal began raining kisses on her face, her neck and her shoulders, leaving heat wherever his lips touched her flesh. With the onslaught of raw passion, Brie's nerves crackled and her head spun. For a frightening moment she felt her soul engulfed with not only her desire but Cal's need, as well.

Instinctively she tried to pull back, but then stopped herself. This is what she wanted. She could no longer play it safe and live life to the fullest. Brie let go of the fear and gave in to the moment.

"Brie, you make me ache!" Cal claimed as drew his hands around her waist and up her rib cage.

When his palms nudged her breasts Brie fully understood the husky words. She ached now, too, deep inside, in places that were unknown to her until she'd allowed Cal Porter's touch. Nothing mattered now but easing that ache.

"I haven't wanted this for a long time," he confessed.

"Until now, I've never wanted it at all," Brie answered.

He laughed, a rough triumphant sound that fueled her desire for him. Then she went airborne. Though startled, Brie clung to Cal's shoulders as he lifted her high in the cradle of his arms and went for the stairs.

As she nuzzled her face into his neck, Brie's head whirled. "I can walk up, you know," she teased.

"Hell, with all the practice I've had over the past three days

I'm used to carrying you by now," he growled.

Three days, her common sense mocked. *Seventy-two hours.*

She was opening not only her heart and soul but also her untested body to this man after less than half a week. How reckless!

Yet how true and honest it all felt.

By the time Cal had hustled her upstairs she'd quashed the blips of doubt. The air was warmer in the loft, despite an open, curtainless window that admitted the cool, arid night breeze. The compact space lay mostly in shadow, with only a wash of moonlight delineating the workstation, a small nightstand, and the edge of a single bed.

Cal set her down on her feet gently, and kissed her thoroughly before running his hands down her hips, bunching up the skirt of her sundress and pulling it to her waist. The air hit her naked legs, sending such an unfamiliar rush of wantonness through Brie's body that her knees weakened, and she was afraid she might not be able to stay upright for much longer. Yet, without hesitation, she responded to Cal's unspoken request and lifted her arms in the air to let him pull the material over her head. A moment later the dress went flying across the room and hit the floor with a delicate whoosh.

Aching for more of his touch, Brie groaned in disappointment when Cal stepped away. Squinting in the dark, she realized he had taken up the task of undressing himself, starting with the buttons of his shirt. Judging from his groans, the job stretched the limits of his patience.

Grinning, Brie set her fingers on the backs of his hands. "Let me take care of that."

He paused, as if considering the offer, but not for long. He chuckled and raised his arms, giving her silent permission.

Slowly, Brie unfastened each button while letting the tips of her fingers slide down his naked chest beneath the shirt. Where she got the notion to play such a tease, she couldn't fathom. Heaven knew she'd never disrobed a man before. It just seemed like a fun thing to do.

Cal stood his ground under the sensual taunting, but inhaled a bit more sharply as she made her way down the placket to his shirttail. When she finished the job Brie slid the material off his shoulder, making sure her fingers trailed the length of his arms to his waist.

Cal didn't move, but his breathing was ragged and his skin was overly warm. She excited him. He wanted her. Recognizing the wondrous power she held over him, Brie felt suddenly giddy and uncharacteristically bold. On an impulse that sprang from pure intuition, she funneled her palms downward, across his lower abdomen, and fit her hands over his arousal.

Now Cal's breathing came hard and fast, and he threaded both hands into her hair. "I think you do read minds, Miss L.A.," he groaned. "Or maybe just damn good how-to sex manuals."

Beguiled by her own audacity and Cal's reaction to it, Brie pressed both palms against his arousal and began a slow rhythm up and down. "Neither," she murmured. "It just seemed like the right thing to do."

But Cal grabbed her wrists and brought her hands back around his neck. "Yeah, Lain said you'd probably know what I like."

That gave her pause. "Lain?"

The question didn't slow Cal. He slid his finger under the left strap of her bra, then the right. "I'm beginning to think my big sister is the real psychic here. She predicted this was going to happen. She even forced me to take a handful of her castoff condoms. What do you think of that?"

"What? What do I...think of that?"

It was hard to think at all when Cal freed her breasts to the warm air and to his touch. Through a haze of ratcheting desire, Brie did a quick reality check. In fact, she *hadn't* thought about protection! Had she completely lost her reason? Or was she just that inexperienced?

Is this what total abandon is like? she wondered. Yes, the answer came. Risky and fraught with dangerous consequences.

"I think..." Brie swallowed, calmed her scolding conscience and answered with her heart. "I think the Universe provided through Lain."

Cal must have sensed her momentary ambivalence. He captured her inside his arms again and held her cheek to cheek. "Because this is *right?*" he echoed her. "Works for me. I'm beginning to appreciate this 'Universe' of yours." He kissed her temple and then her face. "I'm glad no one else has touched you like I'm going to touch you, Brie Quaid. You're mine. I won't hurt you. I promise."

She knew Cal meant what he said. He wouldn't hurt her. Not intentionally. His vow chased away the last of her doubts. The thick, hard press of his desire against her thighs brought her back into the miracle of the moment.

And that was the last clear thought that entered Brie's fevered mind. In the next instant the rest of her clothes were gone. Brie stood naked in the loose circle of Cal's arms as he kicked out of his own jeans and underwear. Then his hands were suddenly everywhere on her body, caressing and working sensual wonders. He guided her down to the bed, eased up beside her and continued the erotic magic.

So many physical sensations from so many places! Rough. Smooth. Gentle. Urgent. Brie gave in to them all. When Cal's hands moved down her stomach and he laced his fingers into the nest of curls between her legs she opened to him as a flower opens to sunshine, as if she'd waited for this her entire life. Perhaps she had. Perhaps she'd waited for this through many lifetimes. Who knew?

Who cared?

Shimmies of release streamed through her body from the center of pleasure that Cal lovingly stroked. The sensations built as Brie lifted herself to meet his probing hands. Behind her closed eyes colors flashed in a wondrous spectrum. And as she felt the first tremors of climax move through her body, she once again felt the fullness of Cal's soul upon her.

But the pain and guilt were eclipsed with hope and joy. He surrounded her, filled her, anchored her to reality as if it were the most natural thing for him to do. He let her fly but wouldn't let her slip away. It was glorious, this abandonment of inhibition without fear.

Then it happened, an overwhelming flood of pure sensual pleasure that took Brie to a place where there was no past or future, only blinding white bliss over which she had no control.

And she didn't care.

Brie clung to Cal, gripped his arms and pulled him on top of her. She wanted to feel him deep inside her before the exquisite tremors faded. She wanted him to feel what he'd done to her, for her. She wanted him to merge with her soul as she had merged, ever so fleetingly, with his.

He needed little prodding. His first thrusts were tentative and more painful than she'd anticipated. But she was new at this, a true virgin in so many ways. Pain was part of the risk, body and soul.

"Deeper," she whispered in his ear.

Cal groaned and did as she asked.

Fire replaced the pleasure, a blaze that seared her, an initiation into womanhood. And then there was pleasure again, the slow movement of Cal's body over hers, chest-to-breast, hip-to-hip, their bodies intimately joined, their soul's touching.

Joy enveloped Brie, both hers and Cal's. She had opened her body, but he had opened his soul. She gave up control, but he hadn't let her get lost. He'd saved her. Just as she had saved him.

As Cal's moment of climax shook him, Brie trembled with the overflow of sexual satisfaction, and something deeper, something even more precious. Acting on little evidence besides pure intuition with a man she trusted, Brie found she could be alive in the moment, joined yet separate, fulfilled yet wanting more. She didn't have to be her mother.

Carefully, Cal withdrew, lifted away from her and pulled the sheet around them both. Then he gathered her tenderly into his arms. Safe, warm and sated, Brie snuggled close, breathing in the heady scent of their lovemaking.

"Are you okay, Brie?"

His words quavered with more of that endearing uncertainty.

"More than okay," she answered, and laid her arm across his waist.

"Then why are you crying?"

She blinked and realized tears had leaked from her eyes. "Oh, that. It's a girl thing. We cry when we're happy."

After a moment, Cal raised his head and landed a searing kiss on her mouth. Then he backed away just enough to let her catch her breath. "And that," he explained seriously, "is a guy-thing. We just keep going after what makes us happy."

Basking in the lighthearted freedom she felt, Brie linked her arms around his neck. "I can make you happy for as long as you want, Cal Porter."

* * * *

The love-starved arroyo toads took up their unified nocturnal croaking. Sitting at his computer station, head bent low and squinting under the intense beam of the desk lamp, Cal hardly heard the persistent amphibian serenade. For the first time in months background noise didn't distract him as he negotiated terms of surrender with Myles Daemon and Company.

The manuscript pages in front of him looked as if he'd opened several veins and a couple of arteries over them, and distributed his blood in frantic jots and squiggles. A creative mind would think he'd made a suicidal attempt to freehand draw a map of the California highway system. He wasn't even sure if he'd be able to read the scrawling edits tomorrow in the light of day.

One way or the other, though, Cal had to get down the essence of his thoughts. He'd awakened near midnight, after making sweet love to Brie, with his mind quickened by a rush of new ideas, snippets of dialogue, and perfect character insights. Though reluctant to leave her alone in the single bed that now seemed perfect for two, Cal found it impossible to ignore the storm of creativity. He had kissed Brie's warm cheek, slipped out of bed and into his jeans, and hunkered down with his leaky pen while she slumbered on her back.

Myles's latest adventure changed shape and direction with the first slash of red ink on page one. Cal wasn't even certain from what creative wellspring the new inspiration bubbled. At times he felt as if he were simply sitting back and taking dictation from Myles, Selene, and Jorge. The characters were making up the plot as they leapt from one paragraph, then one scene, then one chapter to the next.

By the time Cal wrapped up Chapter Seven it was evident Myles had fallen inexplicably but deeply in love with Selene Carter. If Cal stuck to his original story outline and killed Selene in the end, Myles would be forever changed despite the detective's past history of callous disregard for relationships.

Yet, if Cal saved Selene's life and gave Myles a change of heart would his editor buy it? Would his readership accept it?

More importantly, how would Myles emerge from the personality makeover?

"Hey? What are you doing over there?"

Cal started at the sound of Brie's sleep-husky voice and looked at the bed. She lay mostly in shadow, but had shifted from her back to her side. The new angle brought her lovely face into the diffused lamplight. Her eyelids, still heavy with sleep, gave her expression a come-hither quality. Rumpled dark hair fanned out over the plain white pillowcase, though a few thick curls rested on the pearlescent skin of her shoulders.

Cal remembered how her silky hair felt against his skin as she trailed kisses over his body, and the way she made love to him with such innocent abandon. Desire heated his blood again. He grinned, got up from the chair, and ambled over to her. "You started taking your half out of the middle," he teased as he sat on the edge of the mattress.

Her lazy, sexy smile drew him closer. "That's impossible. This bed is too narrow to have a middle."

He tapped his chest. "What? I look like the accommodations complaint department?"

Brie glanced quickly at the computer station and then back to Cal. "For a while there you looked like a man who couldn't write down his ideas fast enough."

Cal squinted. "How long were you spying on me?"

"Long enough," she admitted with another coy grin. "What's up?"

Unable to resist the temptation, Cal leaned over and kissed her thoroughly. He finally pulled away just far enough to whisper against her lips, "You mean besides my libido?"

Brie let her hand trail along his shoulder, down his chest, and come to rest on his thigh. "So soon?"

He chuckled. "Given the right incentive, you bet. Lain stuffed three condoms in my pocket. She had high hopes for you and me. Don't want to let her down."

Brie pushed him back and lifted one brow. "You're the kind who kisses and tells, Mr. Porter?"

Cal set his hands on either side of her body. "She'll take one look at us and know."

Brie grinned. "Maybe you're right. Maybe she's psychic, too."

He peered down at Brie and felt the overwhelming need to wrap his arms around her forever. "I'm beginning to think most good women are."

The gratitude in her chicory blue eyes seduced him nearly as much as her warm and willing body. When Brie edged to the far side of the bed and lifted the sheet and blanket, Cal didn't think twice before responding to the invitation. He unzipped and pulled off his jeans, then slipped in beside her as if he'd been doing it all his life.

She snuggled against his side. "You really did look obsessed over there."

He kissed the crown of her head. "Myles is talking to me again."

"Really? Cal, that's wonderful!" she said with as much enthusiasm as he felt.

"It means unraveling the story from word one," he said with a sigh. "And I had to tinker with Selene's character. But, yeah, it is wonderful. I think I finally reconnected with his character."

"Or maybe you just reconnected with yourself?"

He considered the observation for a moment. "Could be. You still believe Myles is my alter ego, don't you?"

"Sure he is," Brie answered with confidence. "So is Jorge, that idealistic young attorney you called a fool. Maybe they're two opposite but complementary sides of who you are. You use their characters to sort out your own problems. I guess the real mystery is where Selene came from."

Cal pulled her a little closer. "That's a no-brainer. Selene was a fantasy woman I created for myself in college," he said slowly, as if half uncertain he should lay open his secrets. "I gave her all the qualities I wanted in a woman. Back then, anyway."

Brie tensed in his arms. "Was Alicia like her?"

"In some ways," Cal ruminated, "Alicia was smart and talented the way I imagined Selene."

"The way you've written her character," Brie reminded him.

He nodded. "But Selene didn't use her intelligence and wit to scheme and manipulate. Alicia didn't know how to get her way otherwise. That was simply her nature, the way she'd learned to attract and hold her father's attention."

Cal frowned. "I think I always resented that about Alicia. She tried to control me the way she controlled her father, and I resisted that kind of manipulation."

"Like Myles and the women in the first three books?"

"You stand by your opinion, don't you, Miss L.A.?" he teased, and pulled Brie closer. "Okay, maybe I did vent some of my marital frustrations in those first three books. But when I started writing Selene that all changed." He paused. "Selene is even physically different. Alicia had blond-red hair and golden-brown, eyes. She was tall, but not what I would call slender. She had great curves, and she liked to flaunt them."

Brie lay still in his arms. Cal nuzzled her forehead before he went on. "Selene, if you remember, has dark hair and blue eyes. She's medium height and more willowy." He went on pensively. "Like I said, I tinkered with her character. I used to imagine her in a flame-red tailored suit and three-inch high heels. Now she's the sort of woman who would look good in yellow sundresses and sandals."

Brie lifted her head and stared down at Cal as if she was on the verge of some insight she didn't dare articulate. But Cal understood full well. Brie Quaid was Selene Carter, or at least his adult version of the fantasy woman. If it was true that she was his dream incredibly made flesh, and if it was also true that he was part and parcel of his creation, Myles Daemon, then what did the new direction of his story say about his real life?

Might Cal be once again capable of letting himself love?

A definite answer eluded him. Too many emotions competed

for space and attention. Right now, this minute, all that mattered was that Brie's dark hair begged to be stroked. Cal reached up and threaded his fingers through the thick mess.

Her eyes drifted shut, and she smiled with contentment. "I should be so afraid."

"Of what?"

Brie lowered herself into the circle of his arms. "Of what I feel. How intense it is. I've always been so afraid of losing myself, like mom. Then tonight I did lose myself with you for a while." She hesitated. "But I never felt the need to pull back to safety."

"You sound surprised," Cal whispered. "Maybe you're stronger and smarter than your mother."

Brie nodded, but slowly. "Maybe. But all this happened between us in such a short time. I really don't know much about you, Cal, aside from how I can best irritate you."

The wry quip made him chuckle. "It's irritation inside an oyster shell that makes a perfect pearl."

"Well, whatever 'pearl' comes from these last four days should be priceless," she observed. "Be that as it may, tell me something about yourself."

For some reason it pleased and amused Cal that Brie wanted to play this personal twenty questions. "Such as?"

"Hmmmm, okay, for instance do you like ice cream?"

"What kind of a question..."

"Do you?" she persisted.

"Okay, yes."

"What kind?"

"Is this important?"

"Maybe. What kind?"

"Butter brickle. You?"

"I prefer lemon Italian ice."

Cal let out a soft laugh. "Should have known, Miss L.A."

Playfully, Brie gave his shoulder a swat. "Do you dance?"

"Not the polka."

"Me neither. I like to waltz."

"Huh? Are you a throwback to the 19th century or something? What about a nice, sexy slow dance?"

"Those, too," she allowed. "But I love waltzes the best. My mom taught me when I was a little girl, before she started to slide..." Brie cut herself off. "Anyway, I've only really danced it once with a guy in a college gym class. It felt like flying."

On impulse, Cal tucked his index finger under her chin and

lifted her face so he could look down at her. "Then I'll take you waltzing, Brie. We can go flying together."

A smile spread slowly across her face, and even in the shadows, Cal saw the glisten of tears in her eyes. "You've already taken me flying, above and beyond anything I ever expected."

His heart swelled with pride and such deep affection for the woman cradled in his arms that Cal would have promised her the moon and all nine planets. Then he'd somehow make sure he got them for her.

He kissed her mouth, drew from her a deep, hungry sigh. "Want to go flying again, Miss L.A.?"

Fifteen

"It's my job to protect you. That's part of my professional guarantee."

Selene grabbed his arm before Myles could turn away. "It's your job to find out who killed my brother. I thought by now I was more than just your client!"

Her glare accused him. The tears in her eyes condemned him.

Myles's heart whispered the truth. However he'd never trusted that organ. "Let me go so I can do what needs to be done."

Chapter 15, *Murder, My Love—From the Files of Myles Daemon, P.I.*

* * * *

Sunshine and a cool morning breeze streamed in through the loft window. The sweet tune Brie sang in a soft voice while she made breakfast drifted upward to the bedroom. Whatever she had in the oven made the cabin smell like the inside of a bakery.

As he lay in bed, still groggy but eager to face a new day, Cal wallowed in the homey, comforting sights and sounds and smells. The memory of two lovemaking sessions teased from him a slow, satisfied grin, and he made a mental note to pick up more condoms. Soon.

Stretching, Cal eased his way out of bed and spent a few minutes in the bathroom making himself more presentable. Then he put on the pair of jeans he'd worn last night, and hunted until he found a fresh shirt and a pair of clean socks.

That's when he stopped and really looked around at the messy loft. The bed had reason to be wrecked, but Cal frowned at the piles of dirty clothes that had never quite made it to the hamper in his closet. He'd brought Brie upstairs last night in shadow, and neither one of them was focused on the depth of the dust coating his nightstand. In the glare of daylight, however, the neglect of this room was embarrassing. And if he had anything to say about it, chances were very good the bed would get a workout tonight, as well.

He went to the top of the stairs. "Smells good down there," he called. "How much time do I have?"

Brie came to the bottom step, leaned on the banister and smiled up at him. This morning she looked fresh and beautiful in a flowered blue sundress. "Ten minutes."

"I'll be down in five," he promised.

"Creative impulse?" she teased.

He wrinkled his nose. "Housekeeping."

She laughed brightly and went back into the kitchen.

Motivated by the promise of a delicious breakfast and Brie's company, Cal set to work. He smoothed the bed covers and started collecting discarded clothes. As he bent to retrieve a sock he glanced into the bedside wastebasket and decided to empty it after breakfast.

But no sooner had he looked away than he felt a sense of apprehension. Something inside the wastebasket hadn't looked quite right. He did a double take...

And froze in his tracks. Lying on top of paper wads and old tissue was the second condom he'd used last night. And he could tell at a glance it was ruptured.

Cal dropped the armload of dirty clothes, grabbed the wastebasket and plopped down on the edge of the bed. As he stared down into the garbage his heart whipsawed inside his chest. Had the condom broken before or after they used it? Should he tell Brie? Or would he only worry her needlessly? Damn, how long had those things deteriorated in Lain's medicine cabinet, anyway?

He set the basket aside, leaned forward and put his head in his hands. Last night, in taking Brie to his bed, he'd promised without words that she was now under his care. Not that either one of them had to worry about sharing disease or infection. Cal knew he was clean. And holy hell, Brie had been a virgin.

His stomach spasmed. He still couldn't believe that she had so easily bestowed him with that gift. And when he had doubts about his worthiness, she pursued him like a woman possessed. Brie trusted him with not only her physical safety but also her emotional welfare. Now, worst-case scenario, she could be pregnant.

He blew out a shaky breath of pent-up air. Playing uncle to a little girl was one thing, a hurdle he'd jumped and gotten past. But fatherhood? Again?

"Cal?"

He straightened at Brie's call. "Yeah?"

"Your time is up. It's food down here."

"I'll be right there."

What should he tell her? *How* should he tell her? He cared for Brie, more than just in passing, but she wasn't the first woman he'd let down, a list that included Lain, Alicia, and Jeanie. Was he destined to always disappoint and fail the women he loved?

Cal shot up off the bed. Whoa! Love? Where did that idea come from?

The answer blindsided him. *Who are you kidding, Cal Porter? You're in love with Brie Quaid. She got under that tough hide of yours in Olympic record time. You need her more than she needs you, mister. Whatever the consequences of this accident you'll see it through with her. Not because you have to. Because you want to.*

Cal suddenly realized the race of his heart wasn't fear at all for himself, but apprehension about how Brie would react. He could lose her trust. Lose her love. Lose her and all the light she had brought into his dark existence.

Forgetting about the pile of dirty clothes in the corner, he moved to the top of the stairs and stopped. Summoning his courage, Cal forced one foot in front of the other and slowly made his way down.

Brie stood at the counter in the sun-drenched kitchen, with a white dishtowel tied around her waist, transferring hot rolls from a baking pan to a plate. She looked up when Cal stepped off the landing. "Refrigerator rolls," she explained when he took a deep whiff of the air and raised his brows. "While I frost them would you get me a tea bag from my luggage?"

Cal restrained the need to blurt out what he'd found in the wastebasket. Maybe he should wait until after breakfast. He could take her back down by the picnic area, hold her close under the live oaks, and tell her gently and with reassurance what was in his heart. "Sure," he answered and headed for the hearth where Brie kept her roll bag.

"You may have to dig a while before you find the plastic bag," she called out to him. "Don't give up."

Cal found the luggage next to the sofa, but he first reached up and grabbed Brie's sweater from the deer antlers. He could afford to be gracious now, he thought, and laughed to himself. Then he lifted the roll bag onto the coffee table and started to root around.

Brie was right. In her haste to be gone yesterday afternoon she'd jammed her belongings in randomly. The inside of her roll bag looked worse than his bedroom floor. To make the search easier Cal pulled out the two cosmetic pouches, set them aside, and plunged his hand into the nest of cotton and silk materials.

No wonder she wore this stuff, Cal decided, as her clothes slipped sensually over, under, and around his fingers. The materials probably felt as good against her skin as it looked on her body. He moved down, then left and right, but didn't feel the plastic bag.

Cal pulled back his hand so he could unpack a few more items when his palm scraped against something cool, pointed, and hard that had worked its way to the top with all his exploration. A shimmy of awareness caught him by surprise. He really was head over heels for this woman if simply fondling her clothes and belongings made his skin prickle.

Restraining a shiver, Cal started pulling wadded pastel t-shirts from the bag. He'd removed two more before his fingers once again brushed the mystery object. Only this time, the zing of awareness made him bristle.

Vaguely annoyed, he grabbed whatever it was and pulled. A tiny black shoe painted on a delicate, flesh-tone porcelain leg appeared. A doll? Brie didn't seem to be the sort of person who carried around toys. But, then, he'd known her for only four days. What did he really know about her personal quirks? After all, she didn't know he collected 1950's baseball cards.

Curious now about the woman who had wended her way into his life, Cal forgot about the quest for tea bags and carefully extracted more of the toy. At the knee the leg was attached to dark purple bloomers. The second leg appeared. Then the hem of a flared skirt imprinted with a Harlequin pattern...

Cal's knees buckled and he dropped heavily onto the couch. The doll, still clutched between his frozen fingers, came with him. It smiled mysteriously, an expression seared into his brain, seemingly unfazed by the yellowed crack along the side of her face.

Images assaulted Cal. Sunshine. Water rushing over the rocks in Milagro Creek. Laughter. Jeanie's baby-fine brown hair blowing in a warm breeze.

And the doll. Alicia's doll, the one Jeanie squirreled away in the backpack. The one that broke during the impromptu game of football.

Cal opened his mouth. Nothing came out but a low groan of anguish.

* * * *

Brie dipped the butter knife into the small, plastic container and lifted out a wad of gooey orange frosting. She hummed along with the country-western song on the radio while smearing the last roll. Such a perfect moment, she marveled. The sun shone in a blemish-free sky. The air was fragrant with the scent of late-spring wildflowers and the aroma of fresh baking. Her body still quivered with satisfaction from Cal Porter's expert lovemaking. And her soul, for the first time in her life, seemed in harmony with the Universe.

She'd laid herself, her heart, and her body on the line last night and found such pure happiness that even now she trembled at her good fortune. Cal had enveloped her with caring, need, and such total acceptance that declarations, had he spoken them, would have been unnecessary. Mere words couldn't possibly give the right color, brilliance, and texture to what had passed between them.

Better yet, she had sensed the last terrible, dark burden lift from Cal. Their union had set both of them free.

A chill snaked along her arms. The intrusive niggling intuition put her on alert. Brie set down the knife, turned off the radio and listened.

There was silence, except for distant birdsong and the rustle of the grass outside in the morning breeze.

Unease overran the brief moment of contentment when she realized Cal had disappeared into the silence, as well.

Quickly, she wiped her hands on the dishtowel around her waist, then ripped it off and discarded it on the counter. "Cal? Are you having trouble finding my tea?"

The question vibrated with anxiety.

When he didn't answer, she hurried around the counter and made for the sitting room. "Cal?"

As she called out his name, Brie spotted him on the couch. His head was down, his attention focused on something he held with rigid arms between his legs.

Brie stopped short just a few paces into the sitting room. "Cal?"

He didn't respond. He didn't even blink. Anger and confusion, so deep it darkened his features, whorled around him like a vengeful wraith. What had so suddenly snuffed out the new, fragile light in his soul?

Brie's heart slammed against her ribs as she struggled to pull air into her lungs. "Cal," she tried again, and took a tentative few steps toward him until she reached the close end of the sofa. "What is it? What happened?"

His head jerked up. The shock and revulsion in his green eyes made her miss a step. Brie reached for the back of the couch and found her balance as he rose slowly and thrust out his left hand.

"What's this?" he growled with such menace Brie had the irrational urge to back away the same as she might from a coiled rattlesnake.

The terrible emotions reflected in his glare mesmerized Brie for a brace of seconds before she forced her attention to his outstretched hand. Sophie's doll lay in the vice-grip of his fist. He clutched the poor thing so tightly around the middle its head, arms, and legs stuck out like a distorted star. The iridescent blue-green wings were pinned back, and the pretty Harlequin-patterned dress was crinkled beyond recognition.

Brie frowned, irritated by his rough handling of the porcelain and satin piece. "It's a birthday present for my aunt. Cal, it's rather delicate. What are you doing..."

"Where did you get it?" he demanded over her question.

This time his furious tone sent her back two steps. But Brie caught herself, pulled up tall and held his gaze. "I think you'd better tell me first why you're so upset."

"Tell me where you got it!"

She could almost hear his walls of defensiveness dropping back into place. Brie's head spun from the vibration of his bellow, the impact of his anger, and her own implacable sense that a gateway to oblivion had just opened beneath her feet. She clutched her stomach to stem a pang of impending loss.

Perhaps if she soothed him through cooperation he'd explain. "I found it at an upscale resale shop about a month ago," she answered softly in contrast to his fury. "Aunt Sophie has a doll collection, and the price for this one was reasonable because of the cracks in the porcelain."

"Cracks in the porcelain," Cal repeated grimly. "Cracks from a fall."

"Yes, maybe," Brie cajoled.

Cal gripped the doll so hard his arm shook. "Yes, definitely!"

Cold enveloped Brie. She pulled her arms across her breasts in a self-comforting embrace. Fear elevated her voice. "Cal, I don't understand!"

"I made this crack eight years ago. I made it playing football with Jeanie!"

Brie set her hand to her throat where her breath had stalled. "No, that can't be!"

Yet even as Brie denied his claim she "knew" Cal recognized the toy for what it was—Alicia's doll, the one she discarded because of the damage and in spite of her daughter's attachment to it. What did all this mean?

"Answer me, Brie! What does this mean?"

Cal's echo of the question clawing inside her head yanked

Brie out of herself. Her heart ached for him. He looked so pale with anguish and anger. The doll, limp from manhandling, lay in his now open palm.

It didn't make sense. Yet it had to make sense.

Maybe it did. A month ago Brie had combed the resale shop for period lamps and turned down the wrong aisle. Even though she was focused on a specific mission for a very particular client, she honed in on the doll, half buried in a display of gaudier and better preserved pieces. The prickle along Brie's arms alerted her now that she hadn't found the doll as much as it had found her.

Remember, Little Moon Child, there are no coincidences in life...

"What? What did you say?" Cal demanded.

With a pang of fear Brie realized she had gone back inside herself for an instant. "There are no coincidences in life," she murmured.

And then it all played backward—the woman's voice in the cabin, the terror she felt staring into the waters of Milagro Creek, the daytime terrors written on blank walls, the nightmares. It all started after she bought the doll, an impulse buy that she'd tried to send off to Aunt Sophie but came right back to her literally hours before she set out for New Mexico.

The logic hit her with such force her knees almost buckled. "Oh, Cal, that's why I'm here. If that is Alicia's doll..."

"It is," he snarled.

The depth of his emotion made her blink, but she nodded slowly. They both needed their reason and wits to puzzle this through. "Then her energies left a signature on the doll. I picked them up, and that's when my dreams started. Trying to get rid of the dreams led me here."

He lowered his head, and looked up at her through half-lidded eyes. "You're telling me this damned doll worked some hocus-pocus and made you take that wrong turn up the canyon road, and all this has to do with Alicia and Jeanie?"

The wrong turn on the canyon road. A "dead drop" down the canyon face into an inaccessible branch of Milagro Creek A woman's laughter in the cabin. Calling out the name Callan...

Brie swayed with the onslaught of intuition and insight. Her brain hurt from the effort to concentrate, to find a pattern and some meaning. "The pieces all fit. I just don't know how."

Slowly, Cal lowered his arm. The doll hung upside down in his grasp. He slid his gaze toward the wall on which hung the coyote head. He was avoiding her eyes and her unspoken plea for his trust.

His skepticism now felt like betrayal. "I thought you accepted me, Cal. All of me. All of who I am. I'm psychic," she announced with a grit and confidence that came from some unfamiliar source deep inside. "I can tap into lingering human energies by holding objects, remember? That's how I do my job. Open your heart just a little and believe me!"

Cal's expression went blank. "You want me to believe in you? You told me you barely believe in yourself."

"That was true," she answered as she searched her heart. "I didn't, until I came here. And maybe that's part of the answer. We came together to help each other. Neither of us can go forward until we reconcile with our past."

He lifted his free hand in resignation. "All right, then I believe that you believe."

What had she expected? Her father had once loved her mother, but he never fully accepted what made her unique. The "gift of knowing" eventually got in the way of her parents' happiness.

An image of her mother, a lost and pathetic shell of a human, filled her mind's eye. No, she wouldn't end up like that. Ever.

With effort Brie locked both knees and pushed away from the support of the couch. "That's not enough."

The announcement took both of them by surprise. Brie held her breath as Cal stared at her, perplexed.

"I care about you, Brie," Cal finally rasped. "I'm pretty damn sure I'm in love with you."

She wanted to run to him, to fall into his arms and tell him she understood and could live with his doubt. Her mother's image held her rooted. "I *am* sure I'm in love with you, Cal. But it isn't enough," she repeated, and started to turn away before he noticed the tears in her eyes.

He must have moved fast. Brie wasn't halfway around before Cal grabbed her arm, held her in place, and planted himself in her path. His eyes spoke of apology and determination. "Wait, don't just walk away. Let's talk this out. Please."

She peered up at him, though his face blurred in the sheen of her tears. "You don't want to talk about what's most important," she told him. "And I can't pretend that's all right with me."

She latched onto the fist that still gripped the doll. Slowly he relinquished it to her custody, and she pressed it to her breast. "You've spent the last eight years of your life on the edge of despair because you didn't understand what happened to your family. I've spent most of my life on the edge of desperation, running from myself."

Tears ran down her cheeks. "I don't know why I found this doll, or why it triggered the nightmares, or why I'm standing here now. Maybe you're right. Maybe all this is some grand coincidence." She hiccupped a sob. "But maybe everything *is* connected. Maybe I found the doll so I could find you and help you put the past behind you." She bit her lip. "And learn I can't reconcile who and what I am and still be with the man I love."

Cal pressed his forehead to hers and laid his hand against her wet cheek. "I won't accept that."

Brie crushed the doll to her chest. "Neither you nor I may have a choice..."

The air around Brie suddenly sizzled with energy. Her head went light and she swayed backward. When she tried to latch on to Cal to keep from falling Brie realized her hands would not release the doll clutched to her body.

"Brie!"

Cal's frantic call sounded far away. His grip on her shoulders was strong to the point of pain. She didn't flinch. Behind her closed eyes a kaleidoscope of sight, sound, smell, and touch inundated her. *The woman on the beach Brie had dreamed about two nights ago. Alicia, with her strawberry blond hair, topaz eyes, and lush figure. Cal's wife. The cabin. The canyon road. Blinding rain, the screech of tires, the shriek of terror, and the nauseating tumble and spin. Water. All around. Cutting off air and hope...*

Of course. Now it all fit together...

"Brie!"

The shaking cut through the mind-haze. Brie stiffened, opened her eyes and found herself on the couch. Cal knelt in front of her, his face distorted by frantic worry. Her hands still clutched the broken, rumpled doll.

"Brie, what the hell just happened?" Cal demanded.

She peered at him, still a little wobbly, and words came to her mind unbidden. "It's all here, Cal. It always has been."

Cal sat back on his heels while he kept a good grip on her. "What?"

Blinking out of the haze she replied without pause. "The answers. You didn't see because you couldn't get past the pain. I can find out what happened to Alicia."

Sixteen

"Why didn't I see this before?" Myles slammed his fist on the desktop. "I could have closed out the Carter file by the second day!"

"You were distracted," Jorge suggested, and only smiled when Myles shot him a warning glare.

"Get out before I throw you out," Myles ordered. "I need to think."

Jorge sauntered to the door, but looked over his shoulder one last time. "You think too much. Time to start feeling."

Chapter 16, *Murder, My Love—From the Files of Myles Daemon, P.I.*

* * * *

Brie claimed to know what happened to Alicia. She begged Cal to believe her, open his heart and trust intuitions so strong she called them "psychic."

She sure as hell believed in herself. Cal knelt on the floor in front of her and stared into her flushed face. Her blue eyes were wide, and her breath came in short, shallow bursts that made him afraid she might hyperventilate. As she rocked gently back and forth, Brie clutched the doll—Alicia's doll—to her heart with so much intensity her knuckles were white.

He doubted she was even aware of the movement. Though she looked right at him, Brie's focus was obviously elsewhere.

Cal wasn't really sure he wanted to know exactly where "elsewhere" was. Another dimension? The past? The future? How could he buy into this magical, New Age mumbo jumbo?

Maybe he just didn't want to buy into it. After all the years of heartache and frustration, self-doubt and guilt, anger and black sadness he might be on the cusp of actually finding out what happened to his wife and daughter. That's what he'd wanted all along. At least, that's what he'd always told himself as he wrote out another astronomical check for another futile search. Now? Now he was ready to bolt from the cabin.

The truth hit him like a blow to the gut. If he believed Brie had somehow divined what had happened that night he'd have his answers. And in knowing, he might have to grieve the loss of his ill-fated marriage and worse, his child, when little Jeanie still felt so real to him. Could he handle that? Could the joy and light Brie had brought into his life counter the dissolution of all hope?

Brie centered her focus on him suddenly. "Hear her out, Cal."

"Who?" he pressed. "What are talking about, Brie?"

"Alicia. Hear her out."

Cal started and released Brie's arms. "Alicia? I'm not tracking here."

If Brie took offense at his withdrawal she didn't show it. "I...I'm not fully tracking myself," she admitted. "This has never happened to me before. I...I 'feel' someone else. It's Alicia. She's here. I recognize her just as you described from a dream I had Wednesday night."

"Shit, you're talking like a freaking carnival medium here," he blurted.

Brie didn't flinch at the insult. Judging from her rapt expression Cal figured she hardly heard him. "I didn't realize it then, but the doll triggered that vision, too," she went on. "Alicia was on the beach, in a red-and-white striped swimsuit. There was a green beach umbrella. And..." She honed in on Cal again. "A little girl was with her. Alicia was swinging her around and singing."

Brie hummed the melody of a familiar tune Jeanie had loved to hear her mommy sing, and then tilted her head. "Does any of this make sense to you?"

His breath stalled. With reluctance Cal nodded. "We lived only a block from the ocean in Santa Barbara. Alicia took Jeanie down to the beach almost every day. We had a green umbrella. Alicia was careful about letting Jeanie spend too much time in the sun." He pulled stiffened fingers though his hair. "The striped swimsuit was my favorite..."

The bittersweet memories overwhelmed him. Cal rocked back and stood, then paced to hearth. He couldn't look at Brie, not right now, for fear she'd see a coward. "Stop, Brie. Stop now before we're both sorry."

"I can't."

He swung around to find her looking at him helplessly. "I can't stop the images. Or the feelings I'm receiving. It's like something's broken loose inside me. It's terrible, but...wonderful, too." Her voice wobbled. "Oh, Cal, this is part of what I've always been. This is who I am. I can't run from it any more. I have to accept what's happening." She pleaded with her beautiful, innocent eyes. "So do you."

"The past is behind me, or at least it should be," he countered.

"I put it behind me last night. With you."

"No, not yet," Brie whispered. "It's important you listen to me. To her. Alicia has to tell you something."

In desperation Cal held up both hands. "Brie, I don't believe in goddamn séances..."

"She started out for San Francisco, just as you always suspected," Brie talked over him. Her gaze fixed on nothing tangible, and she spoke hesitantly, as if translating to English from a foreign language. "Someone had arranged a flight for her and Jeanie out of the country." Brie frowned. "Mac...Macart? Macar...tan?"

A cold sweat broke out on Cal's forehead as she struggled with the unusual name. She couldn't be saying what he imagined.

"Macartan. Henry Macartan," Brie decided, and then jumped as if surprised. "Alicia's father?"

He didn't have to answer. Cal figured the truth was evident in the way he staggered to the coffee table and took a seat on the hard wood before his knees gave way.

"But she changed her mind," Brie went on doggedly. "She got to her father's house and changed her mind. He...he was angry. He tried to convince her she should leave you, but she..." Brie lifted her eyes. "Cal, she decided she loved you and wanted to try harder."

If Brie hoped the words would soothe him she thought wrong. Cal wasn't sure trying harder would have healed the deep ruptures in their marriage.

Brie squinted in concentration. "Alicia wanted to make a gesture of her sincerity, so she turned around and headed..." She gasped. "Cal, she came here! To the canyon! She was going to call you and tell you to meet her here at the cabin!"

Brie gripped the doll harder and started to tremble. "The voice I heard Monday night was hers. I know that now. That night when she tried to come here it was raining, too. She should have stopped in Los Angeles, but was afraid if she did and thought too much about it she'd go back to San Francisco. It was hard for her to choose between you and her father."

That was heaven's own truth, Cal knew. Henry Macartan played his daughter's emotions like a concert pianist played Chop Sticks, with so many frills and trills the basic tune of manipulation was disguised by the appearance of paternal devotion. Starting with the prenuptial agreement Alicia's father had found every way possible to wedge himself between Cal and his wife. Alicia's dire need for both men left her torn and the marriage unstable.

Everything Brie said was eerily true. Both fascinated and horrified, Cal found himself conflicted between edging closer to her and bolting from the cabin. She held him in place with her steady voice and transfixed stare.

"The storm was so bad," Brie went on, and closed her eyes. "The rain was so heavy it was like fog. Yes, that's it, a right turn." She nodded encouragement. To Alicia? "It's...confusing. Callan always drove when we came here before..."

Callan? Brie had used the name she knew he hated. Who was talking now? Panic strangled Cal's insides. He slid his backside across the tabletop and dropped to his knees in front of Brie. Grabbing her arms he gave her a sound shake. "Come out of it! Brie, come back! Don't get lost!"

Lost in what? his rational self mocked. *Runaway imagination? Neurosis? Hysteria?*

No, Brie was grounded in hard reality. She had practically denied the "gift" others named psychic ability. She wasn't hysterical, neurotic, or overimaginative. Besides, how could she have guessed his given name, or Henry Macartan's name, or the specifics of Alicia's trips to the beach with Jeanie, or the melody of that song she used to sing?

"Brie!" He gave her another hard shake.

"I can't see the signs," she complained in a voice edged with fear. "I can't see the side of the road. The turn has to be close. There. There's the canyon wall. This is the top of the ridge. It's...No, I don't want to die!"

A scream tore from her throat, a shriek of terror, pain, and awful resignation. Brie's head lolled backward and her face bleached of color.

"Brie! Come out of it!" Cal shouted at her.

She didn't respond, yet held fast to the doll.

The doll! Still unsure what he believed, Cal nevertheless ripped the toy from her grasp and tossed it at the hearth. He then gathered Brie into his arms and held her close, trying to fuse his body heat into her icy limbs. She felt so cold and stiff. Like death.

Alicia's death? Had Brie somehow captured the trauma and terror of the moment? And what of Jeanie in the backseat?

Cal shut his eyes against the burn of tears.

Brie moved and groaned. Her cheek against Cal's cheek flooded with warmth. "It's here," she mumbled. "It's always been here."

A surge of hope made Cal gather Brie even closer. "What happened to you?" he whispered raggedly. "My God, Brie, where did you go?"

She tried to lift her arms around his shoulders but couldn't manage to do so. Cal eased her into the back of the couch and brushed the dark hair away from her damp face. Smiling weakly, she let her eyes flutter shut for a few seconds before forcing them open.

"That was my nightmare, Cal," she said in a thick voice. "I was seeing what happened to Alicia eight years ago. She missed the turn at the top of the canyon wall and went down into that remote part of Milagro Creek. Lain told me no one goes there because it's too wild and dangerous for even experienced hikers."

A shiver wracked Brie's body. Cal ran his hands up and down her limp arms. "Where?" he pressed. "Brie, there's never been any evidence of a car going off the road where you say."

"No one suspected she headed south instead of continuing north." She forced the words out while catching her breath. "And did anyone look, really look, before the rain washed all the evidence away?"

Reluctantly, he shook his head.

"Alicia went down that canyon wall, Cal," she insisted, and edged her way into a sitting position. "I felt it yesterday when I went into town with Lain. I didn't know what it was then, but now I do. She's been here all this time. Right here." Brie clasped his arm. Tears stood in her eyes, though she smiled. "Cal, Jeanie wasn't with her."

The air left Cal's lungs. He didn't realize he'd lost his balance until his spine smacked the edge of the coffee table and sharp pain shot into his shoulders.

But he didn't move. He couldn't. His arms hung uselessly at his sides. He felt as if he'd been mentally and physically gutted.

Brie sat up straighter. Though still smiling, her eyes were now uncertain. "Cal, do you understand what I'm saying? Jeanie wasn't in the backseat. She's still alive."

When he said nothing, couldn't pick the words out of the chaos raging in his brain, Brie's smile flattened.

"This is what you've always hoped for," she reminded him. "This is what you've always known in your heart. You knew she was still alive."

"Get out of my head!"

Cal didn't realize he'd shouted at Brie until she jumped and cowered into the cushions. Why that command had filtered through all the mental noise and jumped from his throat, Cal wasn't sure, except that he was seized by a panic he couldn't name.

She blinked quickly half a dozen times. "I'm not in your head. I never have been. Whatever impressions I receive you give off freely. I didn't go searching for them..."

"No." The primal urge to flee gripped him. Cal pushed off the floor and took four healthy back steps before his legs bumped the rollaway bed.

Brie peered at him solemnly. "Why are you looking at me that way, Cal? Like you've never seen me before. You know who I am."

Every muscle in his body shook. Every nerve was poised to run. "I didn't know..." He waved wildly at her, at the room, at the door. "This. That you're some sort of spirit channeler."

Tears spilled onto her cheeks. "You're afraid of me." It wasn't a question. Brie spoke as if she expected as much.

Part of Cal, the man who shared his bed with this sweet, wonderful woman, wanted to stumble to the couch, take Brie into his arms, and deny the fear and confusion that addled his brain. Another part, the near-cynic prosecutor who stopped believing in miracles and magic as a child, screamed for measured caution.

"I don't...I don't know what I feel right now," he admitted, and started edging toward the front door. "I need time alone. Time to think."

Her gaze filled with tears, Brie followed his movement across the room. "The car is at the bottom of the canyon wall, in Milagro Creek," she muttered. "Call the authorities to search for it."

"Sure, later," he hedged, and opened the door. "I'll...do it later. When I get back. I need to go now."

He hesitated, and took a moment to look over his shoulder. Brie wasn't crying, but tears rolled down her face unabated. Again, he felt ripped in two by competing needs. Run back and comfort her, or run away until he found the courage to accept all this on some level and make sense of it. Until he understood, Cal knew he'd botch any attempt to talk with her.

She was strong. She would understand. She claimed to touch his soul, and in some way he knew that, at least, was true. Brie would realize that he needed solitude and time to think more than she needed his assurances.

Cal grabbed the keys to his Jeep from the wall peg and launched himself outside. Without meaning to, he slammed the door behind him.

* * * *

Brie wasn't sure how long she stared at the closed front door, or listened to the dull silence once Cal sped away in the Jeep. She hardly felt the tears track down her face and dampen the front of her dress. She didn't really feel the numbness of shock and grief wear off until her right knee twinged with complaint over the odd angle at which she sat.

With the tingling in her arms and the ache in her muscles came the inevitable onslaught of awful truth. Cal would return. Eventually. But he would never return to her. In exorcising her nightmare and offering him hope that his daughter, at least, could still be alive, Brie had destroyed the glorious happiness she'd found in Cal's arms, in the warmth of his love.

It all happened so fast she didn't have a chance to prepare herself, much less Cal. Brie wasn't even sure what had happened, or why. But when she stopped struggling against Alicia's persistent presence and allowed the energies to flow through and around her, she felt whole and useful in a way she'd never before experienced. For the first time in her life she embraced the gift she'd denied since childhood, and it felt right.

In that moment of accepting and finding her soul's calling, she lost the man she loved. She'd never forget the way Cal backed away from her, shocked and frightened by the flux of psychic energies that allowed her to connect with Alicia's spirit. She hadn't imagined the suspicion and total bewilderment in his eyes. For too many years Brie had seen that same expression overlaid with sadness and regret in her father's eyes when he looked at her mother.

Yes, Cal would return. He might even believe her and call for a search of Milagro Creek's most inaccessible branch. Perhaps he would hold her again, speak of caring and concern, even desire her in bed. But there would always be the wariness and a barrier of misunderstanding between them. Cal could never comprehend the terrible wonder of this gift of "knowing." He could never fully accept it. He could never love her again without reservation.

And Brie knew as sure as the Earth circled the sun she couldn't spend the rest of her days hovering at the edge of the emotional uncertainty that left her mother unstable and unhappy.

She had to take control.

She had to leave and not look back.

* * * *

Cal made a screeching turn onto the canyon road. The county

sheriff's office promised to call back by two. He had five minutes to make it down to the cabin.

Damn, if only he had his cell phone none of this business would have taken so long. He wouldn't have had to rely on a string of undependable public pay phones. He could have called Brie from the Jeep and stayed on the line until she got sick of hearing the ring and picked up the handset. He would have babbled that he'd been an idiot to run, that he was willing to put his already skewed local reputation on the line and ask for a sweep of Milagro Creek's wildest tributary. He would have confessed to needing more time to digest what had happened that morning. But he would have confessed, as well, to needing her love more than he needed to protect himself.

However, the moment Cal pulled up in front of the cabin he knew something was amiss. Maybe it was the kitchen window, closed despite an unseasonably cool, steady breeze that portended another round of thunderstorms. Maybe it was the whisperings of his conscience, assuring him in the foulest language he would have bolted, too, if Brie had treated him with such barely disguised hostility.

And maybe it was his heart, already missing her without solid evidence she was gone.

Cal threw open the driver's door and didn't bother to close it. Hoping against hope, he pounded up the porch steps and glanced in the front window to check for movement inside the cabin. Nothing. The doorknob resisted the twist of his hand. Locked, something he didn't do when he ran away that morning.

With an oath, he jammed the key into the narrow slot and shoved back the door. "Brie!"

Silence.

Stuffing the keys into the right pocket of his jeans, Cal scanned the kitchenette. The refrigerator rolls, all eight of them, still sat on the plate where Brie put them to cool and frost. Moisture collected under a film of clear plastic wrap, and the orange icing was half-absorbed by the now-soggy rolls. Breakfast dishes were piled neatly in the sink to be washed. The coffee pot was turned off, the carafe emptied.

"Brie!" Cal ran to the closed bathroom door and banged on it with his fist. "Brie, are you in there?"

No answer. That door opened without a problem. There was no sign of her toiletries on the counters.

The living room was similarly sanitized. Her luggage was

gone. The rollaway bed had been stripped, and the used bedding was neatly folded at one end. On top of her pillow lay the twisted and crumpled doll.

Cal swore. Common sense told him she had fled. Still, he charged to the back door and flung it open, hoping to find her car. All that was left was the imprint of the compact's tires.

Slumping against the doorframe, Cal gave in to both self-recrimination and a despair he hadn't felt in eight years. He'd found love and life again, only to blow it because of fear and doubt. The memory of hurt in Brie's eyes as he backed away from her cramped his stomach with shame. When she looked at him, recognized his shock, she probably saw her own father. No wonder she gave up on him and left.

He didn't even know where or how to start looking for her. Hell, Neil and Hank, the biker tag-team priest and neurosurgeon had her address and phone number in L.A., something Cal had never bothered to find out. He didn't even know Aunt Sophie's last name.

The telephone jangled. Cal tripped over his feet to pick it up before the second ring. "Brie?" he answered hopefully.

"Ah, no, is this the Porter residence?" a woman replied.

"Yeah, who's this?"

"The Sheriff's Office. I'm getting back to you about the request for an on-site investigation of a car accident that happened...let's see. Eight years ago?" She sounded uncertain.

Cal sympathized, but that didn't stanch his impatience. "How soon can you get out here?"

"Ah, well, that's the problem, Mr. Porter," the woman said. "An excavation of the scene you've pinpointed would take quite a bit of manpower and nearly a fleet of heavy equipment. I'm going to make a wild assumption here that there are no lives at immediate risk."

"The hell there isn't!" Cal barked. "There damn well could be a life at stake!"

"Oh?"

"My daughter, Jeanie," he told her. "I've been told she could be alive. I have to find out for sure."

"Huh?"

"I have to make sure she wasn't in the car." But hadn't Brie already told him that? Why couldn't he just believe? "Don't you see?" Cal demanded in spite of his own quavering. "I have to know who was in that car!"

There was a pause. "I think the officer who took your report must have left out a few important points. You did say this accident happened eight years ago."

"Eight years ago next Wednesday." He gave the word "Wednesday" a verbal stab, not because the date would mean anything to the woman. Cal was reminding himself of an anniversary that had upended his life and plunged him into despair. Only now, after Brie Quaid blew into his life on a thunderstorm, was he seeing a pattern and purpose to everything that had happened over the past years, and especially over the past few days.

"All right, yes, well, you see, Mr. Porter, in light of how long ago this happened, and the fact that our county crews are busy clearing away rockslides caused by all this rain..."

"When are you sending out equipment?" Cal talked over her.

"Three weeks, maybe four," she answered tersely, obviously perturbed by his attitude.

Cal was just winding up. "Three weeks?" he growled. "Maybe four? What the f—"

"I warn you, Mr. Porter," the woman cut in. "Our conversation is being recorded. "If you swear at me or continue this unnecessary hostility, I'll hang up."

Cal beat her to it. He slammed the handset back into the cradle so hard his palm tingled.

Four weeks? To hell with that!

Cal grabbed the telephone handset again and speed-dialed Lain's private number.

She answered on the third ring. "Hey, hello?"

"Lain, I need your help," he said without return greeting.

"Cal! What's up? You sound stressed."

"Yeah, that about says it all. Brie left."

"We covered that last night. Don't come crying on my shoulder now."

Actually crying sounded like a real option about now, but he didn't have the time.

"No, you don't understand," Cal replied. "We came back here. We made love all night long. She was going to stay. And then I made an ass of myself again, so she left. Got the picture?"

He thought Lain sucked back air. "Oh, okay," she finally said after a long pause. "Thanks for sharing. But if you're looking for sympathy, forget it."

"I want her back."

Despite his anger and impatience, Cal's voice cracked with

deeper emotion.

"Lain?" he prodded when his sister said nothing for a handful of seconds.

"Okay, little brother, what can I do?"

For the first time since he woke this morning, still warm in the cocoon of Brie's sweet love, Cal smiled. But only for a moment. "I need you to call Jim Atwood for me. I don't have his number handy." No, he'd thrown it away with all those years of friendship. "But he's still in Sacramento. I think I heard he has an office in Orange County now, too."

"Mission Viejo," Lain put in.

"Is that so?"

"He's still on *my* Christmas card list," she huffed. "So, call Jim, and do what?"

"I want him to track down Brie. I don't know if she went back to L.A. or went on to her aunt's place."

"What's her aunt's last name? Quaid?"

"Sophie is Brie's maternal aunt. I don't have a last name."

"New Mexico's a big state, little brother," Lain warned.

"Uh-huh, and a big problem because I'm a big idiot. Suppose Jim will take the job?"

"He always figured you'd come around someday," Lain answered. "But shoot, I had another two years to go on the bet."

Cal wanted to laugh but didn't have the heart.

"Is that why you want me to call him?" she asked. "You don't think he'd do it if you asked?"

"No, I don't have time to play phone-tag with him. I've got to do something else before it gets dark, and I have to start now."

"The sun doesn't go down until almost nine this time of year," she reminded him.

"It could take that long," he answered with a sigh. Especially without the right gear, heavy equipment, and manpower. "And Lain, you might want to tell Jim he was probably right about Alicia."

"How?"

"She's probably dead."

This time Lain did gasp. "You know this for sure?"

"I hope to by dark."

"Cal, what's going on?" Worry edged Lain's voice.

"I'm finally getting what I wanted. Answers."

But more than the answers to old questions, he needed Brie. What were the odds he'd end up with both?

"'Bye, Lain. Thanks."

Cal replaced the handset and leaned against the counter. He needed some basic gear, if he meant to go full ahead with his immediate plan. Time to raid the padlocked storage shed out back.

He jammed his hand into the right front pocket of his jeans to retrieve his keys. Something else came along with the ring and dropped to the floor.

Brie's moon bracelet. He'd tucked it away last night, intending to fix it before she left. Both of them had forgotten about it in the wild flow of unexpected events.

Cal got down on his haunches and scooped up the delicate talisman. It felt inconsequential in his palm. Is this all he'd ever have to remind him of Brie Quaid, besides an aching heart and lonely cabin?

Not if he could help it.

Seventeen

Selene walked to the desk. Her heels clicked an angry staccato on the wood floor. When she laid down the bank draft in front of Myles, she somehow made the flimsy paper snap. "For services rendered, Mr. Daemon. This is the amount we agreed upon. The terms of our contract are mutually satisfied."

In reflex Myles reached across the desk and grabbed her hand. "I never meant to hurt you, Selene. Trust me."

Her chin went up, and she shook off his hold with a decisive flick of her wrist. "If you can't trust a man with your heart, Mr. Daemon, you can't trust him at all." She turned and left.

Chapter 17, *Murder, My Love—From the Files of Myles Daemon, P.I.*

* * * *

Mental and emotional exhaustion caught up with Brie fifty miles southeast of Saratoga Springs. At a small desert resort town she stopped for a red traffic light and closed her burning eyes against the harsh sunlight. The next thing she knew a middle-aged man was tapping on the driver's side window.

"Hey, Miss," he said without humor, "I'd kinda like to make it through the intersection before I retire."

Confused, she glanced up and saw the light was green and changing already back to yellow. Full minutes had passed and she had been unaware. With horror, Brie realized she'd not only driven on autopilot, but she'd fallen asleep in broad daylight, sitting in her car on a four-lane highway.

She pulled into the nearest motel and got the afternoon rate for a single bed in a stuffy, shabby, ill-kept room. Had she been any less drained and witless, she would have checked the mattress for vermin, or at least semi-clean sheets. As it happened, she simply dropped her roll bag on the stained carpet and dropped herself facedown on top of the faded burnt orange bedspread.

But the moment her head hit the pillow the first sob shook loose, a long, almost silent wail that felt as if it came from the pit of her stomach. Another followed. And another, until she was certain there was no more water in her body. Her head hurt, her eyes burned, her stomach cramped with hunger despite the fact she'd eaten half of a fast food breakfast. To make matters even worse, her right knee throbbed a warning that it might start to stiffen up again.

Nothing, however, matched the depth of hurt in her heart. She loved Cal, and she was certain he loved her in return. But love wasn't enough. He might accept the gist of the message from Alicia, but in the end he didn't accept Brie. The look of near revulsion on his face that morning as he scrambled to put distance between them would be forever seared into her brain.

How could she blame him? Until now Brie had never really accepted herself. The Universe had taught its lesson well this time, and with no shortage of cosmic irony. She'd tried running away from the nightmares and from the wonderfully powerful gift that generated those images. Of course, in doing so she ran right into her real self. She had finally surrendered to the inevitable, but had to surrender, as well, the purest happiness in her life.

Neither did she find much comfort knowing she'd served a noble purpose. Cal now knew where and how to search for Alicia. Certainly he'd redouble his efforts to find Jeanie. Brie "knew" he'd succeed, and then he could close that long, sad, depressing chapter of his life. Maybe someday she could take a measure of pride in that much.

But not today.

As the sobbing subsided Brie wondered how many days, or weeks, or months it would take to start filling the utter emptiness inside her.

Sleep came as it did in the car, quickly and without warning. When awareness returned it did so gradually. Through a haze, Brie realized the air was cooler and guessed it was probably late afternoon. The room still smelled stale, but it was more bearable. A rumble in her stomach told her she needed to get some food, and probably a couple bottles of water. Her skin felt stretched and dry, no doubt from the crying jag.

Reluctantly, she tried to open her eyes, but the lids wouldn't work. When she tried to raise her hand to scrub away the sleep, her arms felt weighted to the bed. Attempts to lift her head made her dizzy.

Then the images started playing in full living and terrifying color behind her closed eyelids. Water. So much water. Pounding and lashing. Thunder. A glimmer of metal. Slipping. Falling. Reaching for...something to hold on to...

Not the dream again! Hadn't she exorcised these demons from her mind back at the cabin? What was happening now? Was she still in danger?

A crack resounded though her skull. She felt no pain, but lethargy overwhelmed her body, blocked her senses. She sank as the air slowly left her lungs. Cal's face appeared through a murky, watery veil. His eyes were wide with surprise...

"No!"

The scream kicked its way out of her brain. Brie opened her eyes and realized she sat in the middle of the bed, drenched in sweat and gasping for air, as if she'd been underwater too long.

No, it wasn't her beneath the water. It was Cal. But he didn't struggle to reach the surface. He was...drowning!

"It's been Cal all along!" she cried as the reality finally hit her. Alicia died eight years ago. Cal's was the death she had been "feeling" and fearing. But why didn't she realize this earlier, before she fled the canyon?

"I won't let this happen!" she shouted to no one but the dispassionate Universe.

Brie lurched across the bed and grabbed the scuffed and dirty telephone receiver. Ignoring the sticky feel of the plastic, she poised her finger to begin dialing, and realized she didn't know the numbers of either the cabin or Cal's cell phone. Frantic, she punched up directory assistance.

"That number is unlisted," a computer generated voice answered her inquiry about the cabin.

She tried Lain's residence and got the same stilted voice with the same unwelcome reply.

"Damn!"

Her third try was the ranch business number. Success.

A man answered in a pleasantly casual voice. "Sutter Ranch. How may I help you?"

"Please," Brie nearly shouted into her the telephone, "I have to talk to Lain! It's an emergency!"

"Ma'am," the attendant replied in a calming twang, "this is the business phone line. Mrs. Sutter can be reached at home."

"I don't have the number," Brie cut in. "Can you transfer me? It's important! My name is Brie Quaid. This is about her brother, Cal."

"Well, I don't know. Maybe you could give me your number and I'll have her call you back."

"Damn it, put me on hold and go find her!" Brie ordered him. "This is life and death here!"

The attendant took a breath. Brie didn't know if he was shocked at her outburst or confused about what to do. He might just hang up. "Please," she begged less stridently. "I can't begin to tell you how important this is!"

"All right, ma'am," he finally said. "Just a moment then, I'll see if I can find her."

The line went quiet. Brie closed her eyes and counted the seconds that stretched into minutes. Her brain replayed the terrible dream sequence, and by the time the attendant came back on she was nearly in tears again.

"Ma'am," the attendant said, "I'm transferring you to the family quarters. Mrs. Sutter should pick up on the first ring."

She didn't have time to thank the man before the line buzzed.

"Hey, hello," Lain answered. Dulcie was chattering in the background. "Brie? Is that you? What's going on? Cal said you lit out this morning..."

"Lain, I've made a horrible mistake," Brie practically sobbed into the phone. "I shouldn't have left, but I didn't know the dream was about him."

"Him? Him who? Brie what are you talking about?"

"I can't explain it all now," she said. "I have to talk to Cal, but I don't have either of his phone numbers."

"He's not at the cabin, Buttercup," Lain answered, her voice betraying worry. "So don't bother calling there."

Brie's heart seemed to stand still. "Where is he?"

"Don't know. He just said he was going to go look for answers. Do you know what that means?"

Images of pounding water and Cal's lifeless face flashed through Brie's head. "The creek. Milagro Creek. Lain, he went to find Alicia in the creek."

"You're not making sense," Lain said.

"Lain, if you really do believe I'm psychic, trust me now," Brie rushed her words. "I know what happened eight years ago. Alicia was driving to meet Cal at the cabin and went off the crest of the canyon road into that isolated tributary of Milagro Creek. I saw it all happen inside my head. I told Cal this morning. I think he went to find out for himself."

There was pause on the other end of the line.

"Lain, I know this is true," she almost yelled into the silence. "I *am* psychic. But Cal doesn't really believe. And I understand if this is hard for you to accept. Just humor me, because I'm in love your brother. For whatever that's worth help me get word to him. He can't go down by the creek. If he does I know he's going to die!"

Lain sucked back air. "I...I believe you, Brie. Honest. But he took off about three hours ago. He's got to be there already!"

Brie closed her eyes, turned inward, and searched for the life force of the man she loved. "He's still alive," she said. "Lain, he's still alive, but you have to get word to him. Call someone. The local law enforcement maybe. Tell them to get a search and rescue team into that isolated area of the creek. Make sure they understand Cal is in danger. I don't care how you do it, just do it. I'm turning around and coming back, but I won't be there for about an hour or more."

"I'm on it," Lain assured her. "Brie?"

"What?"

"For whatever it's worth Cal wants you back. He's got people out looking for you. I think he's in love with you, too."

"I know," Brie murmured. "But love doesn't conquer all, Lain. It's not enough to save our future. I only hope it's enough to save Cal's life."

* * * *

Sweat plastered Cal's clothing to his body. The inside band of his wide-brimmed hat was sodden and uncomfortable against his forehead. The heavy rope slung across his torso seemed to weigh an extra pound with every print made by his heavy boots. In the last half-hour of his hike along the isolated, little-explored tributary of Milagro Creek the canopy of live oak branches had gotten so dense it blocked out whatever sun the gathering thunderheads let through. Though it was only six in the early evening according to Cal's watch it looked to be dusk.

The trek to the foot of the canyon wall had taken far longer than Cal anticipated. Heat and humidity slowed his steps. The crackle of underbrush, the batting of bird wings overhead, and an occasional rattle reminded him he was in territory given over to Mother Nature by humans with far more common sense than he possessed at the moment. The high, heavy boots protected him from snake strike. The battery-powered lantern he carried to help define the unstable rocky bank could be a weapon should he cross paths with a big cat.

But the thick, muggy air sapped his energy. He should have packed more water for what was becoming a long, arduous hike. He had only a swallow or two left in his last bottle, and he didn't dare resort to dipping into the creek, even to rinse his face. The current of this branch ran deep and fast, but the action didn't clean all the detritus from upstream. Twice he'd spotted small animal carcasses bouncing past on the white-tipped water.

The heavy air vibrated. Thunder. Still distant but approaching. As if to emphasize the turn of weather, a breeze gusted and sent the grass and leaves rustling furiously. If he began backtracking now he probably wouldn't make it to the Jeep before another storm swept through the canyon. He could hunker down and ride out a passing shower. A prolonged storm was another matter. The bank here was only two to three feet wide in most places, and slick with rotted vegetation and runoff. The land sloped up steeply from there. If the creek rose fast he'd find himself swimming for his life.

And just why had he put himself in this peril?

Pulling to a stop at a wide spot on the bank, Cal stared into the murky, roiling water. What the hell was he doing out here? Trying to find evidence? Of what? That Brie was right?

As if he needed proof, like a prosecuting attorney at trial. She had been right about everything else. She had his number from the minute she crossed his threshold Monday night. He had been a man so lost in grief and guilt that he had forgotten how to live and love and even write.

Brie had changed that. She'd shaken him up, shaken him out of his despair. Running from her own life, she gave him something and someone else to worry about and cherish. For her he'd been a knight in shining armor and the court fool; benefactor and supplicant; friend and lover.

It didn't matter whether or not she was a psychic or a beautiful wise woman with an incredible power of insight. Her real magic was the kindness of her heart and her ability to give love in spite of her own pain.

He'd accepted Brie's wisdom, just as he'd accepted her into his bed. Somewhere along the line Cal also took her into his heart. He loved her.

Then shouldn't he trust her without proof?

Open your heart, she'd begged him. *The answers are here. You didn't see because you couldn't get past your pain.*

If Brie said Alicia and her car had found a resting place somewhere in this tangle of woods and river, then it had to be true. If Brie said Jeanie hadn't been in the backseat, then he needed to renew the search for his daughter. He'd let the county road crews, with all their fancy equipment, find the car. Tomorrow. Next week. Next month. It didn't matter.

Suddenly, the rope didn't seem so heavy and the air so

oppressive. Cal whipped off his hat, wiped his forehead with the back of his arm, and let out a laugh for no reason. He just felt like laughing at the world. At himself. At the stupidity of standing on the creek bank with a thunderstorm rolling in.

He was going to march out of this lost wilderness, find Brie and beg her to forgive him. He wanted and needed her in his life. He loved her. He would prove that he wasn't like her father, that he could accept her on faith alone.

The decision came not a moment too soon. A few heavy droplets of rain plopped on his overheated skin. Cal barely had time to look up before the wind picked up and the downpour started. He jammed the hat back on his head and did a one-eighty. The lantern swung around with him, and the spotlight swept the opposite bank. Just a little further downstream he saw an unnatural glint out of the corner of his eye. Cal skidded to a halt and automatically made another visual sweep of the area.

Again, something winked at him, something smooth and highly reflective that seemed to bob and weave as the creek water tumbled past it. He squinted into the encroaching gloom, while overhead the roll of thunder grew deeper, nearer, and the rain began to slash his skin.

A shaft of awareness cut through Cal's chest a second before his brain recognized the object—a piece of molded metal that was actually stationary and only appeared to move because of the rushing current. The bumper of a car.

Cal didn't realize his mouth had dropped open until he tasted rainwater. Was this a cruel twist of fate? Just at the moment he'd given himself over to faith in Brie, the object of his search rises from the depths? This didn't happen in real life.

And yet the longer Cal stared at the jut of metal the more obvious its configuration became. Yes, it was the chrome bumper of a car. Maybe Alicia's car. And it was there, taunting him from across the expanse of a very dangerous Milagro Creek.

Cal's knees went weak. He locked them just in time to keep himself standing upright. The car had probably been there for eight years, since the night Alicia disappeared.

He glanced around. Just up the steep bank stood a sturdy young live oak. If he tied the rope around the trunk and then around his waist, and if the creek wasn't too deep at this point, he might be able to fight the current and wade out to see for himself...

No. He didn't need proof that Brie spoke the truth. If he risked his life to touch and see whatever lay across the creek he'd betray his faith in the woman he loved. He wouldn't do that again even if she wasn't here to see the act of faith and love.

Shielding his face with his free hand, Cal did a visual sweep of the area, memorizing rock outcroppings, clusters of trees, anything that could be a landmark for search crews. The rain fell in sheets now, nearly obscuring the opposite bank. Thunder shook the treetops. But he managed to find four distinct points of reference. Yes, he'd remember this place well.

A distant bark cut through the storm noise. Cal jerked his attention from the scan and listened hard, trying to hear the sound repeated over the drum of the rain and shock of thunder. Was there some other fool out here in the lightning, balancing on the dangerous bank, under a canopy of trees?

Framing the situation so, Cal realized just how vulnerable he was at the moment. He had to make tracks back to the Jeep.

By now the creek bank was sodden and even more slippery than before. Gingerly, he set one foot in front of the other, leaving the bumper, his doubts, and much of the past behind him. The future lay ahead. Cal smiled in spite of the sting of wind-driven rain and the anxious slam of his heart. His thoughts drifted to an image of Brie's face...

Pain shot through Cal's right ankle as the heel of his boot twisted in the muck. He looked down to find the ground beneath his feet giving way to the rush of the creek and the pounding rain. In reflex, he tossed the lantern and lunged toward the steep bank. But there was nothing to grip. The grasses and ground covers pulled up by the roots with his clawing. His body slid backward, toward the rushing water.

Cal dug in the toes of his boots, but found no solid hold. Water lapped at his knees. Before he had time to take a deep breath the current of Milagro Creek sucked him in. His face slammed against the bank and snapped his head back. Momentum and the weight of the rope slung over his torso took him down fast.

Though stunned by the blow to his face, Cal realized he needed to cough out the water in his throat and breathe. If he could only touch bottom and push off he might be able to propel himself to the surface. But time slowed, and then seemed to halt. No matter how far he went down it wasn't far enough to find solid footing.

And then suddenly it seemed the bottom came up to meet him. His lungs bursting, his head spinning, Cal set down both feet. The new pain that ripped up his right leg would have doubled him over. The realization he'd probably either sprained or broken his ankle flitted through his mind. Had he not held on to some instinctive wit, he'd have cried out and probably drowned then and there.

Instead, he focused on getting to air and filling his starved lungs first. With all his strength, Cal shoved off the creek bottom with his left leg.

The current lashed him, using the mass of the rope around his torso to pull him downstream as he fought to swim skyward with both arms. He had to break surface. He refused to die because of stupidity. He had a new life to begin living.

Rain! Thunder! Oxygen!

Cal broke the surface of the creek and coughed up water before he drew in a deep, frantic breath of fresh air. But he took only half of what he needed to fill his lungs before the current tore at his body again and dragged him down and backwards. The waterlogged rope seemed to have tripled in weight, but he couldn't divert either the strength or the use of his arms to get rid of it. He simply had to stay afloat and try to work his way back to the bank.

Flailing, fighting nausea and dizziness, he struggled to turn his body around to see where he was going. His right ankle was useless. The mere action of the current pressing against the bone made Cal gasp in agony. Something thick and warmer than the rain trailed along the side of his mouth. He tasted blood, and fought off another wave of sickness.

Making his left leg work for two, Cal made an agonizing turn in the water, just in time to see the chrome bumper dead ahead.

He didn't have time to consider how foolish it would be to try and latch on to the car. Cal pulled both arms out of the water, reached out, and snagged the metal outcropping with both hands. His body snapped out and back, yanked one way by Milagro Creek and the other way by his desperate hold. He rode the current for a moment, testing his strength before slowly hauling himself forward. His arms screamed with the strain, but his elbow bumped something. A tire. Though dazed he could tell it was probably the left front. The car, whatever remained of it, was lying on its right side.

While the water swirled and crashed around the roof, the undercarriage provided a protected, relatively calm pool. Cal threw one arm over the hard rubber and pulled his body into the shelter of the car. Water still splashed into his mouth and hazed his vision, but at least he could breathe.

Yet, he still couldn't let go of the tire long enough to untangle himself from the heavy rope. Neither could he muster the strength to lift himself onto the car chassis. And while the water that flowed around him wasn't as turbulent, it still tugged incessantly at his legs. He'd saved himself only to be forced into a dire choice—let go to be swept away by the current and dragged down by injury and extra weight, or hold on until his strength gave out, he lost consciousness from the blow to his head, and *then* let go and be drowned.

Ironic that he should have rescued Brie from such a fate only to fall victim to the same situation.

Brie. Grogginess settled over him in spite of his efforts to fight it. Cal's eyes drifted shut, his arms lost feeling, and he went still inside. If he had to die he wanted hers to be the last face he saw...

You aren't going to die, Callan Porter. You aren't through with life, and life isn't through with you.

The familiar voice forced him back into awareness. "Alicia?"

His wife's bright laughter seemed to float through his head, surround him.

A little feeling came back into his arms. "Alicia? Am I dead?"

Hardly, my dear. Though for the last eight years I wondered about that.

Cal spit out a mouthful of creek water. "Where are you? Am I hallucinating?"

Some would call it that. Some would call it opening your mind and heart.

"Brie."

Yes, you should listen to her. She tried to tell you I'm here. I've always been here.

"And the cabin?" Cal sucked back more air to keep the grogginess at bay. "You were there, too."

I couldn't leave you. Not just yet. Not with so much left undone between us.

He gagged on water, coughed. "Alicia, I'm sorry."

And so am I. Our choices weren't always wise. The night I left I wanted to hurt you, as I imagined you'd hurt me. I didn't mean for you to waste eight years of your life looking for answers.

His eyes felt heavier. The rope cut deeper into his shoulder, and he shook with a bone-deep cold. "Those years weren't all a waste," he muttered. "I've written three books." His mouth twitched into a weak smile and he tasted more blood. "But you know that if you've been camped out at the cabin."

Yes, I know.

"And Lain's been good to me. She wouldn't leave me alone."

She always was a forceful woman.

"And there's Brie." The cold dissipated for a moment when the image of her face flashed in his mind's eye. "I'm in love with her. I fell in love with her while I was trying to hold on to you."

That couldn't have been easy.

Cal didn't remember his wife being so understanding. Maybe he *was* hallucinating.

Then you have something to live for. Someone to live for.

He nodded. "Yeah, thanks for pointing that out." Cal fought against heavy eyelids. "But I've let go of you, Alicia," he confessed.

It's about time, Callan. Now I can let go of you, too.

Amazingly, Cal understood. Peace stole over him. He no longer felt his body...

Don't you dare slip away now, Callan Porter. Too many people need you.

His daughter's presence filled his thoughts. "Jeanie?" Cal barely felt his mouth move, and didn't know whether of not he actually spoke the name. "Where is she?"

Where I left her. Behind. You'll know where. Search your heart. But there's another.

Brie. This time Cal knew he didn't speak. His lips were heavy with cold, and his facial muscles frozen with exhaustion.

Alicia's laugh trilled through his mind again. *You need her quite a bit more than she needs you, my dear. There's another. Hardly more than a wish and a hope right now. But he needs his father.*

He? Father?

For some reason Brie's image flickered in his mind again. Cal tried to concentrate, but lethargy started to claim him. Far away he heard the crash of thunder and the rain spatter into the creek...

And the barking, that didn't seem so distant anymore.

I can leave now, Callan. Live the rest of your life well and full.

"Alicia, thank you."

You're welcome. Now hold on to that tire. Hold on. Hold on...

"Hold on! Hold on to that tire!"

The warning no longer came in Alicia's soft and cultivated voice, but in a man's commanding baritone as he shouted over the loud barking of a dog. Cal tried to obey, but his head dipped forward. The splash of water revived him momentarily, yet his hands slipped from the mooring.

Then he felt tightness in his chest and the drag on his body. "Brie," he whispered, "I'm sorry. I can't hold on anymore."

As his palms dragged over the tire and hit the creek Cal wondered if his soul would end up here, too, haunting this place after his body was called reluctantly away in untimely death.

"Brie. Jeanie," he muttered, "I'm sorry...Can't hold on..."

"We got him! Easy! Get the collar over here! That ankle needs to be immobilized, too! Fast!"

The rope no longer cut into his shoulder, and rain sluiced down his cheeks into his ears. The loamy smell of wet earth filled his nose. Solid land supported his back.

"Everybody, stay away from the bank! Damn, Phil, keep those two women up there!"

"Like hell I'm staying put!"

The words were those his sister would use. The voice was Brie's.

Cal worked to open his eyes, but the weight of the rain foiled the attempt. When he tried to turn his head a brace restrained his neck. Plastic cupped his nose and mouth as cool, pure oxygen flowed into his starved lungs.

Voices babbled overhead. Hands tugged at his body, lifted him. Where had all the people come from? Where was Brie?

"Cal, hold on!" She was at his side, despite the man's best efforts to keep her back, her voice quavering with emotion.

A hand covered his hand. Brie again. He knew it was her even though his eyes still refused to open. He willed his fingers to move, but that effort failed, too.

"You're going to be all right." Her words seemed to come at him from farther away.

"All right," he repeated, though the words echoed back at him inside the oxygen mask.

"Damn straight, Mr. Porter," the man at his side answered. "You owe this young woman your life."

Cal owed Brie a hell of a lot more than that. And when he could make his mouth and brain work together again, he'd tell her so.

Then he'd ask her to marry him.

Eighteen

"You don't look surprised to see me on your doorstep."

Myles waited, like a beggar with hat-in-hand. But Selene didn't smile. She didn't frown. She didn't invite him inside. Myles thought he should be insulted by her lack of any clear emotion. All he felt was miserably schoolboy nervous.

Finally she tilted her head. "I can't say that I am."

"Why not?" he asked, too fast for her to believe the careless tone of his voice.

She opened the door wider. "Because you're in love with me."

Myles paused, considering, then shrugged. "I suppose I am." And he walked across the threshold.

Chapter 18, *Murder, My Love—From the Files of Myles Daemon, P.I.*

* * * *

Brie drew in a deep breath of the warm, moist air and leaned against the edge of the worktable until the dizzy spell passed. Usually the earthy mix of rich soil, pungent herbs, and budding flowers in Aunt Sophie's greenhouse sensually enhanced the routine of repotting plants.

For the past week, however, the chaotic smells made her stomach pitch and roll, whether or not she'd been able to force down breakfast. This morning she had eaten only a handful of soda crackers and washed it down with a cup of chamomile tea. Still, that little bit of food roiled in her stomach, and she suspected she looked as pale as she felt.

Calmly Brie reached for the bunch of spearmint that overflowed its pot, plucked a leaf and crushed it between her thumb and forefinger to release the oils. Within seconds of inhaling the bright, fresh fragrance her insides settled and her stomach actually growled. If only her body could decide whether to accept or reject food.

Fortunately, she knew, the nausea would pass soon enough, probably in another few weeks. Then the real stomach-churning decisions would have to be made.

Brie pulled off her gardening gloves and laid a hand across her aproned middle. She hadn't had to take a home pregnancy test to figure out one of the condoms she and Cal used the night they made love had failed. The new life that grew in her womb announced itself with morning sickness two weeks ago, only a month after she returned to the sanctuary of Aunt Sophie's house. Already she fiercely loved and cherished the fledgling life.

She had also vowed that if this baby had the "gift of knowing" in any way, shape, or form, she would teach the child to honor and respect the ability, as if the talent were no different than that of a musical prodigy. She now understood, all too well that she could best protect her child by instilling self-acceptance.

But what of *his* father? What would Cal think?

Tears filmed her eyes, and she brought the spearmint leaf back to her nose seeking some sort of visceral comfort from the persistent ache in her heart. In spite of all else that had or would pass between them, she'd always love Cal Porter. She would always miss him, as she missed him now, so much so that she spent much of her day in a mental haze, and sleep often eluded her. Whenever she began summoning the courage to call him, she remembered his expression when she told him where to find Alicia, He realized then that her psychic abilities were real, and he was horrified.

She had stayed at Cal's side in the hospital two full days, only long enough to make sure he'd recover from his injuries. But she hadn't stayed long enough to watch him regain full consciousness or to say good-bye to Lain. It was better that way, a good clean break from a moment in time when she finally found herself at the expense of losing her heart to a man who could never accept her as she needed to be accepted.

How could he accept a child who might inherit her gift?

Still, whatever immediate plans the Universe had had for her were fulfilled. Cal had gone searching for his lost wife, found her alone in the wrecked car at the bottom of the canyon, and now was free to resume his search for Jeanie. He had his life back.

And Brie had found a certain peace of mind as well. At least the terrifying dreams were gone.

The front double doors squeaked open on hinges that had needed WD40 for the past year at least. Sophie was probably bringing her a snack. Her aunt had been watching her closely these past few days, seeming to mentally weigh each gram of food Brie ate or mostly didn't eat. With keen powers of observation and intuition, Sophie was the next best thing to a psychic herself. Brie wondered how long it would take for her aunt to figure out the secret.

She swiped her damp cheeks with the back of her hand, unconcerned that she probably left smudges of dirt behind. Thank goodness the greenhouse was off limits to her aunt's clientele, and she didn't have to put on a brave, happy face for the public.

"I'm back here, Sophie," Brie called out, and was gratified that her voice didn't wobble too much. To hide her bout of melancholy, she set about rearranging some empty clay pots on the worktable. At least the scrape and clatter made it sound as if she were being merrily productive.

Perhaps that's why she didn't hear the heavy, lopsided gait until the uneven footfalls were within earshot. Sophie was either wearing oversized garden boots or...

Brie swung around. The clay pot she was holding slipped from her suddenly numb fingers and crashed to the cement floor. For a moment the dizziness returned, and she squinted to make sure she wasn't having another waking dream.

"Brie, I'm sorry. I didn't mean to startle you."

No, it wasn't a dream. Cal's voice, deep and low, was too real. His presence, not more than six feet away, was solid. Dressed in khaki trousers and a white summer shirt he looked cool, casual, and so handsome. Despite her better instincts, Brie took a step forward to throw herself into his arms. That's when she noticed he tilted to the right and was balanced on a cane. The same cane she'd used during her stay in the canyon.

The moment of surprise brought her back to her senses. How could she touch him again and walk away? Impossible. Instead, she laid her hand to her heart. "Cal." She tried to catch her breath and had to make do with only half the air she needed. "You look...well."

That was the grandmother of all understatements!

He peered at her a moment, and leaned a bit harder on the cane. Then he smiled tentatively. "A couple more weeks of physical therapy and I'll be back to new." The smile died. "Almost."

Protectively, Brie moved her hand from her chest to her abdomen and swallowed hard. "You look better than the last time I saw you," she tried to jest.

He took a shuffling step forward, halted. "So do you. But the last time I clearly remember seeing you was in the cabin, after I found the doll." His green eyes narrowed and seemed to express both sadness and accusation. "When I woke up in the hospital, Lain told me you left again, with no forwarding address." He took another step toward her. "You didn't even give me a chance to say thanks."

She bit her lip to keep it from trembling. "I did what needed to be done," she demurred. "I couldn't ignore what I..." She hesitated, and then lifted her chin proudly. "What I knew would happen if you went searching for Alicia's car."

His brow twitched. Brie thought she noticed the corner of his mouth jump, too, as if he were trying to decide whether or not to risk a smile. "You didn't have to drive all the way back to the canyon to supervise the rescue party."

Yes, I did! her heart called out.

Brie wet her lips and shrugged in a badly affected show of nonchalance. "All part of my full psychic services."

Cal set the cane in front of him, put one hand over the other on the crook and leaned forward. "We'll get back to that part later."

Brie went on guard. "We will?"

"Uh-huh," he said with his usual cocky confidence, and gave the greenhouse a thorough scan. "You didn't tell me your aunt was an herbal entrepreneur."

She rubbed a chill from her arms. Or was that ratcheting desire that prickled her skin? "It must have slipped my mind."

His gaze settled on her again. "Did she hire you on for the summer?"

She gave her head a quick shake. "Just helping out for a while."

Cal glanced at her hands resting on her middle and frowned. "Shouldn't you be wearing protective gloves or something?" he fretted. "Chemicals can leach right through a person's skin and into the bloodstream."

Taken aback by his attention to such a small detail, afraid that her posture might be too maternally protective, Brie dropped her arms to her sides. "Sophie doesn't use chemicals to grow her plants. Every fertilizer and pest control agent in this greenhouse is naturally derived and processed. Even so, I wear gloves." She swiped at the discarded pair on the worktable. "I was just taking a break when you walked in."

She pinned him with a forthright gaze. "Why are you here, Cal?"

Some of the attitude left his stance. "Unfinished business. As I started to say, and in spite of your reluctance to let me be gracious, I thought it was only right and proper to thank you face-to-face for saving my life."

His gratitude sounded stiff and formal, and it left her more cold than warm. Still, she nodded her acceptance. "Then you're welcome. Is that why you came all the way to New Mexico to find me?"

"Partly." He jammed his right hand into the side pocket of his slacks and pulled out her moon bracelet. "I wanted to return this."

Brie gasped, but she didn't move forward to take the precious keepsake. "Oh, my! I thought I'd lost this for good."

When Cal frowned in question, she stemmed the flow of her runaway thoughts. "This was...quite a thoughtful gesture."

Yet, she didn't reach to take it from his outstretched hand. She wasn't sure if she could move closer to him without feeling the inexorable pull of his soul, and she couldn't get lost in him again.

He wiggled the bracelet as if tempting her. "I fixed the clasp as I promised. Sorry if it looks worse for the wear. It was in my pocket when I took the plunge into Milagro Creek."

When Brie only stared at the bracelet, Cal limped to the far end of the worktable and set it down on a relatively dirt-free spot. "I brought the doll, too. It's in a bag in my trunk."

"I left it for you to give back to Jeannie," Brie told him.

He shrugged. "The doll belonged to Alicia, not Jeannie. And you bought it from that resale shop. You're the rightful owner."

Brie allowed herself a rueful smile. "Ah, yes, the lawyer finally emerges."

Cal nodded and cocked his head. "Maybe you can still fix it up for your aunt. Unless you're reluctant to handle it again."

Brie shook her head. "That won't be a problem." She didn't volunteer that once Alicia's spirit had used Brie as her voice that day in the cabin, she'd left nothing of her essence behind in the doll. Cal didn't need to know that. He probably didn't *want* to know that.

"Thanks again, Cal. But you could have shipped the doll to me for a lot less time and money," she pointed out.

Cal leaned heavily on the cane. "I spent a bundle of time and money tracking you down, Brie. The airfare from L.A. to New Mexico was a drop in that bucket."

If he wanted her to feel guilty, he'd done a bang-up job.

"Besides," he went on as if oblivious or unconcerned about her discomfort, "there's something more important I felt you deserved to hear in person." He cracked a smile, restrained and weary, but still the smile she had fallen in love with. "I found Jeanie."

Brie's heart skipped a beat. A laugh of joy bubbled out of her throat, and tears leaked from her eyes. "Oh, Cal! I'm so happy for you!" If only she could find the courage to run to him, hold him close and let him feel her delight at the news. She didn't dare. "How? When?"

He stayed rooted, as well, but let out a breath of what seemed to be relief. "I put my friend, Jim Atwood, back on the case. This time he found Jeanie with no trouble. It seems the night Alicia left

Santa Barbara events happened just the way you said." He paused. "The way you *saw* them happen in your mind."

A flicker of hope licked at Brie's heart. But she reminded herself that her predictions had been backed up by hard facts. This time.

She held her breath as Cal went steadily on. "Alicia's father had Jeanie hidden away in Europe with the family he retained to oversee his properties there. Alicia did change her mind about leaving me when she got to her father's house, but she didn't want to drag Jeanie all the way back down the coast to hash things out with me. That's how Jeanie got left in San Francisco."

Cal shut his eyes a moment, and then blinked them open. "When Alicia went missing, Macartan really did suspect me of having something to do with it. Dear God, Brie, I knew the man despised and distrusted me, but I didn't understand the depth of his fear for Alicia."

He shook off the moment, and focused back on Brie. "Macartan feared for Jeanie, too. He flew her out of the country for safekeeping. By the time his own investigation proved me innocent, he was afraid I'd nail him for kidnapping." He sighed. "He was right. I would have done it, too."

Shoulders slumped, expression pensive, he looked anything like a man bent on exacting retribution. "Now?" Brie asked.

Cal lowered his gaze to the floor. "What he did wasn't right. Henry Macartan wanted to rein in a situation that was spinning out of his control. He loved Alicia and Jeanie in his own way, and that love made him do something incredibly stupid. He should never have kept my daughter from me all these years, and let me wonder whether or not she was alive."

He lifted his eyes. "I'm not sure I can completely forgive him for that. There's no way I can ever make up those years Jeanie and I lost. But he took good care of her, Brie. She's almost twelve, and she's beautiful, intelligent, and poised. She's had the best private tutors and has never wanted for anything, but she isn't in the least bit spoiled. Henry spent more time in Europe these past eight years, to the detriment of his business in San Francisco, just so he could be family to her."

"Henry?" Brie wondered.

Cal shrugged. "Yeah, well, Alicia's father and I have gotten to know each other a little better. We have more in common that we realized years ago. We both try to exert cast iron control over life, generally at the expense of everyone around us. I guess I understand him now, at least on some basic level. Besides, neither of us is the same as we were back then. Jeanie and I lost each other, and it's going to take time and effort for us to find our way back home. Her grandfather is a natural bridge."

He edged a half-step closer. "Since a week after I left the hospital, I've been in France, getting reacquainted with my daughter and trying to explain all that happened in a way that won't hurt or scar her. I can't in all good conscience make Henry out to be some monster that needs to be punished. If I destroy Jeanie's love and trust for him she might not have enough of either left for me."

"You aren't going to hold him legally responsible, are you?" she guessed, smiling her admiration.

His face flushed crimson. "A little psychic razzle-dazzle, Miss L.A.?"

Her heart clenched when he used the nickname she'd come to cherish. Bravely, she shook her head. "Your decision sounds completely in character to me. I think you've figured out the past doesn't matter. There's only now, and the future will take care of itself."

For a moment he only stared at her, and then he blinked, as if taken by surprise. "Do you mean that?"

A shimmy of awareness rippled along Brie's arms as she realized she'd just destroyed the reason for keeping her emotional distance from the man she loved. Still unsure if she was brave enough to risk again, she hedged, "On general principle."

Raising one brow, Cal started a slow shuffle in her direction. She couldn't move backward without betraying the cowardice that left her knees trembling.

"You know, Brie, you were harder to find than Jeanie, as it turns out," Cal told her. "It was like you wanted to disappear off the face of the earth. I put Jim Atwood on your trail, too. Now, that man's good. He even tracked down your two biker buddies from Saratoga Springs."

Her mouth dropped open. "Neil and Hank?"

"Yeah. You had them worried. A couple weeks ago, they stopped by your place in Glendale for a visit and you weren't around to share a root beer with them. I think you owe them an apology."

The edgy tease in his voice put her on the defensive. "I'll see to it."

"You do that. And that decorator friend of yours. Darien?" Cal whistled low. "Jim said the guy was a bulldog in an Armani suit. Very protective of you, Brie. Wouldn't even give out your middle name." He cocked his head. "Which, by the way, I found out from another source, is Marie."

Unnerved by his encroachment on her space, Brie crossed her arms under her breasts. "You could have just asked me. We spent four whole days together."

"If I remember, we had bigger issues than worrying about the exchange of middle names. Or, it turns out, addresses and telephone numbers."

"You needn't have gone to all that trouble, really," she insisted tartly.

"Oh, yes, I did. For all the reasons I've given so far, and one that's more important than all the rest together." Cal took two last steps that put him within arm's reach and stopped. In the warm, moist air his scent enveloped her. "I wanted to tell you, face-to-face, that I don't appreciate being some big-city woman's one-night-stand."

"What?" Brie clenched her fists. "Are you kidding?"

"What am I supposed to think?" Cal prodded. "I mean, true, you are from Los Angeles..."

"Now wait a minute," she huffed. "We've had this little chat about your unfortunate habit of stereotyping people..."

"I promised to take you waltzing," he reminded her. "Do you know how much I was looking forward to that?"

Her breath stalled at the mention of their intimate conversation and the erotic memories it stirred to life. "Cal, I'm sorry..." she started to choke out.

"And then there's the unfinished manuscript sitting on my desk," he interrupted. "You left me high and dry for inspiration and coaching. My editor's a patient man. But he's already postponed my deadline by almost two months, only because part of that time I was semiconscious or on pain pills. I'm up against a wall, and it's your fault because you made me change the entire flow of my story. The least you can do is help me finish the first draft."

Her eyes went wide with disbelief. "I'm not responsible..."

"And what about the baby?"

Though Brie's mouth continued to work, her brain went blank. For a moment, she thought she might lose control of her already weakened knees. "Ba...baby? Wha...You...How could you know? Sophie doesn't even know yet. Did Jim Atwood...no, that's not possible!"

He startled her into silence when he clasped her hand. His eyes were the darkest green she'd ever seen and demanded full honesty. "When were you going to tell me? Ever?"

His touch disoriented her. His words, though soft and low, were filled with hurt and wariness.

Unable to lie or even twist the truth, Brie shook her head. "I don't know. I wanted to, but..."

When her voice broke, Cal set aside his cane and took both of her hands. "But you were afraid of how I would react, knowing that a child of ours might be born psychic," he said matter-of-factly.

Brie sucked back air to clear a block of emotion. "I saw the way you looked at me when I held the doll and..." The memory was too painful to speak out loud.

Cal slid his thumbs along the backs of her hands, sending zings of electricity up her arms, through her body. "That was before I understood."

"Understood what?" she nearly sobbed.

He attempted, and failed, to smile. "Your gift."

In reflex, Brie stiffened and tried to pull away. "You can't understand. You don't really believe."

Cal held on to her gently but firmly. "Oh, no?" he challenged with a lift of his chin. "Not even after I found Alicia's car, right where you said it would be?"

"But you wouldn't take just my word!" Brie accused, angry now that he'd penetrated her wall of defenses and made her so vulnerable again. "You had to go see for yourself if she was there, and it almost got you killed!"

Cal edged his grip up to her wrists and peered deeply into her eyes. "I went there, Brie," he admitted. "I'm ashamed to say it now. Even Lain, my hardheaded, practical sister believed you without question. I claimed to be in love with you, but I didn't trust anything except my own eyes, when your eyes—the eyes of your soul—saw so much more."

He shook his head. "But before I spotted the bumper sticking out of the water, I had decided I didn't need hard proof. I had your word. I trusted your 'knowing.'" He sniffed a derisive laugh. "My own clumsiness landed me in that creek." Cal lifted his hand and brushed his knuckles along her tear-moistened cheek. "And then your gift saved my life. For a second time."

She wanted to believe him. She wanted to give in to the race of desire and need that his touch provoked. Confused, Brie started to stammer that she needed time and distance to think, but the odd cast of Cal's gaze stalled her efforts.

"Something else happened in that creek," he whispered. "Something that I had to pull piece by piece out of my unconscious mind over these past six weeks. The disjointed memories all finally came together last Thursday, when I was in France making plans to bring Jeanie home. Jim called from Sacramento and told me he'd finally tracked you down. Then he apologized for taking so long when my 'intuition' about how to find Jeanie with Henry had gotten such miraculous results."

Cal's hand strayed to Brie's neck, and he threaded his fingers gently through her hair. "That's when all the words and images that had free-floated around in my brain for weeks started making sense." He peered at her with such intensity Brie trembled. "You asked me how I found out about the baby. I knew there was a possibility that morning in cabin before all hell broke lose. I found evidence that one of the condoms had failed."

"I guessed as much," she answered with resignation. "But you made a real leap of logic to guess I was pregnant."

"No logic, leaped at or otherwise, involved here," he said with a wan smile. And then he took a deep breath. "Alicia told me."

Brie stared up at him agog.

Cal only grinned down at her. "Is that the way I looked at you? Damn, no wonder you took off."

"What are you telling me?" she found the wit to demand.

"That while I was hanging on to that car for dear life, half-drowned and regretting my most recent unfortunate life choices, Alicia talked to me."

"She..." Brie swallowed hard. "She talked to you?"

"About Jeanie," Cal said with a nod. "About how I could track her down." He slipped his hand around Brie's still narrow waist and held her protectively. "About how I had to live because my daughter, my unborn son, and the woman I love all needed me." He quirked a brow. "Well, Alicia did say I needed you more than you needed me, but we can debate that point later."

Brie went still inside, a quiet born of the need to believe that Cal believed in her gift, fully and without question. In the stillness she felt the nudge of his soul, a presence so familiar and yet so unlike the dark, sad spirit that had overwhelmed and disoriented her that night she drove headlong into the canyon.

Yes, he was open to her now. Open to all the wonderful possibilities of life. He had his own brush with the gift that had almost sent her into despair, and he believed.

Then, the full impact of what he had told her sank in. "It's a boy? We're going to have a son?"

He chuckled and nodded. "I guarantee it."

"Cal?" she whispered, "I'm afraid this is all another dream."

His mouth hovered just inches from hers now. "Yeah, me, too," he confessed. "I'm still not sure what sort of magic you worked on me, Miss L.A. Interior Decorator. But I sure as hell got all my mental furniture rearranged. Kind of a *feng shui* of the mind."

She opened her mouth to correct his pronunciation and caught herself. "You said it right!"

"I finally got a lot of stuff right," he breathed. "Like now is the right time to kiss you."

He didn't wait for permission. Brie suspected that had something to do with the way she braced her arms around his neck and lifted up on her toes before the last word left his mouth.

She lost herself in the moment, in the tender neediness that left them both breathless.

"Do you feel what I feel?" Cal whispered when he came up for air.

His soul embraced her soul, without reservation. "Yes," Brie whispered back.

"Then you know I want to marry you."

She laughed and kissed his cheek, his chin, his mouth. "I don't read minds."

Cal braced the back of her head with his hand and held her still while kissing her with a depth of passion that left her wobbly. "Neither do I," he murmured against her mouth. "Give me an answer, Miss L.A."

The urgency in his voice, in the press of his body, brought tears of joy to her eyes. "Maybe we could get Father Neil to perform the ceremony down by Milagro Creek?"

Cal leaned back, stared down at her a second. Then he threw back his head and laughed. "Yeah, sure," he finally said. "We'd come full circle at Milagro Creek." He peered at her more seriously now. "I'm beginning to think it is a "miracle" creek. What were the chances..."

"Shhh." Brie laid her finger over his mouth and smiled serenely. "Don't think too much. Just let the magic work."

Cal smiled and pulled her closer. "I can do that."

Brie let his warmth envelope her. "We'll do it together."

Printed in the United Kingdom
by Lightning Source UK Ltd.
113168UKS00001B/208